ARTEMIS
EYE OF
GAEA

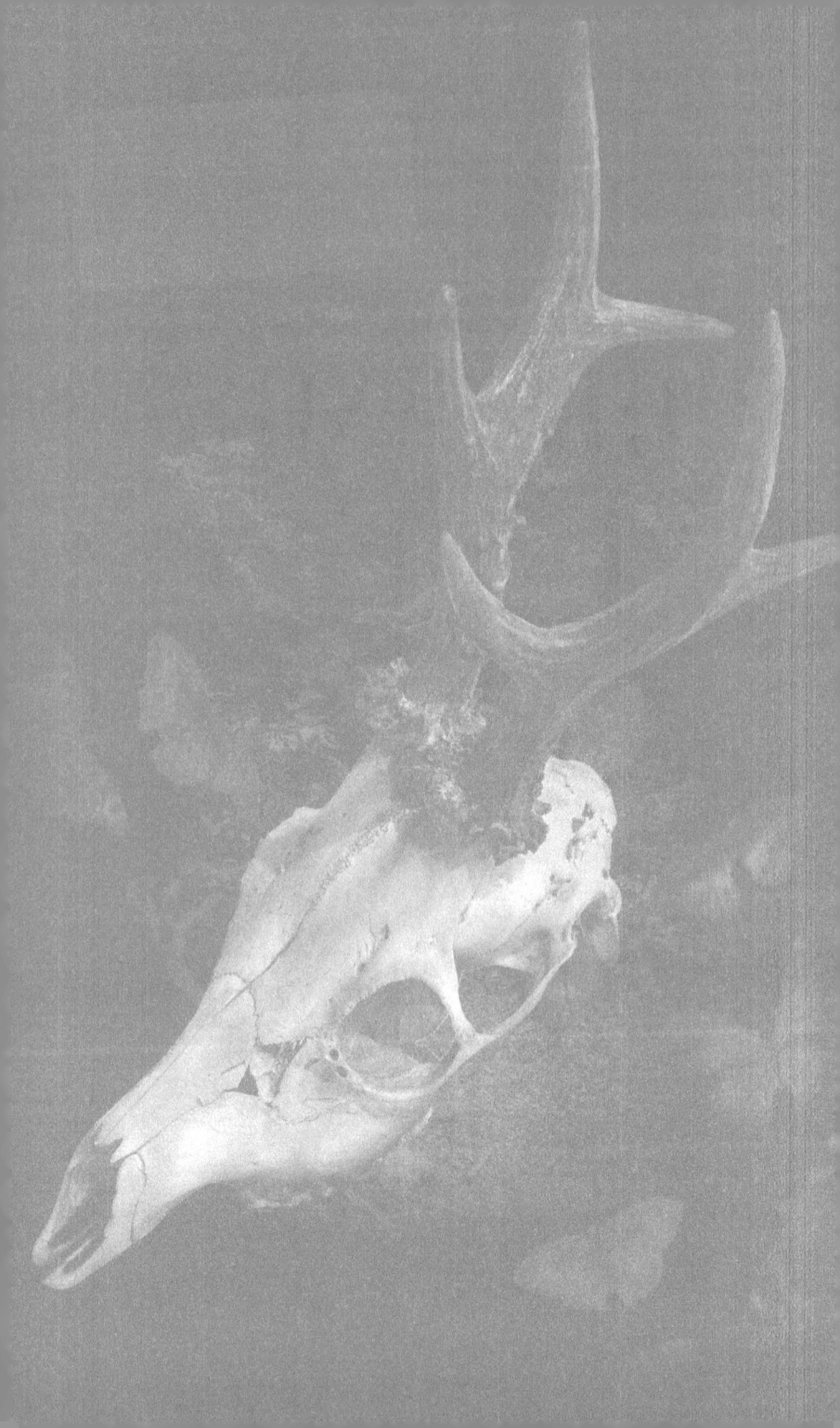

THE CEDRIC SERIES

ARTEMIS EYE OF GAEA

AWARD-WINNING AUTHOR
VALERIE WILLIS

4 Horsemen
Publications, Inc.

Published By: 4 Horsemen Publications, Inc.

4 Horsemen Publications, Inc.
PO Box 417
Sylva, NC 28779
4horsemenpublications.com
info@4horsemenpublications.com

Cover & Typesetting by Valerie Willis
Edited by Kris Cotter

Library of Congress Control Number: 2022931334

Paperback ISBN-13: 978-1-64450-047-7
Hardcover ISBN-13: 978-1-64450-538-0
Audiobook ISBN-13: 978-1-64450-045-3
Ebook ISBN-13: 978-1-64450-046-0

DEDICATION

Thank you to Mr. Justin Willis—my amazing, wonderful, super sexy, Mr. Fix-it-all Husband—who threatened that he better be in every dedication here on out by name... or else! I am not allowed to just say Husband! He also thinks that all my readers should thank him for not insisting I go to bed *every night by midnight*.

I Love You, Mr. Justin Willis.

TABLE OF CONTENTS

DEDICATION V

PREFACE...IX

ACKNOWLEDGMENTS XIII

CHAPTER 1
Egos 1

CHAPTER 2
The Realms of Aether 8

CHAPTER 3
Ball and Chain 18

CHAPTER 4
Inheritance...28

CHAPTER 5
Merrow-folk..37

CHAPTER 6
Controlling Ether...50

CHAPTER 7
Wizard Manannan 56

CHAPTER 8
Strings of Fate and Prophecy Spoken 62

CHAPTER 9
The Art of Shapeshifting..67

CHAPTER 10
Valkyries, Furies, and Amazonians 74

CHAPTER 11
Striking a Deal with Nicholas Teague 80

CHAPTER 12
To Become a Fury...88

CHAPTER 13
Making of a Gladiator 95

CHAPTER 14
The Art of Stealth...104

CHAPTER 15
Minotaur Fight...112

CHAPTER 16
Train with Valkyries..121

CHAPTER 17
We Three Kings..127

CHAPTER 18
Olrun's Fortitude...135

CHAPTER 19
The Bird Cage...141

CHAPTER 20
The Challenger..149

CHAPTER 21
Soul Mates..157

CHAPTER 22
Regrets...165

CHAPTER 23
Dryad's Message...170

CHAPTER 24
The Aqrabuamelu...180

CHAPTER 25
Locked Doors..187

CHAPTER 26
Gaea's Throne...192

CHAPTER 26
War of Roses..199

READY FOR BOOK FIVE?... 203
King Incubus: A New Reign is waiting for you...................203

ABOUT THE AUTHOR 205
BOOK CLUB DISCUSSION QUESTIONS........................ 209

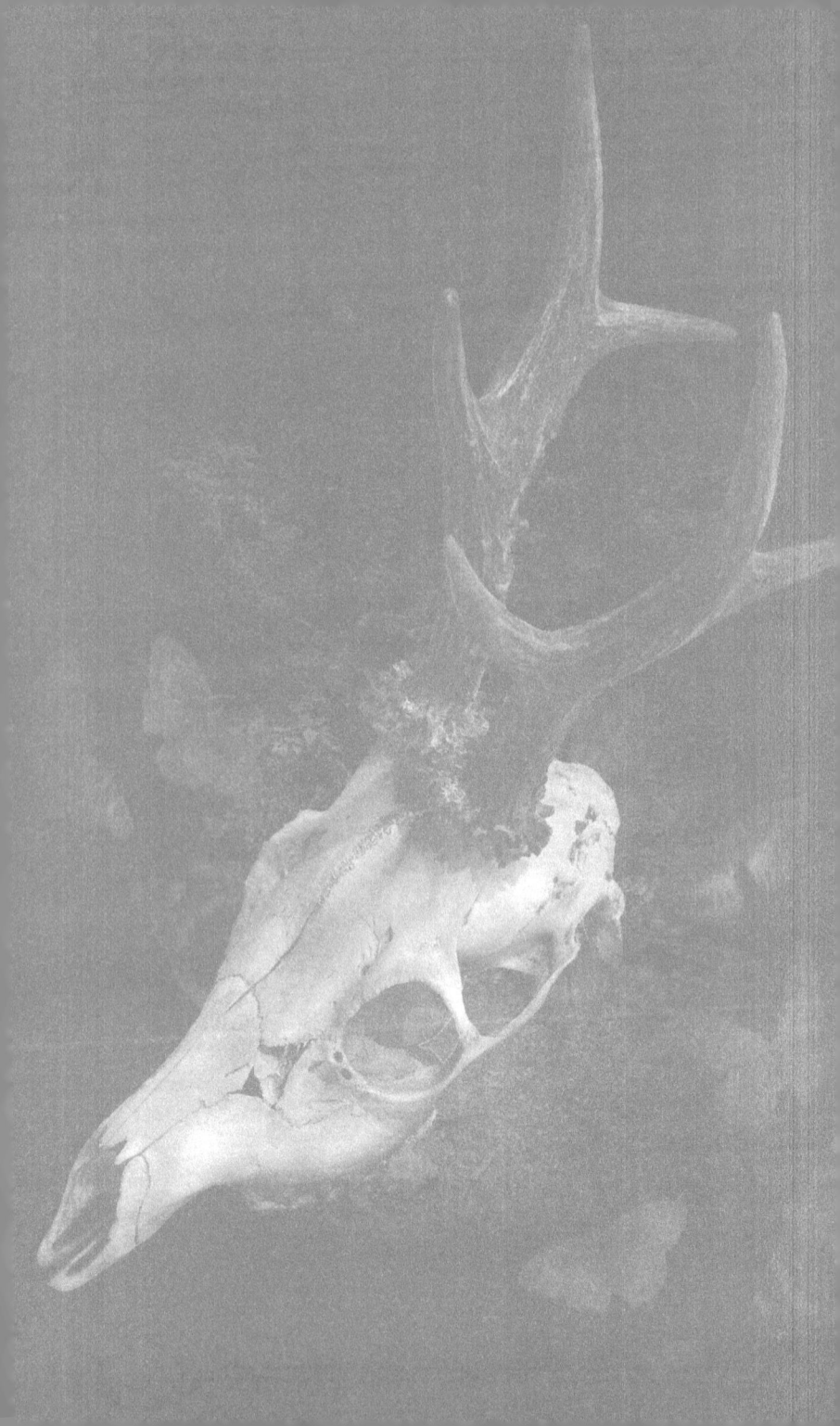

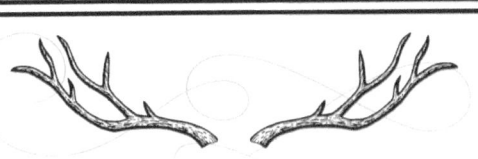

PREFACE

It was brought to my attention that I should take a moment to talk to the readers and fans of *The Cedric Series*.

I wish to share my inspirations for writing this story. This will explain a lot about how I came about creating these amazing ideas, characters, creatures, and events as a fictional work with heavy fantasy and romance elements in the mix. If one really wanted to drag out all its genres, I could label this a historical fiction, mythology, or even an occult and paranormal series. So far, fantasy romance has done this work the most justice for my readers' expectations.

Historical fiction can be applied to several parts throughout the series, whether it's a scene, event, or even a reflection of a character and their on-goings. What do I mean by this? Well, a lot of you might get the Vladimir Tepes, or Vlad the Impaler references, but it dove deeper than that. King Frederic was the First King of Germans and the lepers in those times did indeed have to ring bells and seek refuge in colonies, Cerdanya was a real trade town, and so on. There are a ton of subtle hints here and there because I wanted to bring the unseen, untold side of the history during the Medieval Times to a tangible state.

As far as the mythology side of this series, I wanted to teach you all my versions of forgotten lore, legends, and mythology. I did my best to not use anything that was newer than the 12th century as I dug deep. Some of the concepts woven in with my own perception were hard to obtain and justify. There was a lot of book buying, digging through a Medieval-age bestiary, and though I scoured the internet, it failed me often in my journey for research. As I created and developed each character, I did my best to tie them into one or more myths so that I may weave a wondrous story without limits. At the same time, I wanted some of you to get caught in a conversation or to be sitting in class and have that moment of, "Oh! I know how this myth goes!"

Let me enlighten you all on some of the tales, history, legends, and myths stitched into some of these amazing characters you have experienced so far:

- Cedric takes after a very forgotten and neglected epic legend from the Medieval Times of the Russian knight hero, Ilya Muromets. Search him, check it out, and feel free to compare what you unknowingly learned about this amazing legend. You'll be excited to see a red-haired knight on a black horse as one of the images in the mix. Included in this were some really obscure Romanian beliefs involving early vampire-like stories. The off-shoots involving the strigoi showed less fear toward these vampire creatures, but held a tone of sorrow and remorse. People who became these creatures had not finished living their lives (Including not ever getting married) and met the insane stipulations to come back as one of the undying. Truly interesting, and I can only hope to capture that same empathetic tone I had discovered in my digging.

- Barushka combines a few tales as well, starting with his name drawn from the Russian knight hero tales. Other than that, I focused heavily on the shag foal lores. I was intrigued by the first few variants I stumbled on and found that the internet proved void of information. Amazingly, the hairy phantom horse tales started so long ago. There was no exact date as to when they began. The folklore was mysteriously always there. Adding to my wonder about this lore was the fact I stumbled on a 1927 naturalist journal that devoted a section to them. Even this far forward, it was believed it may be an undiscovered species of horse! Despite that, the one thing I saw reflected in all the writing was that a shag foal approaches lone travelers and scares them so much that they run off to their deaths. Never once did the research say the horse actively killed someone.

- Morrighan, Badbh, and Nemaine were derived from the tales involving the evil sorcerer Calatin. This was an older tale involving them that did not mix the three as one entity. There are no words to describe my frustration and disappointment at how many times Badbh and Nemaine were labeled as alternative names for Morrighan.

Especially when the story of the Legendary Cuchulainn made it clear that they were three sisters, each with unique powers. Seeing that Badbh and Morrighan had earned the title of goddess at some point through the passing of time, I felt the need to give Nemaine her own placement as a goddess as well.

- Romasanta is the most complex of all my characters. His name is taken from a man in history who is not as common as he once was, Manuel Blanco Romasanta. He was the first serial killer to be trailed and as you read book two of the Cedric Series, you will see a lot of that history drawn upon. Feeding off the tragic aura, I pulled in both werewolf and wolf-related myths and lores, wanting to show a more accurate flow through a single entity. It was my intention to bring in familiar aspects and add in the historically forgotten complications that modern book culture has failed to take into account. Those well-versed in mythology will be able to pick out elements on their own, but the amount of lore here is wide. Tales of Apollo and Daphne, Pan and Pitip, Fenrir, versipellis, Romanian beliefs of vampires were caused by a werewolf, Wolf of the Cemetery from Haiti, Romulus and Remus, and so on. There are deep seeds that I only give you teasers of the mythology that is mentioned here.

- As for the monsters, you can say thank you to the Medieval Bestiaries. There are so many wild and crazy creatures in these that are no longer touched that I wanted to bring them to life again. Orms, Jidra, and Aitvaras were a few of the frightening things that travelers spoke of and warned each other about in their explorations. I can only imagine what they may have been based on, but there is a great sense of pride I take in including such monsters in my story. Granted, I have not followed their descriptions exactly and have embellished them with my own imagination, but I hope they make my stories more memorable.

In the end, I encourage my thirsty readers to explore what you've read in my *Cedric Series*. Search the names, look deeper into the scenes, places, and events, and discover these in more detail. My goal is to introduce you to the forgotten lores and history while adding my own perspective and imagination into the mix. May this tale make its mark in your heart and open your world to the legacy our ancestors once talked about over the dinner table so long ago!

Happy reading and discovery!

Valerie Willis

ACKNOWLEDGMENTS

Thank you to my 4 Horsemen "Publiactions" crew! Without the push and drive to get my career out of the mud, I probably wouldn't be able to get this fourth installment out the door. I was down and bummed out that I had missed my initial goal.

To all the writers out there! May you find a tribe that supports you, pushes you, and isn't afraid to get dirty and give you that leg up over the walls that often block our way. Granted Erika, Jen, and Vanessa showed up with sledgehammers and just busted it through. Now, back to working on book five!

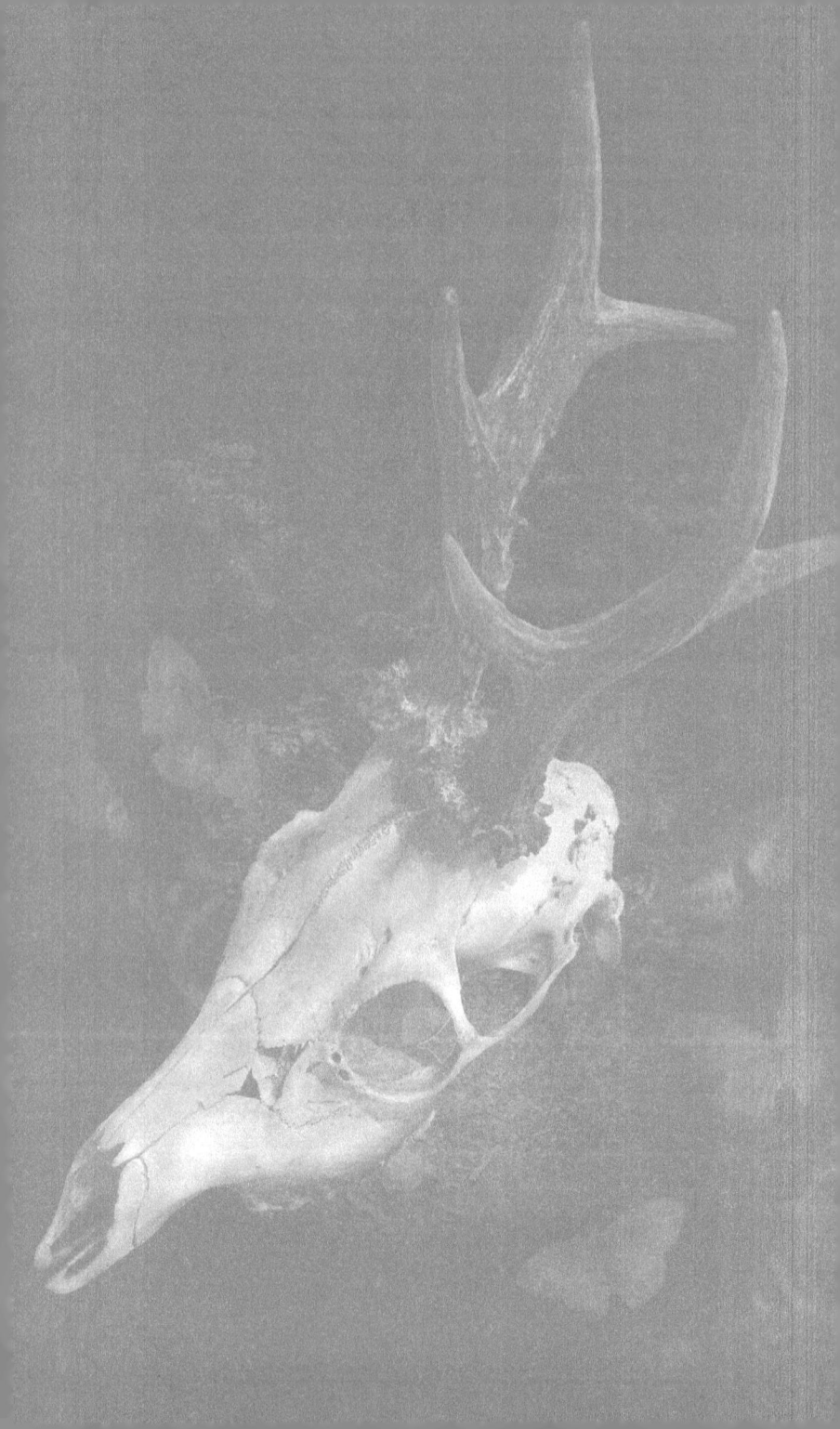

CHAPTER 1

EGOS

CEDRIC

C edric welcomed the bright, warm light as they left the security of the cave behind. Wylleam led them down a path through thick woods while Fenrir kept close behind Cedric at the back of the assembly. The singing of birds filled the air like an orchestra. Flowers and fruit filled every tree they walked past, the air engulfed in their sweet and bitter scents. They had passed through into the realm of Gaea, but were shocked to see not much had changed besides the oddness of the trees and the overwhelming enthusiasm of the birds. The sun was in the sky, dirt at their feet, and they even needed to breathe.

The path wound through the thick forest. Cedric's shoulders and wings would brush against the trunks of trees, making him groan in annoyance. He was engorged with power as if his body took in the thicker magic in the air and absorbed it,. Fenrir chuckled, watching as Cedric tried unsuccessfully to get used to the new, larger version of himself. Wylleam took a hard turn to the right. Anxious to keep pace, Cedric turned too soon, and a horn slammed into a nearby tree, gouging a deep groove into the bark. He cursed under his breath as birds scattered in alarm. Flowers floated on the wind and fruit plopped to the ground all around him, one bouncing off his shoulder. Everyone stopped to stare at him. He gritted his fangs; it was all he could do to not lose his temper. His mind focused on Angeline, wondering where Artemis had taken her.

At least this time she's with someone who will protect her.

"Are you all right?" Wylleam's voice expressed concern, recognizing the signs of Cedric's frustration. Cedric's eyes shot a knowing glare that said, *this isn't the time to discuss it.* "It's not much farther to my cabin. There's an opening in the trees where I live."

Sighing, Cedric nodded. "I look forward to no more trees."

Fenrir, Romasanta, and Nyctimus chuckled until an angry green glare hit them. As promised, they walked about five hundred yards farther in the dense underbrush before a meadow housing a small cabin blossomed before them. Fenrir circled in a thick, grassy spot before flopping down on his belly, watching Wylleam lead Romasanta and Nyctimus through the door. Cedric moved to follow, but Wylleam held up a hand, signaling he was to wait. The door clicked close and Cedric began pacing. After a few rounds, he could no longer ignore the heat of the stare from the golden eyes of the massive white wolf in the field.

Halting his steps, Cedric stood tall, crossing his arms. "What is it, wolf?"

"You seem to be in a rush, even though you've yet to stop and take in this new environment," snorted Fenrir. "You're quite the fool."

Narrowing his eyes, Cedric retorted, "What is there to know? There's ground and trees, a sky and sun. Everything smells the same."

"True." Fenrir wagged his tail a few times. "But you still haven't adjusted."

"I don't have the luxury of taking the time to play with myself," scoffed Cedric, returning to his pacing.

"I, too, once found myself in your state over a female." Rising to his feet, Fenrir shook his fur free of grass. "But if you don't learn to trust in her strength and abilities, she'll never discover them at all."

He stopped, his back to the wolf.

"Struck a nerve with you, didn't I, pup?" Fenrir's voice fell deeper with the next words. "Don't make the mistake I once made in thinking she's incapable of protecting herself, incapable of being by your side, let alone, being on her own."

"What would you know about Angeline?" Cedric hissed over his shoulder.

"That isn't for me to know." Fenrir huffed, his lip curling in disgust. "These are things you should be aware of and if you aren't, then I feel bad for your mate to be stuck with such a naïve creature."

Cedric turned to face the wolf, who had paced ever closer, the heat of his anger rising in his voice. "Are you suggesting I know nothing about her? About the girl I chose, the girl I protected and spent centuries to reclaim from Merlin with my own claws and fangs?"

Fenrir flicked an ear, his muzzle contorting to a toothy grin. "Considering you see her as simply a *girl*, should be a sign as to how blind you are to who she was, is, and will become."

Cedric's arms fell to his side, his hands balling ever tighter into fists until his claws dug into his palms. Fenrir's glare stung, his nose twitching. Blood dripped off Cedric's knuckles, the green grass mottled with red streaks. Fenrir took another step closer, the two of them nose to nose. A silent challenge of strength and resolve built between them. Fenrir was large and more ancient than Cedric, but in this state, this form, perhaps he could indeed face one of the most feared creatures of destruction known to man and demon. Fur ruffled, razor-backed, as if the thoughts and comparisons racing in Cedric's mind were spoken out loud.

"Are you challenging me, pup?" There was a sparkle in Fenrir's eyes as his tail wagged. "Because no one here has ever been so brave to bow up to me since I left Romasanta in the land of the living."

Cedric's jaw twitched, his muscles tensing as he dared to confess, "You did say I need to become more familiar with this form, didn't you, Fenrir?"

Massive jaws lashed out. The heat of Fenrir's breath pushed Cedric back with power and speed as they snapped close. Cedric barely saw the muscles under the fur twitch seconds before in order to evade the answer Fenrir gave. Wings flaring, Cedric crouched and launched himself up. A giant paw fell across Cedric's chest as if swatting a fly. Fenrir had assumed his next action and shoved him down, pinning him to the ground. Teeth ripped into the left wing. Cedric paled. There was no sensation of pain, but something far more haunting. With each pop and crackle, euphoria made his blood boil, and he wanted nothing more than to let the wolf continue the destruction of his flesh. Fenrir tightened his bite, and with a savage move, he shook his head back and forth. Not one blade of grass remained green as Cedric's eyes rolled back in ecstasy. The only sound from his lips was a pleasurable moan.

Satisfied he had made his point, Fenrir leaped off, leaving Cedric struggling with the unnatural pleasure overpowering him. His muzzle and chest glistening crimson as he pranced back and forth. Rolling a shoulder in the meadow, bugs leaped into the air and off to safer patches as Fenrir freed his fur of the sticky liquid. With the blood off, Fenrir jerked back onto his feet and frolicked in circles, triumphant of the quick defeat. Finished with his victory laps, he sat, flicking an ear at the door. No one from within the cabin had made any signs of hearing the commotion.

Breathless, voluptuous sensations waved over Cedric with every move until he managed to roll to his knees. More and more sweat poured over him, and with each pulse of ecstasy, his body healed. Staring wide-eyed, he looked at the grass between his clawed hands, shocked by the burden he had regained. He hadn't faced the struggle rattling through him since he had reached into Wylleam's fireplace so long ago. It wasn't something he thought would ever become an issue for him again in this lifetime.

Dammit! How can I defeat anyone if I can't fight against this over-whelming want for them to... Everything to... Swallowing down his fears, he tried to refocus his thoughts. *Fenrir is right. I need to become familiar with this form, but to want my body destroyed? Never have I realized the depth of what Lillith felt when she wanted me to run her through, as I do now. How long will it take me to keep my sanity?*

"You understand the severity of your state, I see." Fenrir had turned back to Cedric. "Do you understand the situation you're in?"

Grimacing, Cedric could still feel Angeline, far from his reach, in this new world. With each deep inhale, he could even smell her, taste her in the air, and he focused on those sensations. Digging his claws into the dirt, he dared to stretch his injured wing out. It was sore, but the overwhelming desire and incubine lusting had served their purpose in speeding up the healing process. Swallowing, he stood and faced Fenrir, who responded with another wag of his tail. Stretching his wings wide, Cedric's muscles flexed. Taking in a deep breath, he charged at the wolf. Fenrir took a defensive stance, snarling.

Horns knocked head-on with Fenrir's forehead, the wolf holding his ground like a rival bull. As if two rams, they pushed with all their strength to make the other take a step back. Tiring of the struggle, Cedric wrapped his arms around Fenrir's snout, locking his jaw closed. Rearing up, Fenrir shook his head. When Cedric didn't dislodge, Fenrir smashed him against the ground, pinning him between his skull and the earth. Folding his wings tight, Cedric's claws dug deep under Fenrir's bottom jaw. Paws scratched across his wings and back. Each crushing and ripping sensation against Cedric's body added to the arousing thrill taking hold of his soul. Growling vibrated through him, foaming saliva dripping into large clumps across the once beautiful meadow.

Fenrir's paws pulled away and Cedric took a reprieve in breaking from the enjoyment of being ravaged. The bouncing and jolting of where Cedric clung to Fenrir's face was alarming; *the wolf has broken into a run!* Looking over his shoulder, Cedric's muscles tensed, and he held on tighter. Branches slapped across his back, cracking and falling to the ground in their wake. Fenrir's body took long, powerful strides, his speed uncanny and careless. Bark scraping across Cedric's skin came to him like the caress of a lover's touch. Fenrir turned back, angry he hadn't come loose, running ever faster through the thicker trees. Cedric gripped harder, hot blood rolled down his arms, dripping from his elbows. Despite it, Cedric held fast to Fenrir's hot flesh, tendrils of muscles between his clawed fingers.

THUD! CR-CR-CRACK-CK! KA-BOOM!

The wind had been smashed from Cedric's lungs, but his grip stayed. Fenrir ran full steam through the trees—*no! At the trees!* Cedric's back and wings were being pulverized against the branches before being run through the trunks, the wood splintering, the shards stabbing both of them from all directions.

THUD! CR-CRACK! BA-BOOM!

Clenching his teeth, Cedric fought the urge to vocally express the intensity of the orgasmic sensations taking hold. His shoulder blades were like gelatin and the strength in his back muscles was starting to fail. He could no longer hold his wings close to his body. Muscles were shredding, his arms weakening, but the excitement struggled to heal fast enough between impacts. It had its limitations, after all.

TH-THUD! SNAP! POP! BOOM!

Cedric's fingers were losing their grip, his spine exposed under a mantle of mangled flesh and wooden spikes. Wings limp, flailing down the sides of Fenrir's face, were beyond broken. The sounds of the wolf's paws against the ground were as daunting as distant war drums. Fenrir continued charging into yet another trunk. Cedric couldn't contain his shout of elation.

KA-THUD! CR-CR-CRRR-CRAAAAACK! POP! P-POP!

Cedric's muscles grew numb, his arms unable to respond to the command to hold tight. Fenrir bolted into the meadow, skidding to a stop. The force sent Cedric's bloodied, broken form bouncing off his snout and rolling toward the cabin. In Cedric's eyes, the world spun before falling dark. Shaking the debris and blood from his fur, Fenrir snorted, pacing to where Cedric lay. Jaws scooped down, gripping the limp wings tight. A heavy paw pushed down on the gruesome remains of Cedric's backside. With skilled motion, Fenrir ripped the wings free from their owner. As the wolf pranced away, the orgasmic peak of pain brought Cedric awake. Cedric jumped to his feet, filled with the adrenaline burning through his veins.

In the field, Fenrir paused, a sparkle in his eyes. Tightening his toothy hold on the dilapidated limbs, he wagged his tail, claiming them for his prize. Anger filled Cedric at the sight. The smell of his own blood engulfed Cedric's nose with its iron bitterness biting on the back of his tongue. A primal scream rolled out of Cedric's chest, ripping free from his lips. Blind with rage, he ran at Fenrir, who turned to face him. Leaping in the air, his hands clenched together high above his head, he came down on Fenrir with breathtaking power. His fists locked with Fenrir's skull, just above his eyes.

The jolt of the impact made Fenrir's jaw go slack, the wings plopping on the ground where Cedric landed. Standing, staggered and slumped over, Cedric glared at Fenrir through one squinted eye. He was fighting the sensations tearing through him, clinging to his anger above all the desires clawing at his soul.

I can't let the pleasures of pain override my will to fight back. It's going to get me killed before I can reach her again.

The wolf shook his head once, then twice. Fenrir took a wobbly step back. Blood began to pool and dribble down between his golden eyes, which fought the need to cross themselves. Huffing, Fenrir shook his head again and laid down in the dirt where the grass meadow had been earlier. Satisfied the fight had ended, Cedric collapsed to his knees. Leaning forward, he tried to catch his breath, staring down at the wings.

Furrowing his brow, he looked back up at Fenrir. "Was that necessary?"

"It was my trophy." Pawing at his head, he snorted. "I'm not sure if it was worth the headache you left me with, pup."

"How am I going to fly?" He fell to his side, exhaustion weighing down his eyelids. "I have no idea if I can grow *those* back."

Laying his head on his paws, Fenrir closed his eyes, also feeling the need to rest. "They always grow back. You incubus are like cockroaches... unkillable."

"How much longer will Wylleam be?" Cedric's chest rose and fell, slowing.

"Who knows..." groaned Fenrir before they both gave way to sleep.

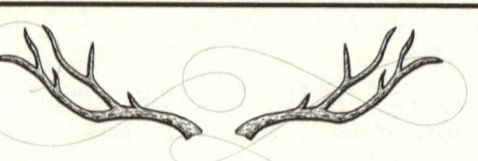

CHAPTER 2

THE REALMS OF AETHER

ANGELINE

Angeline shifted in the chair within the empty grand hall. When they had come through the gate, she had found herself without the rest of the group, greeted by Artemis and her band of female warriors. She had brought her there with a snap of fingers, demanded she sit and be silent. She looked around: a long table ran the length of the massive football field-sized building, making her dizzy each time she attempted to chase the walls to the farthest side. She once heard stories of the grand halls of the Vikings' gods and wondered if this had been what they spoke of. Someplace beyond the walls, birds sang, there was the muffled chatter of people, and there came the occasional bang she could assume from merchants moving or working close by.

This is a village in a wooded area, I assume. Reminds me a little of Raven's Den, just busier. Now where has that old hag scurried off to?

She looked at her hands. They looked foreign to her with their sharp claws, so much like Cedric's when he shifted into his demon form. Her head was heavy with the weight of horns, the aching in her neck building from the cumbersome sensation of keeping herself from tilting too far forward or backward. Her nerves were tight, making her breath tremble in and out of her lungs. Everything about her body felt … wrong. It was similar to how she changed after the battle with the busse, but she had no control in bringing back her human form. Worse, she was too far away for Cedric to help her. In her periphery, she dared not accept the newest feature, the one that had not made itself known in that battle.

Thinking about her new appendages, the towering shadow behind her ruffled. They started to stretch out, but her tension brought them close to her shoulders once more, like two bashful children hiding behind their mother, trembling. Feathers drifted to the floor at her feet and she swallowed. The feathers reminded her of the colors she admired from the wings of a Montagu's Harrier. The sea of matte silver feathers with robust black tips and lines rippled back toward her. *Wings.* She had somehow entered the Otherworld with wings, and something in her gut told her this would prove dangerous.

Am I not human? Was I ever human if this is what I am here in this world of spirits?

"I didn't expect this outcome for you." Artemis had a voice that demanded one's ears to listen. "To be honest, I may have only complicated my own situation with Gaea over the matter. To think the two of you would take in aether and absorb it so sufficiently is admirable ... and terrifying."

Artemis came through the open doorway and slammed it shut behind her with a flick of her fingers. Her face was obscured by a deer skull mask, but it didn't keep her fiery stare from burning through Angeline. She was dressed like a shaman from a time long forgotten. Skin and fur cloth did truly little to hide her sun-kissed olive skin. Her neck was adorned with an assortment of necklaces made of bones, fangs, and even colored stones. In her hand, she wielded a staff that reminded Angeline of the one she had seen Wylleam carry so long ago. Worse was her voice. She knew it, remembered that horrid whisper and laughter it had produced inside her childhood home when she had demanded she consummate her marriage.

How could I forget?

"What's the meaning of this?" Angeline mustered some bravery, knowing well she wouldn't bring her harm. "I imagine you have some demanding need or task for me to cull me from the others like this."

"Such spunk." The cackle rolled from her and she sat on top of the table beside Angeline. "You've come far, my heiress," she hissed, a wild grin peeking out from under the skull. "Welcome to the Otherworld."

Angeline glowered at her. "What did you do to me, to my body?"

"I did nothing." Artemis leaned back on her hands, swinging her legs like a small child. "This is an unprecedented side effect of your magic adopting his abilities, and it's quite marvelous."

"Cedric's magic?" Her heart fluttered. "But he has no magic."

"Come now, I expect you to be a little brighter than this, dear child." Artemis's hair fell down her shoulders in large dreads, beaded and threaded in the way of the ancient tribes. "Let me explain this with something that was lost to the mortal realm long before even I was born. Do you know the story of Aether and Gaea?"

Angeline flinched. She had heard Kronos, or Merlin, mumble the names under his breath. "They're the mother and father of Kronos."

"Ah, true." Artemis waved a hand in the air, a grand gesture of the hall they sat within. "Do you know where you are?"

"The Otherworld," Angeline answered. "The land ruled by Gaea, where faeries and spirits reside."

"Very good. Now, do you know why magic from the Mortal Realm acts so dramatically different here?" She motioned to Angeline's horns and wings, making Angeline reach up and gently run her fingers against the rough edges protruding from her skull. "Why your body has reacted so? Take your time. I prefer you to figure this out. Doesn't help if I always have to answer everything."

"You never give an answer to anything," remarked Angeline, her wings flaring in reaction to her frustration. *Cedric's impatience is rubbing off on me.*

Angeline's hands balled into fists, pressing against her thighs under the weight of Artemis's stare. Closing her eyes, she fought the urge to shout and scream at the witch. Instead of focusing on the riddle offered, Angeline's thoughts spiraled. All the things unfolding in her life, when Cedric first showed up at the castle, and Merlin ripping them apart, every cruel twist and burn had Artemis involved or to blame and there she was, tangible for the first time since the cackling skeleton in her childhood home. Her own father had followed Artemis's command without any regard for how she felt. *The only person I trust with my life, my heart and soul, is the least human creature on this godforsaken...* she bit her lip as if to silence the thoughts.

"You had this in you the whole time, since the first night you laid with him." Angeline's eyes shot up, only to be greeted by the satisfaction that Artemis had caught her attention. Artemis raised an eyebrow, curious, as she watched Angeline's demeanor shift. She had seen a glimpse of this at the beginning, back when her spell had been triggered in Raven's Den. There was nothing more she wanted but to see Angeline's timid nature shattered in order to let her come into her power on her own. Under the fear and uncertainty sat a caged tiger worthy of being a queen beside a king such as Cedric. They were the champions, fated to free the realm of Arcadia from Gaea's law and rule. The problem was one of them was too foolish to quell his temper and the other too slow to rise to the challenge set before her. "The whole time you were imprisoned you could have taken him down, freed yourself."

Angeline gritted her fangs, memories boiling up, the fog of what had happened to her fading. "Shut up..." she growled.

"I'm sure Kronos complained." She began pacing about, speaking in a mocking tone. "Or what was the new name he gave himself?"

"Merlin," she spat.

"Ah, that." Artemis paused, her back to Angeline. "A drop of blood would have banished him. All you had to do was ask Avalon."

"What?"

"A drop, on the book in the library." The tone seemed patronizing. "You only had to listen, to look with your eyes, to use that instinct you ignored so much about everything in your wretched life, girl."

"HE HAD ME IN A DUNGEON!" Angeline's voice shook with the weight of anger and hurt. "I was shackled to the walls."

"Walls that were trying to take you where you needed. Dig deep, you're the only thing keeping his memory spell in place. Show me you can break it here and now." She spun around, the glaring golden eyes hitting Angeline like a slap to the face. "You are my heiress. Now act upon it!"

"You make it sound as easy as breathing," hissed Angeline, tears sliding down her cheeks as her wrists throbbed with the memory of shackles that had marred them for centuries. "Where were you? Why not save me? Tell me, help me! No one came... no one... just my pleasure knowing Cedric was still with me somewhere, still looking. He has always been my only light, even as my lips were sewn shut. Where the fuck were you?"

Laughing, Artemis had sprung a hole in the dam called fear. "Tell me, little witch, were the shackles in the same place on the same wall more than twice?"

Flashes like lightning strikes hit her soul from all sides. The emotions brought her back once more. Angeline played through each moment she had been thrown in the dungeon cell. The darkness slammed upon her with the thud of the door, metal biting and cold against her wrists. With each flash, her eyes sought the chain. *Where? Where had the chain gone?* Her stomach twisted, and she rose to her feet in alarm. More memories and still not once did she see the anchor. A few times the chain had been rung through a loop but no anchor, no final place, not until... She turned to Artemis, her chest aching with fear.

All those centuries... I sat there in fear.

Artemis closed the gap and shoved Angeline down on the chair, her voice hissing in her ear. "When did Avalon let the anchor exist, Angeline?"

How did she know?

"Cedric." The heated tears were only adding to the despair breaking her. "Only when Cedric came..."

"That's right."

"Where... but Kronos... he was the master there."

"Excuses," Artemis scoffed.

"Avalon was under his control."

"Then why did it not cast out the others that day, girl?" Artemis began pacing, annoyed at how hard Angeline hid from the truth. "Look at it for what it was and is. Now tell me, who did Avalon serve?"

After a long, tearful pause, Angeline whispered, "No one."

"Who does it protect?"

"The innocent."

"And did it protect you? Did it not allow Cedric's magic to reach you and keep you alive? Food and water, anything that would allow you to keep going even for a minute longer?" More angry tears fell, and Angeline shook with rage. "Get angry. Now, inhale the air here and tell me why you are more than what you appear. Why has your soul flourished like it has?"

Angeline took in a deep breath, the air there thick and sweet with the smell of fruit and flowers. So much so, it brought a flavor across her tongue and she couldn't help but constantly swallow in response. Her wings shuddered as if excited about her deepened inhale. She paled. Once again, she inhaled deep and held it. Artemis had forced the knowledge into her before they even crossed into Delphyne's barrier with Badbh's spell. She had the ability to pick it all apart, to understand what no mortal should ever hold knowledge of.

"The air," mumbled Angeline.

"Precisely." Artemis slid off the table and walked around Angeline as she spoke. "Aether, the father of all things, was presumably dead. Ah, but this is the interesting part. Before Kronos could swallow his soul, and claim his father's powers and status as his known, they say Aether's body dissolved in the blink of an eye. This gave birth to new magic everywhere. There are many realms, and it reached beyond where even Gaea and Kronos could reach or fathom."

"Dissolved?" Angeline twisted. Artemis leaned on the table beside her. "A god's body vanishing? Soul and all?"

"That's right. Strange is it not?" Fingers gripped Angeline's shoulder, the deer skull brushing against her cheek as Artemis whispered, "He became ether, the essence of magic itself. In the Mortal Realm, it is the lightest, but provides magic on earth. Here, in Gaea's Realm, or more correctly, the Otherworld, it feeds all spirits and magic, so none find themselves weak or starved of magical energy. The Underworld is where his ill-will and anger reside, filling that place with a miasma like no other. Even there, a special kind of being and demons can thrive and feed off the dark ether in order to survive. Lastly, his goodwill and hopes are said to reside in the Heavens or Celestial Realm, but no one has seen or heard from a being from there in ages."

"W-why not?" Swallowing, Angeline could feel her heart racing.

"Rumor has it," Artemis's voice dropped lower, almost inaudible, "that Gaea, with the aid of Kronos, locked the gates in order to prevent Aether's second coming and rebirth."

"B-but..." Artemis let go, her back to Angeline who found the courage to speak up. "But why? Weren't they in love, Gaea and Aether?"

"Were, at one time." She spun around, her eyes glowing under the deer skull. "Gaea and Kronos both became bitter with greed and jealousy. Aether and many of his children had stepped down from their godly positions so that life in all realms could unfold naturally. You can imagine how the current queen and first heir to the earth would feel about this."

Wings flared out and Angeline demanded, "How do you know so much?"

A cackle came from Artemis before she replied, "I am Gaea's right eye until my brother, Apollo, returns it. Oh, wait, what's that boorish name he uses... ah, Romasanta."

"Then why kidnap me and not Romasanta?" Confusion rattled through Angeline. *None of this adds up.* "He has the eye."

"He does." She crossed her arms, towering over Angeline. "I'm very aware, but the issue is that my plans won't go well with you and Cedric sporting such powerful auras."

"Why is that a problem for you?" Every nerve tightened as Artemis leaned in, her eyes wild with amusement. "Isn't this what you wanted? Even commanded of me that day? To consummate my marriage in order for our powers to grow?"

"My dear child," Artemis leaned in, "if Gaea discovers I've been amassing an army to overthrow her, your life will end here, soul and body."

Dread filled Angeline, but it was dethroned in an instant. She lurched forward, breathless from a wave of arousal. Somewhere in this new world, Cedric was fighting. Gripping the edge of the table, her claws crushed the wood, splintering the grooves with ease. Sweat poured over her as heat rose from her core. Angeline's body buzzed with wanton want and she began panting. Another wave slammed her, and she shrieked in orgasmic delight.

"So the plan has moved to the next phase." Artemis's voice was stern as she pulled a blade from the sheath at her side.

"What..." Angeline struggled to catch her breath. "What are you doing?"

"We're just trying to take the edge off." Artemis spun the dagger in her hand. "They'll grow back, with enough time, that is. For now, we need to cut a large chunk of power off of you two."

"Cut!" exclaimed Angeline. "Cut what?"

"Just trimming the wings is all, love." At the very mention of them, they flared out in alarm. "My, and here I thought you were frightened of them."

I will not do this because she demands it of me.

Angeline pulled to her feet, still leaning on the table as sweat dripped off her chin. "Let me get this straight. If Cedric and I are going to be able to escape here alive, we need to do this, right?"

I will choose to do this for myself and our survival.

"I loathe repeating myself." Artemis took a step forward and the wings flared once more. "Look, they hold a lot of magical power within them-selves. If we can knock you and Cedric down a few pegs, it'll make it that much easier to hide your auras to appear as humans, or at the very least, the equivalent of a witch or low-level succubus. If Gaea sees this form, she'll know we've created gods outside her influence."

"Gods..." Angeline's stomach twisted at the thought. "I'm no god."

"And I'm not a daughter of a titan." Scowled Artemis. "They've got to come off."

Leaning farther onto the table, Angeline stretched them out. "Do it."

Again, a wicked grin stretched out from under the skull of the deer. Artemis gripped the first wing with a slight tug pulling at Angeline's back. The cool blade rested at against the back of her shoulder and she waited for what was coming next. Angeline's heart pounded ever faster, a mangled mess of elation from Cedric and the anxiety building. Artemis's fingers tightened, feathers snapping under her grip. The blade slid forward, cutting into the flesh with ease. A moan escaped Angeline and the euphoria of it all made her sick.

"I can't believe you're enjoying this." Artemis ground through the bones and the blade slid through the last of the flesh with ease. "These are heavy. I'm impressed."

The wing hit the ground with a thud. Angeline tried to catch her breath, but Artemis wasted no time to grab and slice into the next. Another arousing shriek escaped her, but Artemis kept sawing her way through bone, cartilage, and flesh. At last, another thud vibrated through the ground at Angeline's feet. She willed herself to look at the pair of bloodstained silver wings on the floor. She allowed herself to sink back into her chair, ignoring the pool of blood that waited there for her.

"What will you do with them?" Angeline muttered, covering her face as her arousal washed through her.

"Does it matter?" Artemis wiped her fingers across the blade, blood painting her fingertips.

"No, it doesn't." Inhaling deeply, Angeline could feel the warm ribbons of blood slowing their descent down her back. "What next?"

She turned and Artemis yanked her head back. Fingers slid across her forehead as Artemis chanted in a rolling growl, eyes glowing gold. It burned into her flesh and the pain of it soaked down to her core. Artemis let go and Angeline found herself screaming from the searing sensation exploding into her veins. She jerked to her feet, the chair toppling over. Inside her soul it was as if strings were being broken, forcibly cut off. It waned, and with it, she no longer could feel Cedric or his pleasure. She paled, gritting her teeth in anger. Before Artemis could react, Angeline landed a fist across the exposed part of her jaw and sent her stumbling back. Artemis's eyes were wild as she laughed. Blood dripped from her chin, Angeline's strength proving she still had power in her body and soul to fight back.

She dissolved our bond!

"Goodness!" She dabbed at the blood and rolled it in her fingers. "You're braver than I thought."

"What did you do to me?!" roared Angeline, marching for Artemis. "YOU BITCH! MY ENTIRE LIFE IS YOUR FAULT!"

A wave of her hand and Angeline found herself caught by vines growing at her feet. She managed to break a few before they tugged her to her knees. Anger poured from her, but she couldn't move as more piled onto her, wrapping around her arms to still her. Angeline's chest heaved. The grand hall had been filled with the smell of dirt and blood, adding to the visceral desire rattling through her.

"What did you do?" Angeline growled, burning her eyes into Artemis.

"I disconnected you two." She rolled her jaw. "It's temporary and will fade away when you two hook up, but it's to buy time and give enough training to counter the aether. Having you two in a magic-rich environment is a liability I don't want to deal with. If you're curious, that pain is almost as bad as the real thing."

Angeline spit across Artemis's feet.

"Such disdain for your beloved ancestor." Twirling her fingers, Artemis healed her chin. "Rest up because you won't have another chance. I'm training you in the ways of the old. At least the horns have faded. We might have a better chance of deceiving Gaea than I thought."

Another wave of Artemis's hand, and Angeline succumbed to sleep. The vines faded and her body thudded against the floor. With a whistle, two female warriors entered the hall, one with skin as black as night and the other pale as snow in moonlight. Seeing the blood and the girl sprawled on the floor, they looked at one another. Giving a worried look to Artemis, they both crossed their arms.

"Sorry, I didn't mean to make such a mess, Ying and Yang." She sighed, walking over to the wings and grabbing them. "Take her to my hut so she can rest. I'll take these with me. Send someone to ... scrub this place with a cleansing spell. I've heard a succubus's blood can leave a nasty curse if left untreated. Forgive me, Nuha and Manah."

"I thought this girl was your heiress?" Manah, the one with obsidian skin, helped her peer Nuha pick Angeline up by her arms. "What on earth did you do? Have you gone mad with jealousy so easily, Artemis?"

"Why does everyone assume it was me?" She was casting a spell to shrink the wings to the size of a songbird's wings. "You all make me out to be a villain of sorts."

"You were the only one with a weapon in here, Artemis," retorted Nuha, pointing at the still-bloody dagger. "And we all know a sapling of a witch has no chance against you. After all, you are a daughter of a titan."

"Go on with you. I am in no mood to argue with anyone of the clan of Kedar." And with that, Artemis disappeared.

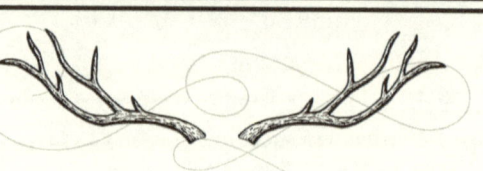

CHAPTER 3

BALL AND CHAIN

CEDRIC

Cedric came alive with a primal scream. His body burned to the core and he couldn't stop the strings of their bond from being cut one after another. Anger fueled him, but Fenrir's paw pressed him to the ground. He wanted blood, and demanded the witch's death as he cursed her name. Wylleam, Romasanta, and Nyctimus watched, unable to do anything as Cedric foamed at the mouth. He was as belligerent as a rabid dog.

"What's the matter with him?" roared Fenrir, the fur standing on end down his spine. "He's gone mad."

"Artemis." Wylleam's ears flattened and there was an angry curl to his lips. "I told her breaking their bond wasn't necessary, but she went through with it, anyway."

"My sister will not bend to anyone's will." The words were bitter as they fell out of Romasanta. "I hear it's the worst pain one's soul can endure. Many never recover from it."

"There's nothing we can do." Nyctimus sighed and took in the destruction around the cabin. "I see you had quite the fight out here. How long has he been seething like this?"

"Only a second before you left the cabin." Fenrir pressed down on Cedric, making him calm further as he panted under his paw.

"What happened to my meadow?" Scratching his chin, Wylleam gave an angry glare at the wolf.

Fenrir flattened his ears and his tail tucked between his legs. "We had some fun, but I think we got carried away."

Romasanta walked over to a chunk of flesh heaped on the dirt. He squatted, poking at it with the tip of his short sword. It was strange to have the need for a sword and proper equipment again. He had been a spearman and farmer long before he and Fenrir shared his body. He pulled a piece of the flesh upward, and it slid off the blade. Skin and bones were mangled into nothing more than fleshy mush. Romasanta furrowed his brow at the near gelatinous gob.

"What in the world is all this?" He stood, pointing with his sword at the ground while giving Fenrir a disapproving scowl. "Did you choke and cough up something foul?"

"That is my prize!" Fenrir wagged his tail and his tongue hung out of his mouth. Under his paw, he shifted his weight off Cedric. "It's proof I won."

Cedric rolled, coughing up blood. He glared at the wolf circling Romasanta. To imagine the two of them were in one body for centuries made his head spin. Wylleam squatted in his view and Cedric frowned. The look on the old cynocephali's face told him that he wanted to talk. Wylleam offered his hand, but Cedric shoved it away. He rose to his feet, eyeing the white wolf one more time before giving Wylleam his full attention.

"What's going on here?" He rubbed his chest, his body sore and healing from the crushing weight of Fenrir. "If I didn't know better, I'd think the old witch knew we were coming, and she's even got you by the tail."

Wylleam's ears flicked forward and he snorted. "She's had me by the tail longer than you've been around."

Cedric winced. "You're joking?" It wasn't the reply he had expected. *Though Wylleam always tells you the truth, you just have to know what to ask.* "Then what does the old hag want from me?"

"What she wants from you and Angeline is for the two of you to make it out of here alive." One ear flicked to the side and he looked distraught. "Romasanta must be the one to give Gaea the eye or all chances to free Daphne from where she is rooted will be gone."

"Right." Cedric had forgotten that Romasanta had waited for this moment to regain his lover far longer than he had walked this earth. *It makes my wait to get Angeline look like a joke.* "So, why the emphasis on Angeline and me? What's the matter?"

"Your auras." Wylleam inhaled, his fur prickling in places. "Your power, and even Angeline's, has grown exponentially. You are on rival with a son or daughter of a titan."

"That's why I was so big." Cedric looked down at himself.

He was smaller. Granted, still beefier than normal, he had lost some height and certainly wouldn't have to worry about banging his shoulders into trees anymore. His horns were still present, but nothing was too abnormal for a normal demonic creature. Cedric drew a deep breath and felt the surge; there was something about the air in this place that fed his powers in ways he never thought possible. He understood the allure of the Otherworld and why so many of the magical beings had fled the Mortal Realm to live and thrive there. Despite that, he would never want to spend his days there. Not like this.

"How do we cut me down to size or keep me there?" Cedric pumped his fists, the emptiness of the broken bond becoming painfully apparent.

"Well, Artemis had insisted on three things." Wylleam scratched his face as if nervous about announcing the list to Cedric. "I don't know how I feel about them, but it seems matters have taken their course, regardless."

Nyctimus patted Wylleam on the back, intruding into the conversation uninvited. "I'll clear the air then. First, it seems Fenrir saved us the trouble of convincing you to part with your wings."

"Right. Though without them, makes traveling harder." Cedric narrowed his eyes at Fenrir. "I could have found the old hag and Angeline faster with them."

"No, not with us four on foot." Nyctimus called a flame forward into his palm. "I still can use magic, so can your shaman friend, but it's not enough to defend against the creatures who live here. Many of them feed on human souls, which puts me and Romasanta at risk of becoming prey. We're humans. Nothing more, nothing less. We will need you and Fenrir if we are to make it to the Grand Hall on *Tir inna mBan*, or as some call it, the Isle of Amazonia."

"Right, and we have to be quick. Time there is skewed, though I imagine Artemis has cast a spell or resource to help with that problem." Wylleam motioned for Romasanta and Fenrir to come closer. "On *Tir inna mBan*, what feels like a year is actually several centuries in the Mortal Realm."

"What else do I need to do?" Cedric couldn't focus on the information. The coldness of his missing bond with Angeline's soul was driving him to do what would be necessary to survive.

"Artemis wanted wings clipped, bonds broken, and..." Wylleam paused, looking away in shame. "And if necessary, take a horn."

Cedric's brow folded. "If you want that, I can break it off myself."

"You idiot!" Laughed Fenrir, his toothy snout earning a sharp glare from Cedric. "They don't grow back. Not even a titan can grow one back once broken. The same goes for sinews and the likes. They contain too much magic."

Romasanta's eyes widened. "Lillith. She lost hers and it's been like that for centuries. Why is that? Don't they fight with them?"

"That's true." Nyctimus pondered on the matter. "I don't know what purpose it serves, but Artemis seems to think they contain enough power to make a difference."

Cedric's jaw twitched, burning the fact into his mind. "Then let's not get that desperate just yet. The wings are gone, and the bond broken. Since we're on foot, I should have plenty of time to work on bringing my aura down to a low-level incubus."

"You seem rather confident about that, pup." Romasanta gripped the satchel at his hip. "Know that more is at stake than just your life and desires."

"I know." Cedric hissed, brushing past them.

Not another word was said to him as he pushed inside the cabin and slammed the door. It was a carbon copy of Wylleam's cottage, and he sighed. There on the old trunk lay a change of clothes and a claymore leaned on the wall. It had been ages since he had wielded any kind of sword, but it would come back to him. *It always does.* He ripped away the last shreds of cloth from his body and welcomed the fresh sensation of clean clothes. Cedric disregarded the dried blood and dirt painting his skin. *I have no time to fret over a bath in a place so dangerous.* Grabbing the overgrown sword, he buckled the hilt across his chest and marched out the door with the same authority he had entered with. Once more, he took in who stood before them.

This feels like the battle against Morrighan all over again.

Romasanta wasn't a sword wielder, and it was obvious in the way he walked and handled the blade. He had spent too long as something other than human. The old wolf would be best for bringing up the rear for defense, but he could still see the path up ahead. Wylleam was a shaman, but it was difficult to know how well he could call forth spirits in a place where they lived freely. Nyctimus had magic, but in a forest, fire was a death wish. Cedric crossed his arms. He would be the front defense while Wylleam led the way.

"Let's go. Fenrir in the back, Wylleam and I will take front," he barked, eager to be on his way.

"Oh, we've taken the lead?" Nyctimus smirked. "Are we all okay with this?"

Romasanta narrowed his eyes, tightening his grip on the satchel. Another awkward and unbalanced shift spoke volumes of how useless and naked he felt in the Otherworld. "It's how I would have done it, considering the circumstances."

He's led us this far, but someone needs to shoulder it. I can't have him sacrificing himself again, so close to getting Daphne back.

Wylleam patted Cedric's shoulder before motioning for him to follow him down the path. Everyone fell in line, silent and on edge. They had worked out all the discrepancies. As they walked through the forest, Wylleam shared with them how the Otherworld worked. It was a cluster of connected floating islands, suspended by a heavy concentration of ether. Many of them could connect to the Mortal Realm in many ways, both intentional and accidental doorways like the one they crossed. All the legends of the faerie realm, the Amazonian Island, the lost city of Atlantis, the far shore, and even purgatory could be found on one or more Tir. The curious matter was each *Tir* had a ruler or guardian of sorts. Wylleam dodged naming the ruler of the current Tir. Many forest-based creatures lived there peacefully with an assortment of fae on *Tir na Nog*, the Isle of Youth.

It could be anyone if I think of all the legends. Galatea? Titania? Perhaps even Pan? Whoever it is, they are turning a blind eye to our passing through for some odd reason. I don't think everyone is bending to Gaea's will anymore, and that notion is dangerous.

"From here, we will be climbing the mountain-like pathway to the *Tirs* residing above us. Technically, we are the bottom *Tir* of this realm, and below us is the Underworld. That place derives off ether made of malice and dwells on miasma. We will need to attempt to go unnoticed through the *Tir Tairnigiri*, the Promised Land. From there, we can reach the *Tir inna mBan* where Artemis is keeping Angeline."

The forest gave way to rocky terrain, and they found themselves climbing a stairway, misplaced on the side of a mountain with no top. Time was a mystery in this new place. No sun nor no moon floated in the sky. The ether-rich air made it so no one felt the pains of hunger or thirst, even the pull of exhaustion and sleep were gone. A fog settled on the path, obscuring their view ahead. They slowed and Fenrir's nose twitched.

Cedric threw an arm out. "There's something ahead." *We both caught a scent at the same time, so at least I know we're going to detect enemies in time.*

He pulled the claymore free of its hilt, his arms aching under its weight. Nyctimus stayed close behind Cedric, a ball of fire providing some light. A shadowy figure of a bird appeared on top of the iron gates that read *Tir Tairnigiri. Heh, iron to keep the fae from traveling farther. Clever.* The fog thinned, and the gate opened. On the archway, a large osprey screeched. The falcon's large eyes peered down at them with curiosity. It was the size of a man, the loud white and brown pattern bright even in the dullness of the fog and its scent laden with magic. Squawking once more, it leaped off and disappeared in a curtain of white. Fenrir snarled and snorted at it.

"Something wasn't right about that," he gruffed. "That was no bird."

"Agreed." Cedric sheathed his claymore, relieved no battle had transpired. "The question is whether they were friend or foe, and why they opened the gate willingly."

"In this place, it's best to assume both." Wylleam pushed the gate open wider so Fenrir could fit. "Welcome to the next Tir, the Promised Land."

Cedric rolled his shoulders and pushed forward. As they walked steadily upward, the fog grew ever thicker. Soon all light was gone, and the world shifted around them in mysterious ways. *We must be crossing into the next Tir, officially.* The sounds of dripping water gave notice to the appearance of stalagmites. Before entering the gate, they had been on an open mountainside, but now they found themselves deep inside a cave as when they first came into the Otherworld. The fog faded, but the fire Nyctimus produced did nothing to take the chill and dampness away. Hours went by, cave walls making themselves known and narrowing to the point that Fenrir had a difficult time getting through. He would knock stalactites off the ceiling.

Wylleam insisted they keep up the pace, and soon they were rewarded with light pouring in through a large opening up ahead. They poured out, squinting at the new world they found before them. Unlike the tall, dense forest from before, this was gentle hills and meadows that wrapped around a large lake. Its waters were cerulean and at the center, a tower shot to the sky. This was the next pathway they would need to climb to reach the *Tir* that would take him to where Angeline was held captive. Cedric marched forward, but halted. He had no clue where to go or how they planned on crossing such a massive body of water.

Turning, he furrowed his brow at Wylleam. "You said we had to get through here unnoticed. I didn't ask why."

This is so far out of the normal for Wylleam. How dangerous is this?

Wylleam's ears flattened. "I can't say why."

"Rather odd reply," Nyctimus cooed, intrigued by the cynocephali's reaction.

"Trust me, it's in our best interest I keep this name to myself." He pushed past Cedric and pointed. "Not far from here, there should be the fishing village of Merrow. We should be able to gain a ride to the tower at the center of Lake Corrib from there."

"Merrow?" Romasanta smiled. "They still exist? They're not a fairy tale?"

"No. Nothing is ever as it seems. Shouldn't you know that by now?" Wylleam huffed, his ears flattened in annoyance. "Your sister may be Artemis, but I see you aren't as educated as she is."

"Ouch." Cedric chuckled.

"I spent a lot of time in the woods, so by the time I ventured to England and Ireland, they were gone." Romasanta dodged their eyes. "Legends say they eat human souls. Doesn't that mean Nyctimus and I will stand out?"

"You're not wrong on that note." Wylleam smirked, an ear flicking, "Considering we have Cedric and Fenrir, I may pass off as a servant and these two as mere snacks for their travels."

"You're joking, right?" Cedric scoffed. "They'll never believe it."

"Why not?" Nyctimus interjected. "They don't know you, you're a new power rolling in and the fact you two," he pointed a finger between Cedric and Fenrir, "could fight like you did and be intact, says volumes. Fenrir has always been feared as a god of the forest, so by default..."

"Don't even give me that ridiculous title." Anger flared in his green eyes and he pointed to Romasanta. "That man is the god among us. Do you not smell it? He's not human at all."

They all froze. Romasanta paled, rubbing the scar on his chest, still marked on his own soul, just as it did on his physical body in the Mortal Realm. Cedric's eyes cut across them all, searching their faces to see who agreed. He swallowed and turned to Fenrir. The massive wolf closed his eyes, inhaling deeply, he held it in his furry chest. His ears twisted back, and he stepped forward and drew air across Romasanta's body. Again, he held the scent within him, breaking it apart. Yellow wolven eyes shot open and fur stood on end down his back.

"Why didn't you tell me, farmer?" A pained expression came across Fenrir's face. "I knew of Artemis, but..."

"And you knew we were twins." Romasanta shot a glare. "I am more human than I am titan." All eyes weighed down on him once more. "Fine. I suppose I am far past keeping this secret. My true name, birth name, is Apollo, but it may be dangerous to use it here. Honestly, it's never been a safe name to use. Unlike a normal son of a titan, my sister inherited the magic two-fold, and I inherited physical prowess two-fold. Granted, it didn't do me much against Delphyne, now did it."

"Fine, but they should be able to tell you're not human." Nyctimus shook his head. "What a mess this little journey has become. Nothing is going according to plan. Artemis and her damn meddling. I suppose the question is whether a titan's soul is tastier than that of a human."

"I'm afraid it does mean you're tastier." Wylleam squatted, pondering over everything.

"It figures. I assume it's the same reason most mages went missing soon after the Middle Ages." Nyctimus scratched his jaw a moment. "Do they treat powerful demons and titans like royalty? Such as those traveling in an entourage?"

"Sometimes, what did you have in mind?" asked Wylleam.

"Well, humor me." Nyctimus cleared his throat. "Let's put Apollo on top of Fenrir."

Fenrir narrowed his eyes. "I am no horse, mage."

"I know, but this is only to get us through here." Rubbing his forehead, Nyctimus reasoned with the wolf. "It was either him or Cedric."

"Never." Fenrir and Cedric shot a look as they answered in unison.

"As I thought." Grinning, Nyctimus continued. "If the merrow are anything like the Soul Cages story, then it can be assumed they know the difference between human and titan to the same level as Cedric's vampiric senses. In this case, if we follow some of the old scriptures from my time as a human, we can easily claim we are taking me as a sacrifice to Artemis. As far as they know, Romasanta is just a son of Apollo or even Artemis herself. No one will question it, will they?" His eyes bounced from Wylleam to Romasanta. "One of you surely has an answer?"

"It should." Romasanta slumped his shoulders, defeated by his own heritage. "I'm willing to do that much. Granted, I would rather claim I am a son of Artemis."

"Ah, that would make more sense." Wylleam nodded as he stood. "Even if they demand some rite to prove it, we are able to do so with my connection on a spiritual level and yours as her twin brother. They may even allow us to cross the way with no payment. Many do this in respect to Artemis trying to win her favor."

"Ah, and, if we dare," nodding, Nyctimus grew excited with the plan, "we can simply ride on the coattails of truth. You are taking me to *Tir inna mBan* to see Artemis. Sometimes mermaids were known to be truth seekers, especially in the Shinto stories. We may run a risk of being caught if we lie."

"And there's the book nerd we know and love." Cedric started rummaging through the pack he was given. "What gives, Wyll? You didn't pack rope?"

"Rope?" He curled a lip at Cedric. "Why would we need rope?"

"To tie up our sacrifice," blurted Cedric. "We have to look like we mean it."

"Uh, rope on a fire mage would be a waste of time." Nyctimus summoned a small flame in his palm and snuffed it out in his fist. "What would they do to lock up a soul here, Wylleam?"

"I can cast something like a soul-linked chain, but I don't recommend it." Wylleam's ears flattened and his fur prickled.

"Why not?" Romasanta didn't need his werewolf senses to see the hint of fear building in the shaman. "What side effect is there?"

"Whoever you choose to be your ball or anchor, will be that for all eternity. You may leave, but the hidden tie will always exist between your souls. It's as powerful as a demon's bond with his mate, and as tenacious as a curse. You will always know where the other is, and what they are feeling." He gave the whole group a grave expression. "It's a forbidden magic taught to me by Artemis, but if you want to take this route, you need to decide who it will be."

She got to him... before all this... before we...

"That bitch!" Cedric grabbed Wylleam, his eyes wide with rage. "She wanted you to cast it on Angeline and me if we hadn't bonded yet, didn't she! DIDN'T SHE!"

Wylleam couldn't look him in the eye. He had exposed the one secret he had hoped to never reveal. Cedric shoved him to the ground, looming over him. His horns were curling tighter and larger, his body fighting against his will to grow no larger. Containing his powerful aura as something smaller was near impossible when his anger bested him.

Now's not the time to be angry. He would have told me before he would do something so drastic. He's not like Artemis.

Spitting on the ground next to Wylleam, Cedric spun on his heel and marched downhill. Fenrir and Romasanta moved to give chase, but Nyctimus stopped them.

"The decision lies with us. Let him walk it off." Looking over his shoulder, Nyctimus watched Cedric sink out of view. "We already know he wouldn't agree to this, so it's for us to decide on the matter."

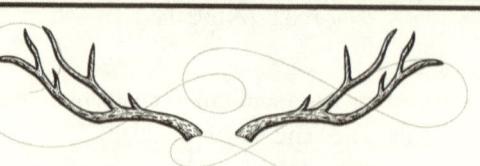

CHAPTER 4

INHERITANCE

ANGELINE

Angeline woke with a cold sweat covering her skin. Shivering, she sat up and held her arms for warmth. She had been put on a bed, but the room was bare of anything else and had no windows. In the center of the room was a brazier with a crackling fire and, above that, a pool of light came in from the hole at the center of the ceiling. She shuffled closer, feeling drained from Artemis's abuse. The heat of the fire was welcoming; Angeline squatted, staring at the flames dancing off the logs.

Cedric and I are no longer bonded. Why does this idea terrify me? Why do I feel so heartbroken over it?

There was a noise at the door, and she stood, facing it. After the events with Artemis, she didn't know whether to be at ease or ready to fight. The door handle turned, and it opened, slow and steady. Angeline relaxed. It was a servant of sorts with a goblet and plate full of bread and cheese. The young girl froze, staring at her as if frightened. Her light blue eyes sparkled like gems and the freckles adorning her face made her adorable even to Angeline.

"Is that for me?" Angeline's eyes fell on the items in the girl's hands, and she nodded. "Ah, thank you. I appreciate that."

Angeline offered to take them from her, but she squirreled around her. Turning, Angeline was thrown by the fear expressed toward her.

I thought I was being held prisoner, but...

A wooden picnic table had appeared near the brazier and the girl sat the items on it and motioned for her to sit. Hunger grumbling in her belly, Angeline complied. She took in the freshly baked bread and tangy cheeses. In the goblet she was pleased to taste a honey mead, something she thought she would never experience again in the modern era. The cold melted away and her anxiety settled.

"I see you still have your appetite." Artemis's voice shattered the sense of security she had earned. "Finish eating. Then I will start teaching you my craft."

Swallowing the mouthful of bread, Angeline glared at Artemis where she stood in the doorway. "I thought you passed on your knowledge?"

"I did." There was a hint of a smirk from under the deer skull mask. "But what good is it all if you've never used any of it? I admit, your talent with the bow is on par with my own, but you had formal training. The spell is meant to regain skills lost, but you still have to know how to use it, train to use it, and, more importantly, do so with confidence."

"The way you manage to insult and compliment me at the same time never ceases to amaze me." Angeline took down the last of the mead. She knew Artemis wouldn't have the patience to let her finish the meal. "Are we training in here or elsewhere?"

Artemis waved a hand, and the girl rushed out, slamming the door. "We'll start in here. The barrier should be enough to keep it here and not disturb others."

With a snap of her fingers, the bench and all items disappeared. Angeline fell to the floor, yelping with surprise. Picking herself up, she brushed off her hip and thighs.

"You could have warned me." Angeline gave her a disapproving scowl. "Or let me stand first."

"When we finish here," Artemis's tone grew dark and edgy, making Angeline's skin crawl, "you'll be able to prevent me from doing anything against your own desires. Granted, this will not be possible in the mortal realm where ether is far thinner."

A smile crept across Angeline's face. "If that's the case, what is the first lesson?"

"Blocking a magical attack." Artemis's eyes began glowing as a ball of fire came to life in her hand. "First, magic you can see."

Thrusting her fingers toward Angeline, the ball of orange flames launched out like an arrow from a bow. Angeline dove to the ground. The flames licked at her shoulder, singeing hair. Dust plumed into Angeline's face, but she rolled, instincts reeling. Another ball slammed the ground where she had been a second before. Crawling and scrambling, Angeline dodged the onslaught, trying to get back on her feet. Rage filled her and at last, she managed to produce her own ball and throw one at Artemis.

Does she mean to kill me?!

With her free hand, Artemis caught Angeline's fireball. Both hands raised, filled with boiling masses of flames. A wicked grin stretched out from under Artemis's mask and she cast them at Angeline. Angeline's attack had only given Artemis another weapon, and she was caught against the wall. Desperate, Angeline let instincts take over, like when she had fought Delphyne. Her arm swung out, not to bat or block the attacks, but in order to sling a shield made of water. The balls connected, sizzling and sputtering out against the water.

I'm in no mood to burn alive catching fireballs!

Artemis straightened her stance. She seemed pleased with the action. Angeline's temper was still raging. She twisted her wrist and balled her hand into a tight fist. The water responded, a spear shape forming. Flicking her fingers out, it launched toward Artemis. Cackling, Artemis stomped a foot on the ground and a shield of earth absorbed the water. Angeline's mind raced as if her eyes were flipping through the pages of an ancient book.

Ah! This might work! If fire can't beat water, water can't beat earth, then earth should be weak against...

Mumbling the archaic words, unsure what she was even saying, she twirled her hand upward and thrust it down toward Artemis. The earth shield fell, but Artemis crossed her arms. Silence fell. Nothing had happened. Panting, Angeline wondered if her lack of understanding the meaning of the words had been at fault.

"Do you even know what you're casting?" Artemis called her out; she knew Angeline wasn't aware of the words she invoked. "Tell me, do you know what element that spell is intended to bring into being? Who it summons?"

Well, I suppose this is part of learning.

Angeline fought the urge to close her eyes. "I thought I was calling... I thought it summoned..." She was searching for the word of a creature she had envisioned, but her knowledge of the non-human world was exposed once more. "Some plant person."

The ground shook and Artemis unfolded her arms. "You can't be serious. It worked? She's never..."

"I don't know what it's called," Angeline confessed.

"You summoned a dryad. Here, of all places." The roof came crashing down on Artemis.

Angeline's back pressed against the wall, her arms raised to shield her face from the debris. The crackling of tree branches urged her to look. There between her and Artemis stood a tree with a woman's face and figure tangled at its core. *Daphne?* It had woven a humanoid-shaped tree with branches extending from her legs and arms, living armor made to protect and destroy. The dust settled and behind the creature Artemis slumped, trying her best not to fall all the way to her knees. Her deer mask was gone, and blood dripped down the side of her face and over a squinting eye. She held one arm; the shoulder shifted forward, signaling it had been dislocated.

The creature looked at Angeline, then spun to face Artemis, confusion building. "Goodness, to think I was summoned here to fight you, Artemis."

"Hello, Hamadryades." Swallowing, Artemis waved her hand and snapped. "Yet when I summon you, I'm ignored. I see how it is."

"You serve someone unsavory, love." She withdrew her roots and branches, shrinking.

The roof pulled itself back together and by the time Angeline looked back to Artemis, her wounds were healed and her mask was in its place. *She looked so much like ... me.* The dryad retracted her bark armor and before them stood a wooden woman, naked, with hair made of ivy. She paced closer to Angeline, looking her over with her moss-laden irises and pursed her glossy sap-covered lips. A smile came across her wooden face and she paced back to Artemis.

"In all my years. This girl summoned me?" she demanded.

Artemis dropped to one knee, kneeling in respect to the dryad. "Indeed, she has, Hamadryades. Neither of us thought the spell had worked and well..."

Hamadryades spun back to Angeline.

Seeing Artemis's position, Angeline also dropped to one knee. "Forgive me. I cast a spell without understanding what it was, well, who it would summon. My sincerest apologies."

"I like her," Hamadryades announced. "Dear girl, you have tremendous power, but that's not why I was summoned."

"She's right, Angeline." Artemis's eyes glowed amber from under the deer skull. "This wasn't a normal circumstance at all. She is a powerful being and can pick what calls to respond to, otherwise summoning magic would be used to entrap many of us."

"Yes, you called for a dryad. Not me in particular." Hamadryades squatted down, meeting Angeline's eyes. "But, it's your past actions that decide whether I would be the dryad to answer the call to someone we trusted."

Angeline's brow folded. Closing her eyes, she confessed, "Forgive me, but I don't know who you are, exactly."

Laughter like the rustling of leaves in the wind filled the room, and Hamadryades patted Angeline's head. "We've watched you for a long time, my child. The way you treated Barushka, cared for the demonic knight despite your differences, and your valiant battle with the golden busse. The trees have watched you give it your all, put your life on the line for others even when all you had to give was your life. We were there when you held on to our branches as a chimera aimed to devour you. We witnessed the night when you stood tall against a horde of werewolves. We saw from the eyes of moss, the struggles you endured on Avalon. Angeline, the dryads know your name and we've waited a very long time for you to call us forth so we may be your sword and shield when you have none."

Angeline's chest ached, and she slid to the ground. Her hands covered her mouth as tears started to fall. *This whole time, I have never been truly alone.* Hamadryades's wooden arms, soft as silk and warm, wrapped around her. Angeline couldn't help but sob. All those horrendous moments, even the centuries of solitude, she only needed to reach out to the magic within her, to the world she was always part of and denied herself.

I have clung so hard to being human, but was my humanity the real reason for the person I've become?

She wrapped her arms around Hamadryades, burying her face into her shoulder. The memories poured over her. Without ever knowing it, the dryads had been watching over her and doing what they could to protect and push her battles in her favor. Pulling away, she managed to still her nerves, and she stood with the dryad. Artemis was still on one knee, silent and unmoved by the emotions and endearment passing between them.

"Is she one of yours, Artemis?" Hamadryades summoned three stumps and a wooden table. "Come ladies, join me for some tea." Flowers bloomed, their petals filled with floral tea as steam snaked into the air. "I want to discuss what my beloved Angeline is doing here, of all places."

Artemis tensed. "Yes, of course."

She sat to Hamadryades's left and waited as Angeline did the same to her right.

"She was here on a journey with my brother," offered Artemis.

"Ah, is this about poor Daphne?" She seemed cheerful, sipping her tea. "That child wasn't a dryad, but we took her in despite the fact she's rooted in one spot by Gaea. Horrible incident."

"Yes, they have Gaea's Eye and are traveling through the Otherworld as we speak." Artemis took up her cup, and after a pause, took her own sip. "Daphne's spell will be broken, but I suspect she will remain a dryad?"

"If she doesn't, she will have to forfeit her life. Gaea is cruel in that way. The poor thing wouldn't be like that if it weren't for... never mind that." A sigh escaped Hamadryades. "So, who are *they*?"

Artemis looked at Angeline, who put her cup down to answer. "It was Cedric, Romasanta, and Nyctimus."

"And you?" Hamadryades finished her cup and the petal tea cup faded away. "Artemis, why didn't you bring the others with you?"

"I was commanded by Gaea not to interfere with *my brother's* journey." Artemis's voice fell flat, and Angeline choked on her tea. "As you very well know, Hamadryades, as the current Eye of Gaea, I can't leave here."

"Ah, but aren't you interfering by having Angeline here and not with Romasanta's party?"

Silence fell across the room. The moss irises were burning with anticipation as Artemis's own eyes glowed yellow. Finishing her tea, Artemis still said nothing more. Angeline opened her mouth, but Hamadryades lifted her tea to her lips, insisting she keep drinking. The glow in Artemis's eyes faltered, and she leaned forward on the table as if drunk. She muttered under her exhale. Angeline tensed, the tea warm in her own belly now suspected as something more than simply tea.

"I would curse you over this trick, Hamadryades." Artemis hissed, anger seeping into her voice. "This is a foul trick you play. It could cost me my life and hers."

"And I can say the same for you. I'm not a child of Gaea, and don't have the shackles of her law to abide by, but my life can be in danger just the same." Hamadryades's green, ivy hair shifted into fiery, red leaves of maple. "Why would you disobey your master and bring this child here?"

"The war." Artemis fought herself and the magic in the tea. "She is my heiress and therefore, my responsibility to protect. I can't say much more. Not until my contract with Gaea ends."

"Ah, I see. This explains a lot of what we've been seeing unfold these centuries." Hamadryades turned to Angeline, who sat empty-handed and afraid. "Angeline will need your aid, but can you really teach a child in this manner? Through fear and abuse?"

Angeline bit her lip, glaring at Artemis. For the first time, the old witch looked helpless.

"I suppose things are complicated when you're the prisoner of Gaea, aren't they, Artemis?" The dryad's words hit heavy.

"And I suppose I'm getting more desperate. Kronos has gained a new power, and she aims to do nothing about him." Artemis aimed to stand, and Hamadryades motioned for her to sit down once more.

Clasping her hands on the table, Hamadryades turned to Angeline with a frown. "She can't even speak for herself nor take certain actions without daring to come under Gaea's wrath. Artemis came here in search of her mother, Phoebe, only to find she was missing. Why and where she went, no one in the Otherworld seems to know and she's even been able to dodge our presence. Part of us fear that Gaea has done something to her, but regardless, we hope she went to seek aid against Gaea's tyranny. It was at that time, Gaea chained Artemis to this world to serve in place of her missing eye, which she had gifted to aid her son in the Mortal Realm. Thus, I'm sure Artemis has been trying her best to do what she can to aid her brother without breaking the stipulations Gaea has placed on her."

"Don't say another word. It's my business, Hamadryades," Artemis growled, her eyes golden under the mask, reminding Angeline of Romasanta's. *Like the eyes of a wolf.* "The less she knows, the safer she will be from this. I need to make sure she makes it back to the Mortal Realm in one piece."

"I understand this," hissed Hamadryades. "You're such a child at times. Angeline, while you are here, let me bestow upon you a weapon." She placed a hand on the table and vines twisted to life across it. "You prefer the bow, yes?"

"Yes. I've had the most practice with that and a dagger." Angeline watched in wonder as the shape took place, the wood the color of jade and artful in its own abstract ways. "It's gorgeous."

"Use magic arrows here in the Otherworld." Hamadryades was standing and Artemis pulled herself from the table. "Magic is the only certain way to fight; leave brute force to the demons. Only they have the blood to compete on a physical level."

Angeline fell silent, glaring at her own hands. *But this shape I took on. With Cedric's blood in my veins, aren't I every bit of a demon as he?*

Artemis paused in front of the door. "She's right. Leave Cedric to be your shield and you must be his sword. He's unkillable, whether he is fully aware of that or not. You, on the other hand, not so much." With that, Artemis left, slamming the door behind her.

"Don't let her scare you." Hamadryades's elegant tea party had vanished, and she turned to Angeline, kissing the top of her head. "You are blessed, don't forget that. Be safe, and learn what you can while Artemis is able to teach you."

Like a plume of pollen, she was gone. Angeline stood in the dark room, alone. Looking around, all signs of the furniture and brazier were gone. She looked to the door, but was unwilling to leave. She was drained, from using her magic and the whole mental game that unfolded between a dryad and her unsavory ancestor.

This whole time, Artemis has been trying to leave this place and still aid her brother.

Closing her eyes, she wanted to sleep. She missed the days when she called Cedric's manor home. The four-post bed with the lion's claw feet and the warmth of a fireplace. Despite all the convenience the Modern Era brought, it was that room and time where she felt most at home. She mumbled the enchantment, her heart racing.

Please, work.

Opening her eyes slowly, her heart ached. Her magic had brought every detail she could recall back to life in the hut. She sat the bow down on the chest at the foot of the bed and walked around. The blankets felt no different from what she remembered all those centuries ago. She gave way to desire, letting herself fall face down across the bed. Pulling herself onto it, she curled into a ball, bringing the blankets and pillow to her. Tears were staining them as she pressed them tight against her face and inhaled.

They smell like Cedric, just like back then.

Her chest ached. She missed him, bad temper and all. She wanted to stand beside him through this journey, and she had failed to do that much. The void where their bond had been stung, and she let her despair rock her to sleep. The nightmares of Avalon would be back, her memories slowly coming back to her and adding to the despair of knowing she could have rescued herself.

If I ever find myself in Avalon, I know what to do. I know I always have options.

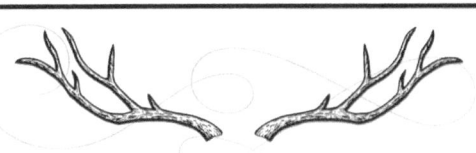

CHAPTER 5

MERROW-FOLK

CEDRIC

C edric had marched straight into the Merrow village without the others. He couldn't shake the sense of betrayal gnawing at his core. He walked down the main street, the village no different from fishing towns of old in the Mortal Realm. The difference was the lack of anyone who looked remotely human or had the scent of being human. Here, they looked similar to people of the mortal realm besides their jagged teeth, jet-black eyes, and webbing on their clawed hands; they were indeed merrow-folk. They paused, all glaring at him as he sashayed through town like he was one of them. A grin crept across his face and he held in the laughter.

I bet Romasanta is thinking he's going to march down here and see half-naked women with fishtails.

He made his way to the docks, and there he could see how far and wide Lake Corrib stretched across *Tir Tairngiri*. The breeze was cool and salty like the ocean, and it seemed strange. A saltwater lake seemed misplaced even here in the Otherworld. From the docks, level with the horizon, the tower at the center of the lake seemed more menacing. Cedric broke his admiration, as the growing heat of unwanted attention irked him. Black eyes from nearby sailors were digging into him and he sighed. They were starting to go on alert, so he turned to a ship where one group muttered in the Gaelic tongue.

"I need to get to the tower." He pointed to the center of the lake. "Is there anyone here who can take me and my group across?"

"Aye, but not us," one answered, scratching his beard and puffing on his pipe. "You'll need to ask Captain Coomara. He's the only crazy one among us willing to take strangers across to the Island of Apples, *Emain Ablach*."

"Right, that place. Of course, stranger danger," scoffed Cedric. "Where is the old coot?"

"Not here," snickered a younger merrow. "I imagine the old salt dog is in the Mortal Realm having tea with his wife."

Cedric's temper flared and with it, horns grew larger, curling tighter. "I'm in no mood for games. When will he be back?"

The laughter had ceased, and fear filled them as the old sailor confessed, "He'll be here soon enough. He never takes long. Fishing is dangerous in the Mortal Realm, even if you're setting up soul cages by the ports."

"Is there any other way to get there?" Cedric eyed them, making it clear he wasn't amused. "Is there any other option to reaching the tower?"

"You could fly there if you had wings." The young merrow's response only added insult to injury, making Cedric's shoulder blades ache. "That's how most of the big brutes pass through here."

"Is there anyone else who can get us across the lake?" blurted Cedric.

The merrows looked at one another, speaking in Gaelic before the third merrow, with one, white eye, spoke. "You can ask the king. Though he may ask a request or some task of you first. It can be dangerous making a deal with him."

Pondering a moment, Cedric looked back at the hillside where he had left the others. "Sure, let's do that. Who is the king and where can I find him?"

"King Manannan mac Lir." They grinned amongst themselves, excited Cedric had chosen this option. The white-eyed merrow relinquished the information with excited haste. "He's probably caught a glimpse of you by now. Just head out to an open field and call his name. He'll come to you. He's good like that."

"Manannan." Cedric thought about the name. *Where do I know this name from?* "Right, I'll do business with him then."

Besides, if I win favor over this Tir's leader, perhaps it'll only make the journey easier.

Cedric turned to leave, but the young merrow called out to him. "Stranger! I must warn you, the task will not be easy."

"Trust me, my journey to get here hasn't been a cakewalk either." He spat at their feet and left without hearing another word from them.

Marching back out of the village, he aimed to travel east of the hill where he had left the others behind. If they were going to keep secrets from him, he couldn't trust them to make the best call here. At least, not the best decision for what he wanted and aimed to achieve while in the Otherworld. As Cedric marched through the trees, he pulled his anger to a calm only to get angry again. In the hum of the forest, not much different from the woods he played in as a child, his thoughts reeled. Every little mistake, every moment he had failed to grasp a clue, beat against his mind and risked him losing this semi-normal form. Despite the rollercoaster of turmoil, he was still having far less trouble now reigning himself in than the night Lillith dragged him out of the bedroom and he shuddered.

It used to be so easy to snuff my emotions out, or was it always this easy before I struggled to decipher my emotions from Angeline's? How far out of focus have I been since her return? I get it now, Romasanta. You're right, I hadn't realized the impact she had on me mentally and, now, it just makes me angry. How can I help her with the trauma, with the past, if I can't tell who the emotions are coming from anymore? Then there's that. Yes, those pains...

Swallowing, he shuddered again. Lillith's glare had been burned into him with its sadness and pity for him matched equally by her rage. He had been dense, but looking back, he realized what it meant. Nausea rose in him. He dare not speak or think his fears. Not until he got her back from Artemis, so he could ask Angeline what he had avoided. The scar, the sensations, the timing; his chest burned with anxiety.

There's a chance Kronos's memory spell might not have hold in this place. It could break with simply a question, or perhaps even Artemis could do something nice for a change. Heh, but would releasing that memory really be so kind? Kronos distorted the physical body, not the spirit. Here, both of us are no longer tied to the physical or Mortal Realm.

The trees opened up into a small opening. At the center sat a boulder, as if the empty circle and forest bordering it had been planned. A shadow flashed across his face, drawing his eyes skyward to a giant osprey overhead. It circled him for a moment and dove down to land on the gray perch. They locked eyes, the bird tilting its head, chirping with curiosity as he stood unflinching. The wings opened, the tips rising high in the sky as it screeched. Again, Cedric did not flinch.

The orm was more impressive than this.

Snorting, Cedric could smell the magic, the fact this was no bird as feathers ruffled. "Are you King Manannan mac Lir?"

The bird huffed, its posture going lax, and it spoke in a deep Gaelic accent. "Aye, though I rather be called Wizard Manannan, or Manny for short."

Cedric sucked on his cheek a moment, realizing why the name had struck him. "A wizard," he echoed flatly.

Tilting his head, the osprey Manannan took in Cedric's reaction. "You've met one of my kind before? Perhaps a magus even?"

"No magus or magi. And I hope I never do." Cedric narrowed his eyes, annoyed at how the wizard hadn't bothered to turn into himself. "Not sure if you can really call Merlin a wizard. He's just a titan throwing a centuries-long tantrum."

"Ah, but Kronos is the titan of chaos and destruction, is he not?" He began preening a feather or two, a bird equivalent to straightening a tie or coat. "And considering there are only three magi in the mortal realm, I suppose I hoped for too much."

Now Cedric's curiosity peaked. "And what does a wizard want with a magus?"

"I have a problem." He stiffened, feathers ruffling again. "A dragon problem."

A wicked grin slid across Cedric's face. "Which one?"

"You! You have met a dragon in battle and lived?" He fluttered off the rock and began wobbling in a circle to take in Cedric. "Aitvaras has been a nuisance for quite some time now."

"Oh yeah? Ha." Cedric's skin crawled with excitement. "Is that not the dragon Fenrir and Romasanta killed?"

"Ah, so that's who sent him back to the Otherworld!" In a blink of an eye, he was a man.

The purple-tailed coat, brown vest, silky green shirt, and golden-rod-colored pants reminded Cedric of Pasco's *Weeping Woman* and he understood how she felt at that very moment. With a huge ostrich feather in his cavalier hat, he was still eyeing Cedric from head to toe as if a man betting on a racehorse.

I suppose if you are going to make a deal with someone, at least make sure they might have what it takes.

His cape fluttered in the breeze and he spoke at last. "And who might you be? A friend of this dragon-slayer Romasanta and Fenrir, I hope."

"Yeah, you can say we're friends for now." Cedric seized the opportunity. "But I'm a dragon slayer as well."

"Oh? Well, who did you face?" A sparkle glinted in the wizard's eye. "Was it a dragon king or Cadmus, perhaps? Or have you faced an orm or pack of wyverns before?"

"I have faced many orm and a pack of wyverns. As for the dragon, her name was Delphyne." The wizard paled at the name and stumbled back, leaning on the boulder. The reaction pleased Cedric and he grinned. "What's the matter, wizard?"

"Dear boy, did you say Del-Delphyne?" Again, the look of weighing everything he was sent a chill across Cedric. "Is that how..."

Cedric narrowed his eyes, waiting for the response. *Could it be it hadn't crossed his mind I'm not here because of death?*

"You can't possibly mean..." Manannan stroked his pointy beard, his eyes glowing with a hint of magic. "You've not truly passed on yet, have you?"

"No. I'm alive and well." Cedric threw out his arms, cocking his head. "Or shall we just say I'm between worlds?"

"Then you passed through Gaea's gate." His eyes darted right and left, reading his thoughts a moment before speaking. "That's why you need passage to the higher *Tirs*, but for what purpose, I wonder?"

Memories of his palm seared by the Eye of Gaea made Cedric swallow. "I'm here to aid Romasanta on a quest. One that Gaea herself has tasked him with doing, though the manner of things seems hard to say if she meant to test him or send the poor man on a suicide mission intended to fail from the start."

"I see, Romasanta." He flashed out of existence and reappeared sitting on the top of the rock. "Is he the man traveling with you and Apollo?"

Cedric tensed. *He's been watching us since we entered his realm.* "Apollo?"

41

"Yes, dear boy, Apollo, the cynocephali, Fenrir, you, and Romasanta is the fire mage, I presume?" Cedric snorted, shaking his head with a smirk.

"Apollo and Romasanta are one and the same." Cedric corrected, seeing confusion build on the wizard's face. "Trust me, he kept that secret for a very long time until it no longer could be kept. The fire mage is Nyctimus from the Lykaon tribe from the days of Arcadia."

"Fascinating," breathed the Wizard.

"So, Manny." Cedric rubbed his neck, having wasted enough time and relinquishing what little information he was willing to reveal. "You have a dragon problem?"

"Ah, yes, I do." He broke from his thoughts and smiled, that blue glow rising in his eyes again. "It should be here soon. You see, I've made him rather mad and until today, I'd kept myself an osprey to mask my scent."

"And which dragon is it?" Cedric visibly tensed, wondering how much time they had left.

"Aitvaras, son of Delphyne." He flinched as Cedric broke into laughter.

"What are the odds?" Cedric snorted at last, the sound of trees rustling and rumbling in the distance. "And it seems he's on his way."

"Oh yes, here he comes. Do you need any assistance?" Manannan raised an eyebrow, entertained by the confidence Cedric carried. "Without your companions here to help, will this prove difficult?"

"Who knows?" Cedric shrugged as the ground shook with the weight of something fast approaching.

I need to let some steam off. Sparring with Fenrir was fun, but I'm itching to kill something. It's been too long since I've given way to my blood lust.

A shriek filled the air, and birds and flying creatures fled the trees from every direction. Aitvaras had caught the wizard's scent. Cedric cracked his neck one way, then the next. He stretched his shoulders back, the shoulder blades still sore from where Fenrir had ripped away his wings. Bitter thoughts flared. *Damn that wolf. I could have used them in this fight.* Inhaling deeply and slowly, he caught the hint of reptilian sweat and sulfur. It wouldn't be long before his aim would bring the dragon to the tiny field among the trees. Manannan started whistling a tune and Cedric spun back to him.

"What in the hell did you do to piss him off?" From Romasanta's story, the few parts he had cared to take in, he recalled how calm Aitvaras had been with him and Fenrir.

"A wager," he replied, straightening his vest and flicking something from his shoulder. "Quite the sore loser, that one."

"What kind of wager?" Cedric could smell the fresh scent of broken trees, the crackling sound growing with the quaking at his feet.

"That he would be too full after he ate a particular pig to even bother to eat me."

It all came rushing to him. *That's right!* "Wizard Manannan mac Lir. Holder of an invisibility cloak, shape-shifter extraordinaire, and once fed an entire village on a single pig. Granted, it's only rumors that I've come across about you."

Manannan stood on the rock, taking off his hat, and bowed deeply toward Cedric. "I see my reputation precedes me."

"It's an old story in the Mortal Realm, not many know it like they once had in the dark ages." Cedric chuckled. *The brass of this one!*

Before either of them could speak, a deer burst through the trees and ran past. The wake preceding Aitvaras's arrival had begun a parade of panic. The chattering of animals drowned out the shrieking dragon still yet to be seen. Squirrels, rats, and other small rodents came washing over the field, rushing past like flood waters. More deer alongside boar and other strange creatures came belting across the expanse. They paid no heed to the strange men, who remained unmoved. When the rush of animals had cleared, the grass and flowers of the little opening had been destroyed other than the small patch under Cedric's feet. The ground came to an eerie calm, the shaking stopping.

"Are you sure you can handle this alone?"

Cedric lifted a hand, waving off the notion.

Through the darkness between the scores of tree trunks, he could see a faint glow of red. The dragon had rattled the whole area in his rage, but now, with his target in sight, he became stealthy. Aitvaras crept closer, the red eyes growing larger. Cedric cracked his knuckles, but the dragon didn't react. The trajectory of his stare locked onto the wizard who straightened his hat and sleeves, like a canary pruning itself, unaware of the cat about to pounce.

Cedric groped at his hip and cursed under his breath. It was a habit to go for his longsword or katana to gauge an opponent, but Delphyne had destroyed his weapons. Worse, he had shed the claymore when he stomped off. Grunting, his skin crawled with excitement. His fight with Fenrir still lingered in his tendons and his body was lustful to experience it all over again. *This will be a dangerous game.* The dragon's eyes disappeared, and Cedric searched the darkness for movement or a hint of red. The dragon's scent was overwhelmingly sulfuric at a short distance and left Cedric's ability to sniff out his location impossible.

"Head's up." Cedric spun at Manannan's words as he flashed off the boulder and was gone.

Aitvaras had taken flight and came diving into the opening. The silence and stealth had caught Cedric off guard; a stark contrast to how he had built up his approach moments before. A heap of black scales smashed headlong into the boulder. *He was aiming for the wizard.* The massive rock exploded into a thousand pieces under the force of the dragon's attack. Rocks pelted off Cedric's back as he turned away to brace against the onslaught of debris. Aitvaras was every bit as destructive as his mother Delphyne, and Cedric grinned. The dust began to settle, and Cedric stood before the glaring black dragon. Unlike in the Mortal Realm, Aitvaras's sight and sense of smell were keen here in an ether-rich environment.

"Out of my way, halfling," he hissed, his mouth opening wide to hint the heat his fire breath could bring. "Stand down or I shall gobble you up with the wizard!"

"That's a shame." Cedric's frown deepened as he shifted to reveal fangs, claws, and horns.

It took an abnormal amount of willpower to keep his size to this manageable height and weight. He needed a form he would be more comfortable and familiar with in order to fight, so he aimed for the physique he knew best. Cedric's tail swiped back and forth with his frustration. *How annoying to have to think so much over this.*

"I was hoping to challenge you, Aitvaras."

The dragon rocked back, sitting up on his hunches as he cocked his head. "What a strange creature you are. I have met shapeshifters, but they always have a hint of animal in their scent. You are something new yet old."

Cedric creased his brow. "And what is that supposed to mean?"

"You were a halfling a moment before." He inhaled deeply, his nostrils whistling with the force. "And now, you are a full-blooded incubus on par with a King Incubus. How strange."

"I am the King Incubus." He spat at Aitvaras's feet, who hissed in response.

"You disrespectful pig!" Teeth snarled at Cedric, a reptilian tongue flickering at him. "Do you know who I am?!"

"The son of Delphyne," Cedric replied coolly, catching the dragon's attention. "The dragon that I slayed to gain access to the Otherworld."

Cedric's tongue still lingered on the last syllable when Aitvaras launched himself forward. He was smaller than Delphyne, but just as foreboding. Snapping jaws came flying toward Cedric in a flurry. Swooping his arms in, Cedric took a chance to wrap himself around the dragon's snout, forcing the jaws to stay closed. He gritted his fangs, his thoughts spinning in a panic. *I may have quelled fang and fire, but now what? How can I possibly do damage and hang on? He's much bigger than Fenrir...*

Aitvaras shook his head, and, sitting up, his claws rose to pluck Cedric from his snout. It was a poor start. A long claw dug in between ribs on Cedric's left side and another curved over his right shoulder to pierce his chest. With a hard yank, pain and pleasure struck Cedric, and he forfeited his grip. His body went sailing, bouncing and knocking between trees before hitting the ground.

Inhaling deeply, Aitvaras roared. "How could an imbecile like you ever defeat my mother?!" His words shook the air, his anger rising.

Pulling to his feet, Cedric marched back to the opening to stare down the red, gleaming eyes. He reached down, grabbed a rock, and flung it with all his might. Aitvaras didn't flinch. The rock connected and Aitvaras cringed with a shriek. The dragon had misunderstood the action, the aim. Cedric grinned.

I need an advantage. One eye down should create a sufficient blind spot to give me some openings.

"You cretin!" Aitvaras roared. His claw fell away from his closed eye and blood teared down the side of his snakelike face.

Cedric ran forward, but Aitvaras threw out his wings and with a single thrust sent a wall of dust and dirt between them. Halting, Cedric ducked down, listening. The ground vibrated, but unlike the orms he had faced, he couldn't tell the direction the large dragon stepped. Inhaling, he took in the earth-laden air and there he could smell sulfur and reptilian blood. A flash of fire lit a portion of the dust before another huge gust sent the curtain of dust thicker and taller. The sunlight dimmed and another flash from the other side of Cedric roared bright before dying out.

He thought he could gain an advantage by blinding us both.

Curious to test Aitvaras's sense of smell, Cedric dug claws into the palm of his hand. The moment fresh blood met air, a ball of dragon's fire came barreling in his direction. He sprinted to dodge, the heat licking at him as it exploded where he had been squatting a second ago. Grabbing rocks, he smeared them with his blood and tossed them to the right of the dragon. Another flurry of fireballs aimed at where they landed. Cedric ran forward in Aitvaras's direction. It would be his good side and he'd have a chance of being seen, but he had to see how much the dust blinded his opponent.

The sun penetrated the curtain of dirt just enough to make out the black bulk of Aitvaras when Cedric closed the gap between them. Another toss of a bloodied rock caused an intriguing reaction. The dragon's head had spun in his direction the moment his palm opened and released the rock from it. Instead of locking on Cedric, the head followed the rock, releasing a stream of fire to follow its flight. In the glow of it, Cedric saw why.

The fool closed both eyes! He can't use all his senses at once!

A wild grin grew on Cedric's face, and he ran alongside Aitvaras from tail to neck. He leaped, his right claw aiming for his prize. Sulfuric blood splattered across his face as he pressed his fingers down and into Aitvaras's eye socket.

"If you aren't going to use it, then I'll take it for myself." The dragon stumbled back, shocked.

His weight shoved him into the very hole he had left behind from the boulder. He rolled to his side, only making Cedric's task easier, more leveled, and balanced. His fingers cupped under the eyeball, confident he had palmed it, he yanked back. The slurp and pop of the attached muscles sent excited chills through Cedric. Fearing another encounter of claws as Aitvaras roared in pain, Cedric leaped off and away. The dragon rolled and thrashed, his claws holding his face as his tail whipped about, wild and frantic.

Cedric opened his palm, the eye growing smaller until at last the flesh dissolved to ash. He blew it away, leaving behind a red and orange gemstone like a blood-stained opal. He thumbed it, rolling it around, the power in it hot in his hand. Aitvaras's cries had stopped. Like a Komodo dragon, he was crawling his way out of the crater, blood streaming down his face on both sides like tears of blood. Cedric held the gem up, letting the sunlight hit it and it looked like frozen flames. The cloud of dust was settling, sulfuric dragon's blood rendering anyone's sense of smell useless.

"COWARD!" wailed Aitvaras. "Come back and fight me!"

"I haven't gone anywhere," mused Cedric.

The dragon froze, realizing Cedric had stood there, waiting and watching. His heartbeat was loud in Cedric's ears, speeding up with each passing second. The satisfaction of killing the dragon's will to fight fueled his smirk.

"I'd heard stories about gems made from dragon and demon eyes, but this is the first I've ever encountered obtaining one."

Aitvaras hissed. Left with only his ears, he lashed out. "How dare you steal my sight for your entertainment!"

The swipe was shy of its target, and Cedric laughed before answering. "Oh no, not entertainment. I go for the eyes often, but I wonder why this time was different?"

Anger biting at his soul, Aitvaras pounced in Cedric's direction. He was too large to dodge him, and Cedric readied for the inevitable impact. A heap of black scales came down on him, but he had overshot. With Aitvaras's soft underbelly landing across him, Cedric rammed horns and a claw into the dragon, unwilling to drop his newfound trinket. Warm blood poured down over him, hot like fire, and steam rolled out of his gut. With another mournful shriek, the dragon rolled away, no longer able to stand.

Licking the blood from his fingers, Cedric could feel his wounds healing. The aching in his ribs, the stinging in his lungs, and the open puncture in his chest faded. His green eyes gleamed with pupils sharp as a cat's. Walking with uncanny calm, Cedric stopped at the edge of Aitvaras's snout. He was breathing shallow and fast, death coming slow and agonizing. Squatting there, the dragon had started so intimidating, but now looked pitiful.

"You should have given up," Cedric mumbled, earning a curl in Aitvaras's lips. "Your mistake was blinding an opponent and yourself without knowing who you were up against. You depend on your sense of smell too much. Did you not learn anything from your last death?"

"Romasanta was a trickster," hissed Aitvaras.

"He's a tactician," corrected Cedric. "The tricksters are Manannan and Pan. Romasanta and Fenrir, those two will go into a battle knowing there is no way they are going to live and walk out by the skin of their teeth because of their wit. They use every ounce of experience and knowledge. I've seen Romasanta look a hundred moves beyond an enemy days before meeting them and not knowing what he's facing."

"He's a coward!" Aitvaras tried to lift his head but failed. "A COWARD!"

Cedric punched his snout, silencing his rebuttal. "A coward doesn't sacrifice himself time and time again for others! I've only done that for one other person in my life. You, you're something vile that feeds off the greed of mortals, so how do you know what anything beyond cowardice looks like?"

Dust blew up around them as Aitvaras's breathing grew anxious, his heart beating faster.

"That man went against the Mother of Dragons knowing very well he wouldn't see the end of that battle."

Chuckling built up in Aitvaras and he pressed his fist into him to silence him.

"But he lived because we care. His self-sacrificing has pulled us all together and we will make sure he sees the end of this impossible quest, even if it means I have to die. You can rest in peace, knowing your power will become mine. In doing so, you will be serving your greatest enemy."

The breathing grew slower, Aitvaras squirmed, trying to rise, moving his head away from Cedric's fist. "What are you!"

"A demonic knight." Cedric found the pulsing vein in the dragon's neck, raking the black scales away like one would do scaling a fish. "An abomination who feeds off all things."

Inhaling, panic shook the dragon, his body and energy betraying him. "It's true! Aether has come back to wreak havoc! He's here to avenge his death! The prophecy! THE PROPHECY!"

Enough scales had been stripped away to leave the raw flesh soft and the vein loud in Cedric's hungry eyes. "What nonsense are you going on about, snake?"

"The end of times... the second coming of Aether to seek revenge on Kronos and Gaea for the crimes they have committed on his children and the world! Aether has come to consume us all!"

"SILENCE!" roared Cedric, digging his claws into the soft flesh to calm Aitvaras. "Who the hell is Aether?"

Silence fell over the dragon, his life slipping and time running out. Cursing his luck, Cedric dug his fangs in, drinking the pungent liquid, taking in the dragon's power and soul as part of his own. It was ten times more powerful than Boto's had been, but he needed to be stronger. Another long draw brought the last of the dragon's power into him.

I need to regain the power I lost. No, I need to surpass the power I had. If I was this powerful before facing Delphyne, none of it would have happened...

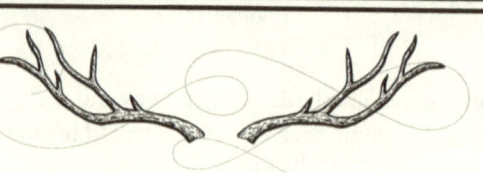

CHAPTER 6

CONTROLLING ETHER

ANGELINE

Angeline sat at the table in her small hut, glaring aimlessly at her half-empty plate. Casting magic had proven to be taxing, and she was thankful for the immortal flesh Cedric's blood had granted her. It all made sense why casting spells as a human had been a dangerous feat. It drained the body. She had passed out eight times trying to keep from using too much power. At this point, she simply wanted to sleep.

"Wake up, let's start again now that you've nourished your body." Artemis appeared out of nowhere as if flashing in and out of reality without warning. "To your feet."

Artemis had set up an obstacle course of sorts, involving drawing water from a barrel, filling a canteen, and pulling only a drop to create a spear made of ice. When they had started this attempt hours ago, she had made it seem trivial, but Angeline discovered how volatile her own magic could be. Not once had she managed to draw water from the barrel yet. Not without breaking, crushing, or even exploding it like a lit powder keg.

Looking at the barrel, Angeline inhaled and held her breath. She threw out her hand, chanting the ancient tongue of those who came before the Greek gods. The panels of the barrel shook, water sloshing over the rim. She furrowed her brow, tensing as the metal rings moaned under the strain. She huffed, letting go of the chanting, and the barrel fell apart.

"Again," Artemis demanded, flicking a finger to pull the water barrel back together as if nothing happened. "You can use far less magic with the same results. Right now, you're trying to drink a barrel of water when you only need a sip from a glass to be satisfied. Both will quench your thirst, but one will overwhelm you."

"Right." Another wave of exhaustion rattled through her. "Maybe I'm just too tired."

"I don't care." Artemis sat in Angeline's chair, picking scraps from her plate and eating them. "Again."

Angeline broke her stare of disdain from Artemis and started again. She took in her breath and held it. Raising her hand—

"Stop doing that," interjected Artemis.

"Doing what?" Angeline exhaled and the barrel exploded.

"That." Another twirl of her finger and the barrel was back to normal. "Magic is part of you, like any other part. You keep holding it in your breath and it makes you build up far more energy than needed."

Swallowing, Angeline lifted her hand and started chanting, trying to remember to breathe steady and slow, imagining the magic riding her breath out of her body and into the barrel. Again, it wobbled, water spilling, and the wood creaking.

"You don't want the barrel."

"Ugh." Angeline stopped, but this time, the barrel sat in one piece.

"See, I solved the first problem." Artemis spun around, leaning an elbow on the table as she crossed one leg over the other. "But why do you keep aiming for the barrel? I said to fill the canteen with water."

Angeline's face flushed, her thoughts recalling all the tries; the truth in Artemis's words cut deep. "If you noticed this, why didn't you say something sooner?"

"Ah, first you needed to realize the strain magic places on the body. You never know when you'll be on your last leg, and it just may kill you to cast that last spell."

Annoyed, Angeline changed tactics. "What were my instructions again?"

"Draw water from the barrel, fill your canteen, and then create a spear of ice from only a drop of water." Artemis lifted an eyebrow, repeating the instructions the exact way she had done the first time.

Twisting her lips, Angeline glared at the skull mask. A smile crept across Angeline's lips and she realized what she had been doing wrong. Grabbing the canteen, she uncapped it. With a huff, she marched across the room, filled it with water, capped it, and as a drop of water began to fall from the canteen, she caught it in her palm. Blowing softly, magic stretched the water from her palm, hardening until it became an ice spear.

I was overthinking the instructions and assumed it all had to be done by magic. This is an exercise to only use what is needed when there's no other solution.

"Exactly what I wanted." Artemis stood, motioning for the spear. "You figured out what the lesson was meant to be."

"Don't use magic until it's unavoidable." Angeline tossed the spear made of ice to Artemis. "You never told me I had to use magic, nor did you say I couldn't. I simply had to complete the tasks given to me. Only the last step required magic."

"Right." She weighed it, checking the staff for bends.

With a firm motion downward, the blade stuck into the hardened floor with ease. Flurries from frozen humidity cascaded to the floor, but not a single ice chip or crack showed on the weapon.

"For as little magic you used, this is as strong as the ones I've made. I'm impressed, my heiress."

"You did make the point I should be able to get the same results with very little magic." Stretching, Angeline stifled a yawn.

"That I did," snorted Artemis. "Rest some, and afterward you may pester the Valkyrie or Amazonians to teach you a thing or two in their ways of bow and blade. You will find no greater warriors between heaven and hell."

"What about learning magic?" Furrowing her brow, she watched as Artemis waved her hand, changing the room into Angeline's preferred bedroom from the Romulus Manor. A smile crawled across her face. "I have given you all my spells by force, and the only lesson I had to teach you is learning flow and recoil. From here, it is how you see fit to use the gifts you've been bestowed by me and by your precious Lord Cedric."

She opened her mouth, but Artemis faded away like dust in the wind. The lesson was short; her hopes for learning magic shattered in an instant. Once more, the old hag left her feeling abandoned and her thoughts wavered to Cedric. Falling to the bed, she pulled herself on and curled into a ball. If Artemis would not teach her further, then she would have to make herself acquainted with the spells stored inside her mind. Use them on some level to know how much they take from her, how useful the outcome may be. She would prepare for the worst.

How I miss those nights in the taverns and brothels... how I regret not being more forward with my feelings... Where are you, Cedric? Your Lady awaits.

Her dreams took her back to the dungeons of Avalon. She lay there, in a memory long forgotten to her, and listened. Drawing a slow breath, she could feel the icy wet cobblestones under her, the weight of metal shackles made her wrists ache and skin burn. She exhaled, her lungs rattling. Blinking, she wondered if she could have some control of the moment. Mumbling a chant, she broke herself from the memory, the enchantment she only could label as a dream walker.

It was more than enough to break the shackles and allow her to sit up. She looked at the scratches on the wall; this was several years into her imprisonment. *Could it be pushing ten or more?* At this stage, her lips had been sewn shut, that too had faded, and her anxiety fell away some. Her eyes chased the chains and found they disappeared into the depths of the dungeon. She couldn't follow any farther. Spinning back, she wondered what part of the night it was, if Kronos had come and gone already.

Marching to the door, she stared out the tiny, barred window. The hall seemed to shift in constant motion. Someone tugged on the back of her shirt and she spun in alarm. There, a young girl with one green and one brown eye stared at her. Swallowing, Angeline let herself lower to eye level, baffled at the girl's presence.

"You're here. You found your memories." Her voice sent chills through Angeline, so familiar and haunting. "We don't have long before he knows."

"Who are you? What are you doing here?" Angeline searched the room behind her. Pulling the girl's hands to her, she too wore shackles. "How do you know about my memories?"

The girl threw herself against Angeline, hot tears soaking her shoulder. "He's cast a terrible spell on me, Mommy."

Angeline's world fell away. She sat up, holding the scar on her stomach. Bile boiled up in her throat and she slung herself over the edge of the bed, vomiting. Tears of rage fell, pain ripping her heart into pieces. A primal scream rolled out of her, building as it grew until the very air and room shook with the ire of pain, and despair filled her soul.

Artemis appeared, a snap of her fingers silencing her voice. "What in the world has invoked this primitive use of magic?"

Angeline's eyes met the mask and she allowed her to speak. "He fucking took my daughter from me."

Artemis pulled away the mask. They could nearly pass as twins. She paled, crouching to the floor, gripping her heart. The yellow eyes grew glossy, a look of sheer pain unable to grasp the level in which burned in Angeline's soul.

"Did you know?" Angeline was pulling herself to her feet, sweat painting her body. "DID YOU KNOW!"

"I DID NOT!" Artemis's voice shook the room this time. "I didn't think you two could conceive and—"

"He has her. He's cursed her."

"The world will suffer if he's intending to use your offspring as a vehicle. There is dangerous magic outside his mother's reach in that child." She stood, whistling.

"Yes, Mistress." Manah had appeared. "What may I do for you?"

"We need your guidance." Artemis summoned a table, motioning for them both to sit. "Summon Hamadryades. We will need any information she may have on the child."

"Does Cedric know?" Angeline's panic consumed her. "What will he think of me..."

"Trust me, he does not." Artemis twirled a hand and a goblet of red wine appeared. "You know he would have bypassed this expedition to hunt the child down if he knew. Drink. Calm yourself. You will need to control your emotions if you are to regain everything he's taken."

"My, the strings of fate on this one are quite knotted." Manah's eyes rolled back, the white eyes unnerving as she hummed in a language beyond Angeline's knowledge. "Many doors are still left to be opened before you'll find her, and when this day comes, a new fate will be decided for you and yours."

Angeline choked back the harsh liquid. "What is this?"

"An elixir crafted by Nuha to dampen one's emotions. You will need it to prepare for what will unfold." Artemis sat, rubbing her forehead. "Kronos was too many steps ahead of me again. I don't know how this time will unfold, Manah."

Manah's eyes turned back to the brown irises and she sat. "We are not without options this time."

Another gulp of the foul liquid and Angeline felt the calmness unfold. "Are you saying this isn't the first time we've been here?"

Artemis sighed, shifting to face Angeline. "No, but it's the first instance that you and Cedric have conceived a child. I'm not sure how or why it happened this time, unlike all the other times, but it's strange. No magic was involved."

Angeline could feel her heart swell. "How could I forget her like she never existed?"

"On some level, she would have to will it herself as well. It's all about timing, and she may prove a clever girl. Now, summon Hamadryades. We have much prying of her lips for keeping this quiet."

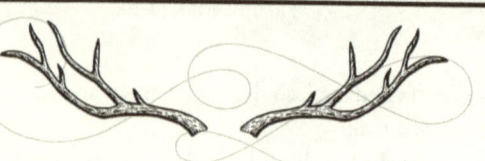

CHAPTER 7

WIZARD MANANNAN

CEDRIC

Cedric sat on top of Aitvaras's carcass, scavengers circling overhead and peering at him from the edge of the clearing. He rolled the gemstone in his palm, pondering what power it could possibly hold or how to best use it. *Maybe Angeline can use this for her magic.* Yelping from the scattering wildlife brought Cedric's eyes to the purple and yellow peacock called Wizard Manannan. He broke through the brush and broken trees, leading the familiar faces of Wylleam, Nyctimus, and Romasanta. Fenrir shadowed them from behind, his nose twitching in the air as his fur prickled. Closing his fist around the gem, Cedric huffed, shoulders tensing. Part of him didn't want to see them again, still hurt by the secrets they kept from him, instead of simply asking.

How long will they take me as daft? I'm no child.

"A-Aitvaras?" Nyctimus paled, looking to Romasanta and back to Cedric sitting on top of the black scaly heap. "You couldn't have."

"Couldn't have what?" Cedric narrowed his green eyes, betrayal and unease still biting at him. "Kill a dragon on my own? Why not?"

"Pup!" Fenrir leaped over the others, tail wagging as he sniffed all about the dead dragon and Cedric. "You've done well! I'm proud to have you in my pack!"

Shoving the wet, snorting nostrils away, Cedric fussed, "Calm down! If you think something like this would take me down, you were mistaken, wolf." With a lick across Cedric's arm and face, the rebuttal continued. "Are you mad?!"

A great roar of laughter unfolded from Romasanta, causing everyone to freeze. They glared at him, baffled at the reaction. The sound of it foreign, but a warm welcome in the man who seemed to be in a constant state of despair. He caught his breath, leaning on Nyctimus's shoulder before he finally revealed what had him so tickled.

"You should be glad I contained that beast within, Nyctimus. Could you imagine having a puppy the size of a castle courtyard running amuck, bounding around, licking us every time he was pleased with us?"

Nyctimus started laughing. "No, I don't want to imagine the troubles we would have endured if he had been in this form."

"I'm no pup!" snarled Fenrir, growling and barking. "And you better be glad I was stuck in the farmer. I would have eaten you all if it weren't for him!"

Romasanta scratched his jaw, smirking. "True, Fenrir. You did try to eat me and that's how all this started."

A snort came from Fenrir, and after a long pause, he confessed, "I can't say I really regret the time we spent together, Farmer. I just wish I had been able to save her at the start."

Romasanta's smile fell into a heavy scowl. "I could have tried harder myself."

"It wouldn't have mattered. You're not a killer, not like me and the wolf." Cedric hated seeing that weight of guilt in Romasanta's eyes. "Let's go. Take us to the tower Wizard."

"Call me Manny. Let's try to keep the wizard thing to ourselves, shall we?" Weighing the newcomers in his land, he was curious. "But first, tell me more about why you've crossed the threshold into this realm?"

What smiles and chuckles had filled the air came to a bone-chilling stop. They all looked at one another until every pair of eyes came to rest on Romasanta. Manannan furrowed his brow, seeing the satchel Romasanta gripped tighter in response to the prying eyes. A grin grew but quickly faded on Manannan's face when he sensed something he hadn't been in the presence of before. He paled, reassessing the men before him before he dared to ask.

"Did the Oracle let you in? Willingly?" Manny visibly swallowed.

"Yes," answered Fenrir.

"You're here to return the Eye, then," he stated bluntly, Fenrir's fur prickling as he bared his fangs. "Oh no, I have no want or need for something so vile. You see, I am a wizard who serves oracles, seers, and the like."

"Vile is an understatement." Nyctimus scowled at the satchel, a red glow growing, steam rising from the bag. "By the gods, it's going to start up again."

Pulling the bag off, Romasanta abandoned the smoldering leather satchel. "Stand back, the eye is up to no good again."

Everyone stepped back, giving the bag a wide berth. The leather caught fire, sizzling and sputtering as the stone burned through and sunk into the dirt. After several minutes, its glow dissipated. They all looked at one another, wary of even approaching the cursed thing. Manny cleared his throat and flicked a wrist. They watched as dirt wrapped it up and a glass jar formed over that before restoring the leather satchel.

"There, it should be safe for now, but we may want to visit the dwarves for a proper container." Manny crossed his arms, not daring to come near it still. "You see, Gaea is watching and listening through that blasted gem."

"So, she knows we're coming," Romasanta grunted and dared to strap the satchel back on.

"Any time that happens, you're getting a taste of her infamous short temper, my friends." Manny scratched his cheek. "Seeing how you're reacting; this isn't the first you've pissed her off on some level."

"Shit." Cedric began to pace. "For someone who wants their eye back, she's doing her damnest to kill us over it."

"You see... about that." Manny lowered his voice. "It seems no one has told you."

"Told us what?" Nyctimus narrowed his eyes.

"That her only interest is helping Kronos to succeed."

Cedric and Romasanta shot a look at one another.

Wylleam cleared his throat. "First, before we go any deeper into this. I suppose it's time to reveal what Artemis's situation and plan have been. It seems all of us are only a piece of a much larger puzzle and we're not aware of what the aim of the game is meant to be."

Cedric's face reddened with his building anger as he fought it back. "Never did I see you being such a keeper of secrets."

Flattening his ears, Wylleam motioned for Romasanta to abandon the satchel. "Let's leave prying eyes and ears behind for a moment, shall we?"

Romasanta dropped it to the ground; he and Cedric were hot on the old cynocephali's heels. Manny smirked, intrigued by this group and the discovery of information unfolding. Nyctimus rubbed his forehead while the other two huffed. Fenrir laid down, quiet. There were two in the group who knew what had transpired and what was still to come.

"Come on, out with it." Cedric barked and began pacing once more. "It seems you and the overgrown puppy know what's going on. If not for me, you two at least owe Apollo an explanation."

Wylleam inhaled, gripping his staff firmly as he whispered, "Gaea is hoping Kronos will summon her to the Mortal Realm. If this happens, the end of mankind will be upon us. You see, no one knows where Kronos has gone. He is not dead. Though he had bonded to a mortal body, Titans don't exactly die."

"Then what became of him after we attacked?" Romasanta demanded.

"All we know is that he constantly had plans and failsafe. He knew that body would eventually wear down."

"May I interject?" They turned to Manny. "What sort of body did Gaea cast Kronos into?"

"A wizard." Nyctimus tapped his lips in thought and added, "A powerful one named Merlin. Do you know of this man?"

Manny's eyes grew wide. "She had him possess Merlin?"

"Are you deaf? Yes, Merlin," Cedric scoffed.

"Did he gain access to Avalon, then?" He sounded shaken by the thought.

"Look, I think we need to let Wylleam finish what he has to say." Romasanta's eyes glowed in a familiar yellow and they all looked at him, confused. "What?"

"Your wolven powers seem to be still there, you just haven't been angry enough to use them." Nyctimus snorted at the idea.

"R-right." Wylleam shook his head. "As I was trying to say, he hasn't passed back into this realm. Regardless, we have the upper hand by bringing the eye here into the Otherworld. Artemis and the Oracles have been working to overthrow the timeline again."

"Again?" The panicked look on Nyctimus said volumes. "Does this mean we've lived through this once before?"

Wylleam averted his eyes.

"I suppose this explains the havoc and rewritten timelines I've seen in the Mortal Realm," Manny chimed in, stroking his goatee. "In fact, that chaos is the reason many magical creatures have come here to live."

"Son of a bitch." Cedric marched away. With his hands on his hips, he looked skyward. "Is this the first version of me?"

"I don't know that." Wylleam looked to the ground under the weight of his own shame. "I do know Artemis has tried to counter Kronos and Gaea many times. The problem is Merlin's magic is responsible for the timelines rewinding and changing. Giving Kronos access to such a rare ability had to be intentional to buy him time."

"That's why they knew," Romasanta mumbled to himself, his shoulder shuddering.

"The goal is to give her the eye. She will *have to reward* Romasanta or lose favor with her subjects. Daphne should be freed, but the Dryads will ensure no harm will befall her." Wylleam paused as Cedric spun, rage in his face.

"Are you implying there would be a repercussion to the reward after the hell she put him through?" His chest heaved.

"Yes." Romasanta knew the answer. "She is a woman of her words, but unforgiving. Daphne will have to decide to become a dryad or become a human whose life ended centuries ago."

Nyctimus paled. "You're going through with all of this knowing she never intended to let her live her life free of any curse?"

"No soul deserves to be ensnared in the way she is." Romasanta avoided eye contact with anyone.

"But don't they serve Gaea?" Cedric's voice made the group flinch.

"They do not. I, too, was caught under her curse until I was thrust into Romasanta." Fenrir had stood and walked closer. "Many of the creatures have found a way to break free from her tyranny while here in the Otherworld."

"Exactly. The Oracles and many creatures outside Gaea's reach have all aided many in this feat. In the meantime, many of the Greek gods who would oppose her have gone ... missing. Even the titans have gone into hiding or are working under aliases. Regardless, an army to oppose her is being pulled together." Wylleam snorted, shaking his head. "The catch is finding someone strong enough to face Kronos and even Gaea head-on." He met Cedric's angry glare. "That's where you come in."

He paled. "You've got to be fucking kidding me. You're all going to thrust me onto the front line for a fight I want nothing to do with?"

"Yeah, that's just it. There's not a soul in this world who can convince you to join our cause." Wylleam turned to Manny. "Now, I know you are close to the Oracles, so I must ask if you intend to join our quest to return the Eye to render Gaea blind to what may pass in the Mortal Realm?"

Manny laughed, looking at the hodge-podge crew before him. "Seeing that you need a proper guide here in the Otherworld, I will join you all the way to the doors of Gaea's gate. As for after that, I don't know if I will brave visiting the Mortal Realm just yet."

"I need time to think about all of this. Rest and plan where we go from here." Cedric stomped off, his blood boiling and mind racing.

Abomination. Created to become a weapon against Kronos and Gaea, but he knew and wanted me, or Angeline, as a replacement vehicle. Wait, the question should be why he stopped seeking us out. If he's not dead, and he hasn't tried to reclaim Angeline... then what did he gain that is better?

His stomach twisted.

If this isn't our first encounter, then what's different about this time?

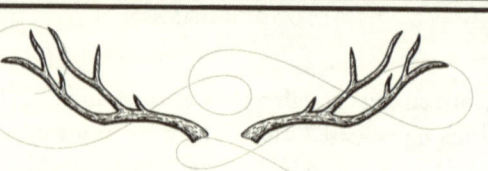

CHAPTER 8

STRINGS OF FATE AND PROPHECY SPOKEN

ANGELINE

"**W**hat have you brought me back here for?" Hamadryades bloomed from the floor and froze the moment she saw the state of Angeline. "What have you done this time, Artemis?"

"Nothing. Though I appreciate the credit." She motioned to an open seat. "This timeline had borne unexpected fruit, and I believe you are aware of that fact."

Hamadryades peered at Manah and arched an eyebrow high. "I suppose she's remembered the child, at last."

"He took her." Angeline couldn't hold back the tears, even with Nuha's elixir in her system. "Kronos has my daughter."

"Yes, and no." This time, her ivy hair shifted into a pink cascade of cherry blossoms. "She's a clever one, and yes, we have been aiding her when it's safe to do so."

"How?" Artemis demanded.

Hamadryades turned to Artemis and snapped her fingers. In an instant, roots erupted from the floor and pulled her into the ground. Manah smiled, but Angeline stood in alarm. Seeing Manah's betrayal, she swallowed and slid slowly back to a sitting position. Wild-eyed, she looked to Hamadryades, wondering what her motive could be. The silences lingered for quite some time.

"Now that Gaea can't hear us, please continue queen of the dryads, Hamadryades." Manah bowed to her deeply, and every nerve tightened in Angeline's body.

"Yes, where was I?" A flick of fingers brought tea cups into existence once more. "Cleo is a clever girl. Though she has been freed from Kronos's immediate grasp, her body was marked as his next vessel the moment you gave birth to her."

Angeline's heart ached. "How can I undo this?"

"You'd have to find a way to kill something greater than a god." She blew the steam from her floral cup and sipped it, calm and collected. "You'll have to find the means to kill a titan and Gaea herself."

"No one can do that." Angeline's tears started to fall faster. "I forgot her, and now I can't even hope to save her."

Hamadryades started to cackle. "Dear child, she doesn't need you to rescue her. She simply needs you to fulfill your destiny."

"My destiny?" Angeline's brow folded as she wiped the tears from her face. "What destiny?"

"The one string of fate that says you will bring the end of Kronos." Manah's eyes rolled back, her eyes white, and chanting filling the room.

A cold wind blew through, but this was different from the time Artemis had appeared to her as a pile of bones. All light pulled away, the bed and fireplace fading to darkness. Angeline's heart raced. Golden threads stretched all around. Voices whispered in all languages; creatures moved beyond the darkness, but no light would reveal who or what they were.

She shifted to chase a thread across the room and realized one was tied to her wrist. Reaching for it, Hamadryades stopped her, shaking her head, and Angeline abandoned the notion of removing it. Following the thread, it crossed and knotted with one that glowed red. Her mind whispered, *Cedric.* She watched as they crisscrossed, knotting with others and faded beyond where she could focus on them.

Manah's voice took on an ethereal and foreboding tone as she spoke the prophecy:

"And Kronos reigned,
Over all titans, even Iapetos,
All men, earth and otherworldly,
Best offspring of Gaea and Aether.

"The punitive satisfaction, bound
Both Kronos and Mother dearly loved.
Tyrants for the Greeks, fierce kings
Overweening, impure, adul-
terous, and altogether corrupt.

"For men, there shall be no more rest from war.
Terribly will he abuse the city of Avalon,
And every land the sun looks down upon,
He alone will rule, east and west.

"Have been finished Kronos will complete
Two hundred years, twice twenty and twice two,
With nine months added; then by the Horned King,
Smitten will he be by the sharpened brass.

"He will make a widow of thee in little time,
When many warriors, many overthrows,
And murders, deaths, and deadly feuds
Miseries of conquests there shall be returned.

"In confusion with a horse and man
Cleft by force of hands, fall in the plain.
And then another He shall rule again,
The sign of his name in the number ten."

Manah collapsed to the floor. With that, the wind sucked back to the realm whence it came. Angeline shook, rubbing her wrist where the threads of fate had tied her to this fate. Hamadryades offered her the cup of tea once more as a consolation prize. As much as she wanted to refuse, she feared these beings she found herself in the presence of. She took it from her, sipping lightly to discover the flavor very different from before.

Artemis is far less intimidating after this encounter.

"My, I haven't been to a good prophetic chant in quite some time!" The dryad was far too happy for what had unfolded. "It seems the Sibylline Oracles spoke about something like this before, to some degree."

"I don't understand a word of it." Angeline took another sip. Her heartbeat became calmer and her nerves let loose. "Cleo. Why do I feel I've heard this name before?"

Hamadryades smiled to herself. "Here, keep this amber ring with you. It will keep the memory of the prophecy for you, but be wary of who you share this with. Gaea has many eyes and ears in this realm and yours." A sapling grew from the table, a single rose budding, blooming, and bearing the golden gemstone ring within. "What would you like to know?"

"What is she like?" She took the ring and slipped it over her thumb. "What kind of person has she become?"

"She is a good blend of both parents, with the tenacity of her father and the patience of her mother." With another wave of her hand, roots plucked Manah from the floor and laid her on the bed. "The magic and powers she holds are only matched by the combined powers of you and yours. There are no signs of the demon side, though. If there had been, this would have become far more dangerous of a betting game and given Kronos access to the Underworld. If he gained the ability to use miasma, no realm would be free of his aimed tyranny. Thank Hades for keeping that gate firmly locked."

"Why would Hades lock Kronos out of the Underworld?" Angeline scraped her memories. She had found a book on the old Greek and Roman gods in the Romulus library. "Isn't Kronos his father?"

"Yes, but Hades is a justiciar, through and through." Hamadryades cleared her throat, both their tea cups refilling and heating. "Honestly, it may be the incident when Kronos chained him to Cerberus, trying to force his way in until he succumbed to Aether's miasma."

Angeline took another gulp of tea, unsure what to say in response to that information. "Why hasn't she come to us?"

"Now that is an important question." Hamadryades placed her cup down and frowned, cupping her face. "We can't seem to convince her to seek you or Cedric out. She's much like the Oracles. Perhaps she sees something we cannot. Instead, she is focused on only one goal; to end Kronos and Gaea."

"That's no way to live." Angeline stared at her reflection in the dark brown liquid. "Vengeance can't be the answer."

"Ah, but she sees it as protecting you."

Another swell of emotions attempted to rise and at last, she felt Nuha's magic burn in her belly to snuff it out. "I should be protecting her."

"Worry not. You have your memories and if you keep dreamwalking you might see her, get to know her." A smirk grew on the wooden face as she stood. "You see, in some ways, she is like Artemis, selfless to a fault and makes enemies out of her allies in order to push things forward. She riled Romasanta once before. Perhaps while you are here, she is seeking out an ally or putting in place a solution to aid you on your return. Have faith."

In a cloud of yellow pollen, the Queen of Dryads was gone. Artemis was sitting at the table once more, blinking as if caught in a daze. Manah groaned, waking from her own moment. The teacup in Angeline's hand gone, making her feel as if she had imagined it all except for the amber ring flashing of the fireplace's flames. She sighed and waited.

"Where did that old tree run off to?" Artemis stood, remembering now what had transpired. "Drag me into the dirt and think I wouldn't notice being placed at the table like a doll! HAMADRYADES! You mossy bitch!"

Manah stumbled to her feet, holding her head. "Does she often invoke the powers of others so easily?"

Artemis jerked her mask off and threw it across the room in anger. "She's playing games again. By the spirits... what did she say? Where is your daughter?"

"She doesn't know." Angeline's body felt heavy, as if her magic drained from her. "And I think she used my magic to do all the work." Stifling a yawn, she wobbled to the bed, wanting the comforts of the bed that smelled of her beloved.

"So be it. Do not call on her a third time. It may get dangerous." With a snap of Artemis's fingers, Angeline found herself alone in the room once more.

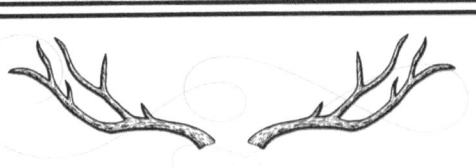

Chapter 9

The Art of Shapeshifting

Cedric

Cedric came back to where he had left everyone and came to a halt. His eyes bounced between the gathered group of men. Fenrir was missing, and a new man matching him in build and height narrowed his yellow eyes at him. With blond hair and tanned skin, a fanged smirk grew on his face. No one seemed alarmed by the warrior and, though nothing smelled off, the visuals before him sent a chill over him.

"Where'd the wolf run off to?" He didn't break his stare at the stranger.

"I'm right here," the man replied, puffing out his chest. "This wizard has proven himself useful!"

Cedric tensed. "Are you all mad?"

Not one pair of eyes would meet his. Except that of the excited wolven ones with their fanged grin. He came over, giving Cedric a hearty pat on the back. A look of dread washed over Cedric and he shoved the arm off. He gained his distance from the new form and strapped the claymore and its hilt back onto his back.

"Fine, if you all think this will make traveling easier, I'll play along." Snorting, he yanked on the last strap and buckled it. "But we can't go around here calling him Fenrir, now can we?"

"Relax, relax." Manny patted Fenrir's arm, which might as well have sent an unseen tail wagging. "We'll just shorten it. Fen sounds like a good name for our Nordic warrior."

"F-e-n," Cedric drawled.

"Yes?" replied Fenrir.

Groaning, Cedric refocused. "So we need to go up that tower to get to... where again?"

"Above us is *Mag Rein*, the Sea of Spirits. This is the southern territory of the *Mag Mell*, the largest of all the *Tirs* in the Otherworld. It was once home to all the Greek gods, but..." Wylleam shook his head, making his ears flopping loudly. "Let's just be thankful that under these circumstances, it will work in our favor."

Nyctimus cleared his throat. "You mean there are still some Greek gods left?" He shot a look at Romasanta. "But it's safe to assume their connection to Gaea directly is the only saving grace."

Cedric turned his attention to the wizard. "I killed your dragon. Now help us out of here."

Manny bowed deeply before them. "It will be my pleasure to join you on this marvelous journey. If you may, let us make our way to Lake Corrib, and we'll make our way to my tower, posthaste."

The wizard seemed delighted with inviting himself into their entourage, and not a single one of them was willing to oppose him. In just the short time they had encountered him, he had shapeshifted, granted shapeshifting, pissed a dragon off with an undying meal, and knew more than they did about the stone they carried. Cedric followed close behind the wizard, everyone else falling into line behind him as they had done before. Cedric stole glances over his shoulder; the intense wolven stare and occasional sniff in the air seemed awkward in Fen's human form.

Shit, do I look like that when I take in a scent? Cedric grimaced and looked back at the wizard, his thoughts unraveling. *And this wizard, he knows a lot about the Otherworld, far more than Wylleam. I supposed there's a difference between a shaman who communes with this realm and someone who lives and travels between the realms. Regardless, we have no choice but to trust him. To think, that bitch has been listening to us, even trying to prevent us from traveling farther. I can't help but think Barushka would have been handy after crossing the realm. Being a shade, he would have been a sight to see.*

"You okay?" Manny cast an eye back at Cedric. "That's a rather intense face you have on."

With a half-hearted smile, he retorted, "Just wondering if I can trust you."

"Look, I don't know where or what will happen to you all when you are before Gaea's throne, but the least I can do is give you every chance at succeeding."

"I thought you said you weren't going that far with us." Cedric lifted an eyebrow.

"I'm not, not unless you want to send her over the top." Manny scoffed, flicking a finger so a lute would appear in his arms. He began plucking a sultry tune, the sound of the instrument a sort of magic to hide their conversation. "I am taking you to a place where the greatest craftsmen thrive. They are forbidden to make a god-slaying weapon, but they aren't banned from making weapons from materials given to them by creatures of this realm."

"God-slaying weapons," Cedric echoed the idea of it, sending his heart racing. "I thought those were all fables."

"Oh, they are certainly not." Manny strummed more boastfully. "All of them have been cast to the mortal realm. After Kronos got his hands on Excalibur by way of Arthur Pendragon, when poor little Nimue had no clue the boy would hand it over to someone else. Anyhow," he picked out a hard stanza on the lute before continuing, "god-slaying weapons were handed to the most trusted and powerful. Both human and otherworldly. Most are now only obtainable through blood magic or by facing someone like Salamandra. Nasty lava lizard, he is."

"So these dwarves, they technically can make something just as useful if given the right supplies?" Cedric's jaw muscles twitched, giving the wizard-turned-bard a stern look. "Are you implying what I think you're implying?"

He stopped and turned, picking the chords again. "Why, my curious creature, you have supplies, do you not?"

"I have a stone from a dragon's head," he snorted.

"Yes. And a horn." He eyed the top of Cedric's head. "Now, all you need is magic-imbued metal or something of that sort."

Cedric's eyes widened and he spun to the group, his expression bringing the others to a halt. "Wylleam!"

"What's the matter?" His ears stretched tall and he glanced behind Cedric, expecting something to be happening. "Is there trouble ahead?"

"The soul link. How does it work?" Searching his mind a moment, he voiced his assumption. "Is there a tool involved?"

"You mean these?" Nyctimus pulled an elaborate chain out, the incantation scrawled on each link between two cuffs.

"Give them here." Cedric took a step forward.

Romasanta stepped in, pushing him back. "What do you intend to do with this magic?"

"Destroy it." They looked at one another.

"I thought it couldn't be destroyed so easily?" Nyctimus tightened his grip on it. "That the link is permanent."

"The link it makes between the souls and the caster can't be broken. It is merely an enchanted tool for casting a difficult spell made to mimic something that happens under the right conditions." Wylleam flicked an ear in annoyance. "Do you really intend to destroy them?"

"Fucking give them to me. I can't tell you why or how." He shot a look at the leather satchel and they all held their breath. "Just trust me."

Nyctimus tossed them to him and snorted. "Well, it's not like we need them anymore. Plus, they were intended for you."

Huffing, Cedric shoved the chain in with his other prize. "Wizard, how much longer until we are at the lake's edge?"

"Just down this hill, gentleman. Enbharr and boat should be waiting for us already." He continued marching, strumming on the lute.

"How long will it take us to get to ... wherever the dwarves are?" Cedric caught up with Manny, wanting to learn more from him. "And what do you get out of helping me?"

A coy smile formed on his face, and he avoided making eye contact as he slid his fingers on the neck of the lute. "Gaea has interfered in my business one time too many times. She doesn't like the charitable folks. As for the dwarves, we've got to get across *Mag Rein* and head west to *Mag Mor*."

"Forgive me, my Gaelic is nonexistent. What is *Mag Mor?*" Cedric couldn't deny he favored the Otherworld and its rather blunt naming system.

"Grande Plain," Manny replied.

"And once we hit this plain, exactly how do you intend on getting us to the dwarves?" Cedric scratched his temple, the trees clearing to reveal a boat with a bough made of solid brass.

"Well, about that." Manny's lute vanished as he slid down the steep embankment leading to the water's edge. "We'll have to travel by foot unless we can commandeer mounts of some kind."

Cedric followed close behind him, but came to a halt. A thickly muscled, dappled gray horse came into view. It shook its black mane, flashes of green bulrushes catching the light as water sprayed from the motion. If Barushka had been there, they would have been the same height and build. It cantered on top of the water until it met Manny on the shore. Petting his nose, the horse snorted Manny's hands off and neighed at Cedric, baring canines. It made Cedric shake his head, blinking his eyes.

"Is that a kelpie?" He couldn't hide the impressed tone in his voice.

Smirking, Manny sidled and gave a proper introduction. "This is Enbharr, a longtime friend of mine."

The beast snorted sea foam from his nostrils and a voice fell from it. "I've told you, we're not friends. This is temporary until I can repay my debt for freeing me from Murphy Castle."

"I've told you, you owe me nothing." Manny scoffed, rubbing his forehead.

"I will pay it back." Another massive shake of the mane sent an eruption of sea foam flying.

As the clumps fell to the ground, a thin and pale figure stood in the place of the Kelpie. The intense stare and naked body revealed Enbharr had no gender. The flat plains contradicted being wholly male or female. The long-lashed purple eyes were hypnotizing above masculine sunken cheeks, riding over a thin cupid's bow, lips only obscuring the alignment further. It fascinated Cedric to see a creature who had no desire to choose, or perhaps kelpies never needed to identify themselves as either, content with what they were and fierce. He locked eyes with Enbharr and they hissed, just as fang heavy as the equine form.

"Do you insist on making every magical animal shapeshift to human form?" Cedric fussed at Manny.

The wizard laughed, throwing up his hands. "Kelpies have always been able to do that. How else would they lure someone like you to the lake in order to drown and eat you? I recommend staying clear of its mouth, in either form."

Cedric huffed, waiting for the others to catch up. It wasn't long before they heard the cracking of twigs, the other four coming down the bank. Cedric crossed his arms, gauging the expressions on his companions. It seemed everyone had their eyes on the bulky brass ornament of a boat that would be their way of travel, except Fen. If he had a tail, it'd be wagging. His eyes were on a different item.

That idiot is going to get us killed waltzing around as a human. I can feel the waves of arousal wafting off him. Last thing I need is a dead forest god killed trying to mate with a fucking kelpie.

Fen's eyes were wide with excitement, his eyebrows raised high on his face. He puffed out his chest with a wide grin. The gait shifted to a march and before he could pass Cedric, Cedric reached out and gripped his arm, throwing him back a few steps. Cedric sidled in his way and snorted. A scowl ruined the playful stare.

"Out of my way, pup," Fen demanded.

"Oh, no you don't, Fenrir." Cedric narrowed his eyes. "I can feel the lust coming out of you. It's not interested."

"How do you know?" he growled, the sound still menacing as ever as it rolled from his chest. "I will greet her and—"

Cedric interrupted him, "It'll eat you, you damn mutt. That's a kelpie."

Fen blinked, confused, as he sniffed the air and Cedric covered his face. "Oh, it is a kelpie."

"Let's try not to hump everything in sight now that you have a human body." Cedric spun around, walking away.

"How else does one build a proper harem?" Fen marveled.

Romasanta approached, landing a heavy hand on his friend. "Let's just try to get back what I've lost, and maybe you can ask Nyctimus about how he did it."

"It's not a harem." Nyctimus snorted, brushing past Romasanta with a smirk. "They just so happen to live under the same roof, is all."

"Harem," shouted Cedric over his shoulder, chuckling.

"It's a harem," Romasanta concurred.

"Not one of them is my slave," Nyctimus defended, his posture stiffening.

"But you have slept with many of them, yes?" Fen cut in and everyone fell silent.

With the weight of eyes on him, Nyctimus's face turned red. "I'm not going to discuss my private life with the likes of you all." He motioned to push his glasses up on his nose, but he had lost them long ago and flustered over it.

Cedric locked eyes with Romasanta, nodding. "Harem."

A great roar of laughter left them as Nyctimus puffed out his cheeks and stomped toward the boat. To be back on a quest, living a life they had left in their past, had given them some freedom to be themselves. Cedric inhaled deep, holding it there.

I may be pissed at them, but I know they are all doing their best to survive no different than me. Can I really be so angry over that much? After all, they chose not to chain me, not to do things in the way Artemis had asked. There is some level of trust and respect in knowing that.

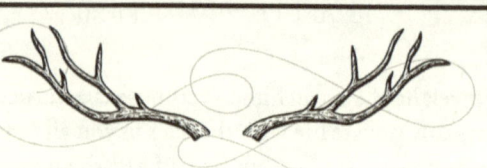

CHAPTER 10

VALKYRIES, FURIES, AND AMAZONIANS

ANGELINE

At last, Angeline ventured from the safety of her hut. Tiring of the nightgowns and simple medieval dresses she had been thrown in, she had used her magic to dress in the way she had loved best. The outfit she and Cedric had crafted for her to be a lady ranger, where everything functioned solely to aid movement and placement of weapons. Artemis had left her items in a chest by the door, and in it, she had filled with relief gripping the old chimeran hilt dagger. The black blade hummed with a terrible curse, something that would make any enemy feel pain threefold, and what it did to something that survived its bite was still unknown to her, to anyone. Happy to have her feet in fitted leather boots, she threw open the door.

The sky there was blue, the weather mild, with a cool breeze to break moments when the heat of the daylight licked at her skin. Women of all cultures filled the bustling village. Many carried a weapon of some kind along with an insignia, whether it be their clothes, jewelry, or even a tattoo. She shifted her new bow on her shoulders and at last spotted Manah talking with Nuha. They were the closest *friends* she had with the state of her being there. Clearing her throat, she marched toward them and they faltered in their conversation as she came to a stop.

"I want to learn more," she announced to them, heart racing.

"That's quite the grand declaration." Nuha nodded and arched a brow. "But more of what?"

Angeline blushed. "I'm sorry, I'm terrible at this."

Manah leaned into Nuha. "She's not the social type."

Nuha nodded. "I see that."

Angeline's temper crept forward, goading her to be braver. "Look, this is the Isle of the Amazonians, right?"

"Yes," they responded in unison.

"They are great warriors, the best ever to grace both realms. I want to know more about how to fight like them. To strike with arrow and blade like no other has on the Mortal Realm since the ancient times." She stood tall, like a soldier at attention. "I've been trained. I've even had spells cast, but what good are they if I don't know why or how to use any of it properly and with practiced skill?"

The two of them looked at one another and after a moment, Nuha made her an offer. "Who would you like to train with first?"

Angeline blinked, not sure. "Forgive me, but I don't know much about where I am and who is here."

Manah smirked. "Nuha, you have to remember she didn't come here and face the trials like the others."

"Oh, forgive me, Lady Angeline!" The pale face flushed pink. "For this, your options are the Valkyries, Furies, and lastly, from which the island is named, the Amazonians. You see, this island is ruled by three queens, including your ancestor, Artemis."

Angeline swallowed. The little girl's reaction that first day in her hut seemed not so farfetched. "Who are the other queens?"

Nuha blinked, surprised by the question. "Have you not heard of Freya and Alecto?"

"No, I am not familiar with them." Angeline grimaced. "In fact, I don't know much about Artemis, either."

Eyes wide, the two warriors looked at one another.

"Well, we can just say I've lived a long, sheltered life. Mostly against my will." She furrowed her brow, shifting. "Who should I train with?"

"What fighting style or weapon would you like to master? The bow there? Perhaps the dagger on your hilt?" Manah motioned to the cursed chimeran blade.

"You know, I would like to know how to use this better. My mentor didn't get to teach me everything." She pulled the dagger free to show the blackened steel. "And I would like to discover what sort of magic this possesses."

"My, that is some interesting magic." Manah leaned in to have a closer look.

"You should seek out the Furies. Surely Alecto or one of the three sisters will be able to sense what sort of miasma paints this blade." Nuha squinted, leaning in for a closer look. "It's been ages since I've seen a dagger with a chimeran hilt. They're highly sought after."

"They are?" Angeline smiled. "This was a gift from my ... husband." She abandoned *lord,* for a more favorable term. "We fought the beasts together, in fact."

"Really?" Nuha became excited. "My, I suppose magic helps."

Angeline frowned. "No, I didn't always have or know I could use magic. Being a natural for the bow, I aided Cedric in many battles from afar. He taught me some maneuvers with a dagger, but I think they were intended more for cleaving men and not monsters."

"What have you faced?" Nuha's eyes chased the dagger back to its sheath before motioning Angeline to follow. "Please, tell me more of your battles."

Manah followed close behind Angeline. "Nuha is always hungry for stories."

The smile crept back onto Angeline's face once more. "Let's see. I have faced a lot of monsters like werewolves, chimeras, heliodromos... I did take down a busse alone."

"How big?" This caught Manah's attention. "I have hunted many in *Mag Mell* for the fae. They can get quite aggressive."

"Yes." Angeline looked around for something to compare. "This one, it was taller than the hut there, fur golden..."

"The golden stag of Arcadia!" The two halted, spinning to her in disbelief.

"I'm not sure, maybe?"

"Impressive." Nuha looked Angeline up and down. "What strength you must be hiding in that tiny frame."

"In my defense, it was a test, and I nearly died." Angeline didn't feel worthy of their awestruck glares and thoughts of the lust she felt when Cedric had found her made her face flush. "Granted, I'd rather face a monster or animal than an enemy who can think and feel."

"I'm impressed daughter of Artemis. You are full of surprises," declared Nuha. "Worthy of earning many blessings for making it here to the Otherworld!"

Manah's eyes sparkled as they started walking once more. "What foes of that kind have you faced? Those capable of feeling and thinking."

"Boto and Lillith, I suppose." Another halt disrupted Angeline's steps. "You know them?"

"Are you mad?" Manah baffled.

Angeline looked at them, confused. "I'm not one to be attacked and not defend myself. Granted, Boto was killed by my husband long ago and Lillith, well, we're allies."

"Your husband, who is he?" Nuha rubbed her chest as if soothing a case of heartburn.

"Lord Cedric du Romulus."

The two warriors looked at each other, shrugging, and Nuha replied, "Never heard of him. Strange."

"You don't know the king Incubus?" Angeline looked at them, concerned. *Shouldn't the Otherworld be aware of someone like that? Or has Cedric kept himself hidden while searching for me? Could this mean...*

Nuha blinked, her eyes shifting in a way that made Angeline shudder. "Incubus? You're married to a demon?"

Angeline fell silent. *Should I be keeping such information to myself? Are demons not a welcomed kind here in the Otherworld? Artemis did say there was an Underworld below this realm, one filled with malice. Is that the realm incubi come from?*

"What are you doing loitering in front of my hut, guardians of Artemis?" They spun to face the voice that cut the air itself. "And this one?"

The woman was tall, muscular even under the black cloth and furs wrapping around her body. Her face had been painted white, red lines running down her cheeks like bloody tears, and piercings reflected the light from her brow, nose, and bottom lip, adding to her savagery. The hair on her head fell in large dreads threaded to mimic snakeskin and the ends of each strand was adorned with a snake skull, fangs flaring. On one hip hung a pair of sickles, on the other a dagger bearing a similar hilt as Angeline's. Angeline's heart skipped a beat as the woman's long legs closed the gap so she could lean down, nose to nose with Angeline.

"Well, well." She smirked, her canines making it clear she was not just another creature, but a predatorial god of sorts. Her eyes jolted Angeline, white irises with dark rims. "It seems you, Miss Ex-Mortal, have been trodden on by the gods on more than one occasion."

Angeline closed her eyes, not wanting to even think about the fact she was standing right there, right then, in the Otherworld, just for that reason alone. Between Kronos and Artemis, she had been beaten and bruised until broken beyond oblivion. Despite it all, she still moved forward and did everything to forge her own path.

"Well? Are you not going to answer me, Angeline?" Hearing the woman drop her name made Angeline's eyes snap open. "Surprised are we?"

"This is Alecto," interjected Nuha. "As we were saying, she leads the Furies, but she is also the one who passes judgment on gods who perform injustices on mortals."

Angeline's anger spiked. "Where were you when Artemis threw my life in turmoil?"

"Well, how about we speak in private about what has happened?" She motioned to her hut door.

"Oh, a private session with Alecto," Manah breathed. "You shouldn't say no to something like that, daughter of Artemis."

Angeline weighed the guardians' eyes and turned back to Alecto. The giantess lifted her brow high with a quirky smirk on her face. Angeline bit her bottom lip and marched forward. *Everyone here seems to know more about me than I do about myself. Artemis, Hamadryades, Manah, and now this Alecto. I want answers now, not later.* The hut entrance closed, and Angeline came to a halt. Much like her own living arrangements, this tiny hut was much bigger on the inside. It seemed more fitting for a Viking queen inside than a Greek god.

"Let's talk, Ex-Mortal." Alecto brushed past her, bumping her as she strode toward a heavy oak table and sat. "I suppose you are wondering where I've been; why hasn't the great Alecto come swooping in like a harpy and passed judgment, no?"

Crossing her arm, Angeline sat unamused. "I am curious why I have caught your attention at all."

"Ah, now that's a better question!" She laughed, pouring herself something to drink. Then she took a gulp. "First, let's talk about when you lost your mortality."

"I imagine the night in the cabin when we..." Her face reddened, that time with Cedric still lingering like an erotic dream in her mind. "So, where were you when Artemis came to me in that ill-mannered form in Raven's Den?"

"Ah, what if I told you that was an act of desperation to protect you and yours?" Alecto smiled behind her cup. "And ever since, the fight with Lillith, the encounter with Kronos, Beelzebub taking a shot at you, and even Boto. All of those battles were enough to summon me as judge and protector. Ah, but that one fateful night thwarted us both."

Swallowing, Angeline's chest tightened as her pulse raced. "Both?"

"You see, I have been hunting Kronos for some time." Alecto set her cup down and pulled Angeline's dagger from her fur cloak to admire the blackened blade.

Grasping at her side, Angeline found the sheath bare. "Give that back."

"I will." She stabbed it into the table, her knuckles white as she gripped the hilt. "But you must promise to train as a Fury, swear legion to me, and bind us as kindred spirits."

Holding her chin high, eyes on her blade, she had heard Cedric in situations like this and she would reply the same, "What's in it for me?"

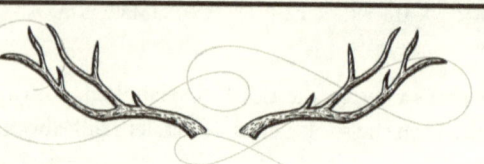

CHAPTER 11

STRIKING A DEAL WITH NICHOLAS TEAGUE

CEDRIC

Pushing through a crowded market, Cedric rubbed his nose. An orchestra of smells new and familiar filled the bustling streets. He grew nostalgic from his youth and the time spent in places like Cerdanya, haggling with the Kerretes for better prices on exotic wares. Manny buzzed back and forth from one stall to the next, and much to Cedric's surprise, many were happy to see the tacky wizard. Cedric furrowed his brow, taking it all in: a centaur running an apothecary shop, an old woman weaving textiles with her six arms and thread-like spider's silk, and a pair of alfir women selling handsewn dresses, with pointy ears and skin glowing like the summer sun.

So many in one place from a variety of regions. It seems surreal...

"Hey." Cedric locked eyes with Manny as he returned to them. "What the hell is all this?" He motioned across the market. "In the Mortal Realm, none of them would dare let the other live in the same territory, and here they're shop buddies. What gives?"

Manny looked back and laughed. "You can't be serious? You do realize the Mortal Realm is where they send their criminals. It's like the Wild West of others by a longshot."

"Great, we're the Otherworld's idea of 19th century Australia. Sure, just unload all the convicts. They totally won't figure out how to band together and create their own society." Nyctimus rolled his eyes, scratching his jaw. "I have to admit, I wasn't expecting Greek centaurs, Japanese yōkai, and Nordic alfir all in the same place."

"Oh?" Manny gave them a baffled expression. "What sort of uncivilized life you must live. Speaking of which! Cedric!" The purple and yellow peacock-of-a-wizard threw an arm over Cedric's shoulder. "You like fighting? Right?"

Brushing the arm off, Cedric grunted. "I like to kill and eat things, yes."

"Eat?" Manny blinked and Cedric pointed to his fangs.

"These aren't for show." Smirking, he crossed his arms and his jaw twitched. "What did you sign me up for now?"

"N-nothing." Manny spun and motioned for them to follow him down a back alley. "I just, well, this place can be unpredictable at times."

"You don't have to lecture us on *unpredictable*." Romasanta grabbed Fenrir's arm and pulled him along, far from the centaur he aimed to approach from behind. "At the rate this quest has gone, I given up predicting anything going down a straight and narrow path. Much like the life I've lived thus far."

"Romasanta." Fenrir frowned. "I wanted to sniff that creature."

"Dogs are dumb," blurted Enbharr. "You especially."

The kelpie's statement brought the group to a stop. The growling coming from half the party filled the air like thunder rolling through the sky. It had taken everyone's insistence to get the stubborn creature to wear a robe. Enbharr crossed their arms, expressionless and unmoved.

Cedric looked skyward, huffing a sigh. "We're going to get nowhere with these two in tow."

"Enbharr, that's not polite. These creatures are our guests." Manny rubbed his forehead, trying to be diplomatic. "You can't insult them like that."

"I was only stating the truth." Fearless, the rather smaller body of the kelpie pushed past the angry scowls of Fen, Romasanta, and Nyctimus. "Besides, they are your guests, wizard. Not mine. I find guests annoying and often choose to eat them."

Cedric shook his head, annoyed and fighting to keep the building temper from boiling over. "Where are we going?"

"Ah, down into the caves, near the arena." Manny took the opportunity to redirect and ran with it, picking up the pace as they traversed down haphazard steps. "The weapons smith that can help us is down there. Perhaps you can acquire some proper gear, so you don't stand out so much."

"You could have just snapped some into existence for us," Cedric scoffed his rebuttal.

"That's not how magic works," snorted Nyctimus. "It has to come from somewhere."

"Right, some prior knowledge and access to the materials." Manny took a turn and more steps zig-zagged downward, the air growing cool and dry. "But it's not like alchemy. We just need enough magical prowess and universal understanding. They say magus can alter the world and rebuild a creature. It's quite frightening to know such a person exists, but more than one existing is much more intimidating. As for the rest, we have to know how to do it by hand to summon it by magic. That's why many of us tend to be specialists."

"Can't Gaea do that?" Nyctimus sped up, coming closer to join the conversation. "Where does a magus compare to the mother of many gods like her?"

"Well, to be honest, they..." Manny's eyes fell behind him to the satchel hanging across Romasanta. "They are unparalleled." His eyes met Nyctimus and signaled to be quiet. "We're almost there, but be prepared to barter for your equipment."

"I prefer bartering, but I don't think we have much to trade with." Wylleam flattened his ears, everyone giving a shudder to think the eye had been listening, prying into every moment.

"That dwarf, he'll work something out, but I will say, it may be an unpleasant task of some kind." Another turn and the cavern was heating up; a red glow was cast from lava or a large forge.

"No offense, but anything is better than dealing with the kelpie." Romasanta sent everyone chuckling.

Silence fell over them, stolen glances to the satchel making it clear no one wanted Gaea to know anymore what it was they aimed to do. Soon the air became thick with steam and heat, humid, the air tasting metallic with each inhale. They heard loud pings of metal clashing, both from the arena still far below and where they circled the edge of a tunnel more like an orm hole. Manny waved them into a shop, and they began to pile into the tiny shopfront.

"Well, if it isn't Manny." A dwarf with no beard came from the back, short and stocky, a leather set of goggles obscuring his glare. "The wizard who owes me materials."

"Oh, finally someone who knows you better," mumbled Cedric.

"Look, I have brought you someone who can complete the tasks you have requested of me." He motioned to Cedric and he cocked his head at the wizard. "Mr. Nicholas Teague, I present you the king incubus, Cedric du Romulus. A dragon slayer, devourer of souls, and—"

"Head of the Vampiric Order, the Hero Ilya Muromets, Bringer of Death, and Slayer of Demons," added Cedric. "I knew you had signed me up for something."

"How are you with fighting godlings?" The dwarf approached Cedric, taking in every detail as he lifted his arms, checked his hands, and kicked a shin.

"Careful you little twerp," growled Cedric.

"Well, he has all his fingers, unlike the last one you brought me."

"I can attest he'll grow them back," Nyctimus snickered.

"Regeneration? Really?" Nicholas hummed, kicking the other shin for good measure. "I see. Sturdy and handles pain well."

"What godling am I dealing with?" Cedric sidled away from the dwarf, snarling.

"Ah, first, if you are indeed Cedric du Romulus, then Hamadryades has delivered something here in anticipation of your arrival." He disappeared into the back and all eyes shifted to Manny.

"Don't look at me! I just know the Oracles wanted me to get you here." He winked.

"Does everyone decide what path my life will take?" Romasanta was starting to get angry, crossing his arms. "I have had my fill with gypsies and oracles. I'm including wizards in that."

Nicholas Teague hobbled back, a wooden box in hand. "She said to give you this weapon. But I'm not sure what good it would do a warrior."

"Is that what I think it is?" Nyctimus came closer and looked at Manny. "Can we trust this will work?"

Manny nodded his affirmation and they motioned for Romasanta to approach. Cedric opened the box, the black velvet interior laced with old magic. Retrieving Gaea's Eye from the dirt-filled container, Romasanta placed the gem delicately inside. Cedric closed it and the box grew vines, wrapping tight and weaving into a braid reminiscent of Celtic knots. The tension and relief hit the entire crew, besides the dwarf and kelpie, at once.

"What in the blazes is wrong with you lot?" Nicholas marveled.

"Gaea was using that gem to spy on us," Manny announced. "It has been difficult to block her sight and ears this whole time while in its presence. Not even I could conjure magic strong enough to oppose her."

"Well, Hamadryades is a creature Gaea doesn't dare oppose or trifle with. If you have that old dryad's blessings and box, you must be a powerful fighter indeed." A wicked little grin grew on his face. "I need you to enter the arena as my champion. You see, we win gold and rare materials in these, and I am running out of supplies."

"What am I fighting against?" countered Cedric.

"Oh, just a minotaur." Manny shrugged.

Clearing his throat, Nyctimus intervened. "Does this one have a name?"

"Yes." Manny wouldn't meet any of their eyes.

"And that name?" Romasanta eyed Nyctimus and Cedric.

"It doesn't matter, I need you to kill the damn thing," grumbled the dwarf. "If you do this, I will let you keep the equipment, might even owe you a favor at the end of this all."

"No." Cedric's answer made everyone flinch. "The name or you find a new champion, Short Stack."

"I don't think formal names are needed in an arena fight." Manny was talking faster, nervous.

"The name, dwarf." Cedric walked closer and bent down. "It wouldn't happen to be the godling known as Asterion, would it?"

The wizard and dwarf looked at one another, narrowing their eyes. Silence took hold as everyone waited for the answer they already could assume was true. As if they hadn't been in a compromised situation, it now twisted into a new dilemma. At last, Romasanta approached Cedric and waited for him to stand. When he had his attention, Romasanta patted Cedric's shoulder a few times, inhaling deeply and blowing it out before he at last spoke.

"Well, Pup. Know that we all appreciate the hard work you've devoted yourself to during this quest. Go make me proud. You deserve any rewards this one offers."

A swift inhale came from everyone.

"Are you out of your damn minds!" Cedric roared, spinning back to the dwarf. "You, short shit! You are going to make me two weapons to my liking, even if I have to fucking slay half the creatures in this godforsaken realm to make it happen! You can keep my leftovers for all I fucking care! And you!" He spun to Manny. "No more dealing me out like a personal street fighter to make fucking bets on! What did you bet half the town? That I would lose or win this fucking fight with Asterion?"

Nyctimus's eyes widened. "Is that what you were doing in the marketplace?"

"Wow, you caught me." The wizard grimaced, rubbing the back of his neck. "You're not as dumb as you look."

"No. Cedric has his moments." Romasanta nodded.

"But I want to fight the bull-man," Fenrir pouted.

Cedric gave the group a silencing glare before turning back to Nicholas Teague. "You and me, in the back. Let's discuss the terms."

The dwarf finally lifted off his goggles, scratching his chin. After a moment, he nodded, and Cedric followed. His shoulder bumped into Manny and Cedric pushed him back.

"Not you, wizard," Cedric growled.

"R-right." Nodding, he backed away. "How bold of me to think I was part of your business."

In the back of the shop was a far greater room with several forges. Each seemed to have its own billow attached, each fueled by a variety of sources. One had lava flowing through it, another seemed to run on wood and coal, and there seemed to be one running off a ball of fire magic. Cedric paused, mesmerized by the forge. He had seen many things, but this blacksmith had the knowledge and the equipment to match. Nichola Teague smirked, walking up beside him to admire his own forge for a moment.

"Is that magic?" Cedric asked.

"Not exactly," he laughed. "That is a dragon's fire forge. One of the last in existence."

"And where would there be another?" He followed the dwarf to a crafting table filled with blueprints and scrolls.

"Rumors say Avalon."

"Of course. Avalon," he drawled.

"You been there?" The dwarf tilted his head, eyes wide with a look of surprise.

"Yeah. Honestly, it's my headquarters of sorts in the Mortal Realm." Weighing the dwarf's expression, he relaxed and let himself smirk. "But we don't have anyone good with blacksmithing. If you know a guy, we'd gladly take him in."

"The best blacksmith was always Badbh."

Cedric visibly cringed. "You got to be kidding me."

"You know her?" The dwarf poured water into a goblet for himself and chugged it.

"Friends." Shaking his head, Cedric double-backed to why he really wanted a private moment with the dwarf. "I need a god-slaying weapon."

"It's good to need things." Nicholas nodded with a smirk. "But we've been banned from making such weapons for hire or sell."

"I'm offering to trade labor and materials," countered Cedric.

"I was hoping you saw that opening."

"And I need something made for my wife." He dug in a satchel, pulled the gem he had taken from Aitvaras, and set it on the table. "A dagger with this. She's a sorceress of sorts, and I was thinking it might help."

"Dragonite." Pulling his goggles back on, he gave the gem a closer look. "This is strong enough to build myself a new forge with... and you want it in a tiny ass blade?"

"If you can't rise to the challenge, I suppose I can go to Badbh when I get back—"

"I'll do it, but I need some very specific materials. Do you want her to be able to use this as a mana supply, or cast dragon spells and fire?"

"Both."

"You're getting greedy." Nicholas frowned. "This is going to need materials from a fucking titan or high demon from the Underworld, and even then, a blade that won't break under magical pressure, like feathers from a stymphalian."

A shudder rolled through Cedric. Tilting his head, he let his horns grow and form. Nicholas took a few steps back, reaching for a hammer on the anvil behind him. Cedric's eyes glowed, the green bright with catlike pupils. Fangs were making themselves known until, at last, he reached up.

Gripping one horn tightly, he tugged. The snap echoed through the room. He dropped the broken horn on the table, shaking off the transition.

Nicholas narrowed his eyes, picking up the horn to inspect it further. He kept looking back at Cedric, his brow knitting deeper as he spun the horn. At last, he scrambled in a bucket of contraptions, pulling them out to measure and ting on the appendage Cedric had given him. Content, he had checked and checked again, Nicholas pulled the goggles all the way off and laid them on a table. He searched the air for a moment, and at last, settled on his next words.

"You've got to be the first titan I've ever met, not blood-related to Gaea."

Cedric nodded, jaw twitching, as he looked away for a brief moment. "So I wasn't wrong in thinking something very big has happened to me."

"You do know this weapon might take you down, but..." He stared down at the dragonite and titan horn, clicking his teeth. "If you and yours can eventually knock that bitch off her throne, I'll do it for free."

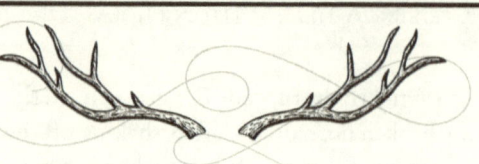

CHAPTER 12

TO BECOME A FURY

ANGELINE

Angeline panted, sweat dripping off her chin as she continued to kneel. Every fiber in her legs burned, the weight across her shoulders had been increased slowly, calculating. When her legs would begin to shake, they would wait before adding more weight and ice-cold water would be splashed on her. At first, it seemed torturous, but the burning of her body soon welcomed the reprieve. She had learned her first lesson; *don't lose your balance.* Alecto had cut her arm the moment her palm touched the floor. Looking at the other Furies, many were scarred with lines running in long rows across their skin. They were badges of tribulations they had encountered in training.

Swallowing, she rasped, "How long am I to do this?"

"Until you stop shaking." Alecto poured herself more wine. "Though, you impress me, Ex-Mortal."

"I don't feel impressive," she hissed, trying to adjust the wooden pole lying on her shoulders.

"You should," Alecto reassured, sipping her wine. "You've only earned one strike on your arm from me. And better yet, almost a day has passed in mortal terms since you started."

Angeline inhaled deeply at the idea she had lost track of time, thanks to the searing burning ache of her body under duress. "When does this stop?"

"I've already answered that," she chuckled. "You like being redundant, don't you?"

Two furies with eyes dark walked in, their faces covered in skull masks. Angeline focused on the slashes painting their arms, like a ladder from the shoulder, down to their wrists. Shifting her glance, she saw the same towering lines etched into their thighs, shins, and one had some on the tender flesh of her abdomen. More weight filled the ends of the pole, buckets hanging filled with rocks and a metal she could only imagine could be lead.

Closing her eyes tight, she willed her burning legs not to shake. The wood pole creaked, digging into her shoulders, sending a rivulet of blood trickling over her shoulder and between her breasts. Inhaling deeply, she steadied herself and thanked Cedric for making her the undying monster that he had made her into.

Wait, if only I can get that trick to work now...

Sweat glistened over her skin as at last the pain shifted to pleasure. Releasing the air from her lungs, she had finally invoked the ability. She had feared it had been only due to their connection and solely Cedric's doing.

Finally, some relief... though it doesn't mean the destruction and havoc will end anytime soon. This is nothing compared to what Kronos spent centuries doing to me.

Her gaze met the two women who stared at the single cut on her shoulder, the badge of red fading to a pink scar. Angeline side glanced and frowned.

I see why he fusses. The idea of being excited about the pain heals. This could be dangerous. Still, the cut should have been completely gone. Now it matches the older strikes on these girls, which means I know who marked even them.

"I see. A mark from a Fury stays for life?" Swallowing, she attempted to adjust the wooden pole, only to shred her flesh.

"And I see you finally used that bonus skill you've been struggling with." Alecto raised a goblet and made a hissing sound to dismiss the gawking eyes. "Artemis can teach you about magic, but it is force of will to tame the rest of you."

Another drip of sweat fell from her chin. Arousal washed through her, and all she wanted was *him*. She fought to not roll her eyes back as the burning in her legs shifted to how she felt when Cedric slid his hand across them. There was only the desire to straddle him on her bed and lick the salt from his skin and taste the bittersweet flavor of his blood on her lips. A visceral desire to tear the world apart in order to satisfy herself on the flesh of her one true soulmate in this life and the next.

The heat of her sexual desire flowed from her like a wildfire. With it came a new awareness of the bodies who had come and gone. She could sense, almost smell and taste, the way her untamed succubine abilities had stirred their bodies. It was this taste that had healed her, the sampling to feed from another's sexual desire and the ability to prompt it to rise in such rapid ascension. Alecto, on the other hand had pushed this heat off her with her own magical aura. Angeline's thoughts reeled with the idea she could use this to protect against other auras and the times Cedric had demanded a room with his own.

I need to remember this sensation. It could prove useful one day.

At last, she rasped to Alecto, "I wasn't sure if it was even a skill I possessed at all. Sorry if it's affecting anyone who comes too close."

"You noticed their stares."

Furrowing her brow, she was starting to relax, to let the weight of everything lay stiff across her body. "Y-yes. And I noticed the scores of scars."

"Most will fill their arms and legs while performing this first trial. They are jealous and in awe of you." She leaned forward and began picking at the meat on a platter. "You see, no one has ever carried that much weight. They envy your perseverance, Ex-Mortal."

Angeline stifled a short laugh. "Survival. That's all it's ever been. The will to live. No pride in that."

"Ah, but look at you now." She gnawed on a chunk and swallowed. "No longer killable or crushable. I would say it's worked in your favor thus far."

The wooden pole creaked some more, splinters breaking from it. Angeline shifted, and it was enough to goad it into snapping at last. The buckets hit the floor, the ground shaking under their weight. Angeline nearly fell forward, her hands daring to touch the floor. The cut on her arm was enough reminder to rock back, recovering her balance. At last, she looked at Alecto, too afraid to stand.

I am way in over my head. This too will be about survival if I am to make it through the Justiciar of the Gods' training. But I want this. She slays and tortures those whom people worship. That's the power I am willing to reach for, and maybe I might be worthy of being by his side for eternity. No longer useless, no longer sobbing, no longer weak.

"Come, sit and eat. Drink." Alecto motioned to a chair across the table from her.

Angeline didn't move a muscle. "Have I completed my test?"

"Indeed," smirked Alecto, watching as Angeline hissed as overstrained tendons moved in the opposite direction, since she began the task over a day prior. "You did very well. Only a single strike on your shoulder."

"So, the point was to stay steady until the pole gave way?" Angeline furrowed her brow, looking at the stones and broken wood scattered across the dirt floor. "That's a lot of weight to hold, human or not."

Alecto chuckled, pouring water into a goblet and offering it to Angeline to make her come closer. "You are the first to squat until it broke. You should celebrate this while there's a moment to catch your breath."

Angeline paused a moment before taking the goblet, staring down at the water with a hint of suspicion. "All those marks on their bodies though..."

"Yes, but you see, those strikes are for falling down." Alecto pushed a platter of meat toward her and she sat, sucking back the water, no longer able to hold back the want to eat and drink. "We only add weight when their legs stop shaking, you see. It's a test of will and endurance, and it's designed to test each girl to their own limitations."

Angeline choked on her water.

"Not everyone comes through here with immense strength like you and I, Ex-Mortal." She refilled the goblet, urging her to drink. "Rest now, refuel. I look forward to seeing how you fare in the next test."

"How many of these trials will there be?" Angeline began tearing a chunk of meat from the bone, wondering what beast she would dine on in this strange realm. "You had pointed out most of the marks came from this first trial, which means I could still fail at this stage."

Alecto nodded. "Clever girl. Granted, the next discussion is more of a review of your triumphs and tribulations while you lived in the Mortal Realm."

Angeline choked once more, this time on her food, and scrambled for the goblet.

"Your fear discussing this... but I don't know if you realize the full spectrum that the Oracles have seen, of what is yet to come and long since passed. Usually, the next trial would be to hunt a busse, but you took down the cream of the crop from what I've been told."

Swallowing her food, Angeline had to know. "Are they always as large as a tree?"

"No," Alecto snorted. "They are bull-sized deer with a temper to match. The one in the Black Forest was the legendary Golden Stag. I'm shocked someone so green was able to take him down at all."

"I had some training..." Her appetite wavered, a flush of arousal waving through her as she remembered how Cedric came to her at the end.

"I see, so that did give you quite the advantage. Good." Nodding, she once more magically had Angeline's dagger in hand admiring the black blade. "Remember the difference between your mortal self and now. You're going to need that later. As for the final ceremony, I deem you worthy of my blessing. Granted, not a full Fury yet. No, this is something I rarely give, access to me and my tribe, yet not bound to our cause."

"Why not? What if I like your cause and want to take part?" Her eyes watched her beloved item, abandoning all want for rest if it meant she could rush over the table to take it back. "I like the idea of punishing gods and goddesses who do wrong to mortals sort of mission."

"Of course, you do, Ex-Mortal." Alecto's voice seemed to purr as she stabbed the dagger into the table between them. "But you are destined for far greater things. You're a child of the Oracles, designed to set nature right and that, in itself, serves the Fury well."

Angeline swallowed as Alecto's eyes glowed and the room darkened under her monstrous aura. It crawled and scattered in ways that made the shadows distort, as if taken hold by some kind of infestation. Angeline pushed back with her own, blood boiling with a wanton heat that licked at Alecto. A wicked grin, sharp-toothed like a beast, parted Alecto's white lips until the pink of her gums broke them apart. The food at the table began to rot rapidly under Alecto's power, and every joint in Angeline's body tightened with a sense of alarm. She abandoned the food in her hand, pushed back the goblet.

All this talk about destiny and oracles. When do I get to decide how I defeat my enemies for myself instead of being every fucking immortals' plaything or broken tool?

In an instant, Angeline's fear shifted to anger and her aura grew with it, pushing back Alecto's miasma with one of her own making. A shudder rolled over Alecto, and at last her aura retreated. There was something lingering in Angeline's senses as the hairs on her skin raised in a mangled mixture of arousal and hunger for something more than food or drink. Her own aura had dared to push past Alecto's own and a hint of lust escaped the ancient goddess. The tension in the room shifted. That was how Cedric's aura worked, and again, she'd felt Lillith's sting threefold. Alecto had looked away from Angeline and released the dagger, as if contemplating something.

"Your willpower is amazing, dear." She bit her bottom lip and met Angeline with a softer gaze; another hint of lust sent a wave of excitement through her. "I have not felt that level of lust in a long time. Not since my days of learning about the mortals and enjoying the pleasures of the flesh. For that, I will gift you one favor, a favor that follows your soul and cannot be touched or corrupted by any god or magic in the known world. This was something granted to me by Aether himself."

Angeline stiffened as Alecto rose to her feet. The way she paced around the table was grace and stealth. Not a sound or movement made without purpose. She towered beside Angeline, and she swallowed her nerves, looking up. Her hair made a haunting sound as the skulls slid and knocked into one another as she leaned down to cup Angeline's face. Much to her surprise, Alecto pressed her lips firmly against hers. First, she felt the silken heat of her tongue slide between them. The succubine desires goaded Angeline to deepen the kiss, thrilled and hungry to feed on the lustful whims Alecto offered her.

A jolt rocked her, Alecto held her face like a vice as something long crawled out of her mouth and into her own. Legs, long-bodied and hard-shelled, it scurried across her tongue and clacked against her teeth. She tried to close her jaw tight, but it was too late. The taste of blood as its tendrils forced their way down her throat. At last, Alecto released her, and she fell back, coughing and gagging. Something crawled inside her flesh and soul, burning like hell's fire. Nausea and panic rolled through her, but neither brave enough to take hold of the situation. Laughter rolled from Alecto.

"Unpleasant, that bug of mine."

"What the..." Her throat and voice failed.

"That is what you will use one day to call me to your side, when you've met a foe, no, a god of some kind you can't punish and wish for it to be done." A whistle rang out as Angeline's vision began to blur, the searing heat making her sweat more so than the training had. "Once it's found a spot and settled, it'll stop burning. After that, we'll see if you can manage to sneak into Freya's hall, past all those Valkyries, and draw blood on the mother of all ice queens. And then, just maybe, you might change my mind about making you an official Fury."

Angeline's skin began to blister. Receiving Alecto's blessing could kill any ordinary person at this rate. She coughed up blood, certain the cause wasn't the creature boring its way into her soul, but the fever cooking her internal organs. Collapsing, her eyes rolled back, and everything fell dark.

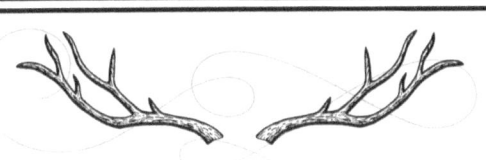

CHAPTER 13

MAKING OF A GLADIATOR

CEDRIC

Cedric stood in the battlement room, snorting at his sponsors Nicholas Teague and Manannan Mac Lir. Behind them, Romasanta walked around, observing the competitor and the selection of items for fighters to use at their leisure. Many of the weapons smiths and armorers had tables set up, inviting them to buy or even represent a certain item. This was a moneymaker for the Otherworld nobility, and worse, was modeled after the gladiator battles of the ancient Romans. Cedric had ignored the conversation they had wanted to carry on with him, focused on Romasanta as his jaw tightened on occasion.

"We mean it, you brute." Nicholas shoved Cedric and demanded his attention. "Whatever you do, you keep that helmet on."

"Why?" he snorted. "It's not like half of these fighters don't have horns."

"You don't understand the trouble we'd be in if they discovered we entered an incubus into the fight." Manny leaned in again with the arm over Cedric's shoulders. "You can't tell anyone. And worse, the idea we pulled someone from the Mortal Realm to compete."

Brushing the wizard off, he grunted, "You didn't pull me from there. I came here on my own."

"If that's true, then we will feign ignorance." Nicholas began unlocking a massive chest behind his vendor table. "I made you a special helmet, but you'll need to choose what gear you want. You survive this fight, I might make a tailored set for you."

Cedric watched as the lid fell open, the variety of armor piled together, mixing centuries of styles. "So tell me, why the ban on incubi?"

"First off, they're creatures of the Underworld. They prey on everything, frequenting the Otherworld and causing trouble." The dwarf began pulling items out, laying them out on the table for him to better pick from. "But the real trouble is that they're unkillable. Only able to be killed by one of their kind."

"Right, but that doesn't mean we're undefeatable... we just revive like a cockroach." Inhaling, he held it as he sucked on his cheek. "You make all these?"

"Of course." Nicholas gave him a disgusted expression. "Now pick your armor and weapons. Time is running out."

Cedric glanced back to Romasanta, watching how he held the gladius and swung it. The look in the old man's eyes reminded Cedric how much seeing these items brought back a mix of emotions far deeper than his own. Romasanta slid it into the sheath and handed it back to its maker. They insisted he buy it, offering one price, and lowered it as he walked away. The twitching of the arm muscles and balled fist said he had wielded a weapon much like it for some time. He met Cedric's gaze and shrugged at the battlement room.

"Tell me, old man." A smirk crossed Cedric's face as he grabbed Romasanta's shoulder, leaning into his ear. "How long did you fight in those arenas for House Romulus? Decades? Centuries? Or were you there for that thousand-year or so rise and fall?"

Grunting, Romasanta shook his head and peered around the room with hungry eyes. "Leave it to you to see that in me."

"You've done this, so I need a favor." Cedric nearly choked on the last word, something he hadn't wanted to say. "I need you to be my advisor. They may be the sponsors, but we both know I'm useless without a proper battle master to set me on the right path."

"You want advice from someone who's been there." He met Cedric's gaze, his eyes dark as his past pulled into the present.

"I don't know what to aim for and these fools are throwing everything and the kitchen sink at me in equipment." He flicked the Roman-style helmet, altered to accommodate his horns, complete with crest. "They already have me looking like a fool in an officer's helmet with a broken horn."

"Why did you break your horn?" Romasanta narrowed his eyes as Cedric rolled his. "I see. A gift for her when you cross paths, hm?"

"And now who's reading the other like an open book?" They both cracked a smile. "Now, tell me, old man, what will you have me do?"

"You'd do well as a *dimachaerus* because you can take damage. We will double down on agility and striking power." He marched over to the dwarf's table, pawing through the items. "Too heavy, too long. This is fucking worthless here..."

"Who the hell died and made you the expert, you pissant?" The dwarf spun from his digging, his face red with anger.

"Ever hear about the oldest mortal gladiator?" Grabbing a leather *pteruges*, he shoved it into Cedric's arms. "Lose the pants and wear this. You want to be near naked in battle."

"The one who died at the age of ninety after surviving a hundred-fifty battles?" Manny leaned into the conversation, excited to share his knowledge of the Mortal Realm.

"It was more like a thousand-five-hundred battles... and I feigned death at ninety only because I lost track of time." Romasanta took a step back, frustration knitting his brow. "I can't say I don't love the fight, or even that fleeting moment when the last tendril of life lingers before you snuff it out. For the longest time, I blamed that on Fenrir, but this all came after he left me."

The wizard and dwarf glared at one another in disbelief until Manny spoke up. "And how long did you participate, good sir?"

"I suggested the *bestiarii* only because I got tired of eating humans." Shoving past the dwarf, he dug through the chest and cursed under his breath. "Where are the greaves, the shin guards and sandals, small pint?"

Crossing his arms, he snorted. "I don't work often with leather."

Cedric and Romasanta shot a look at one another and Cedric hissed, "Then who can we buy them from?"

"Wait..." Romasanta dove to the bottom of the chest, emptying the contents to the floor in a big scuffle of metal pinging and banging. "These. At least this *galerus* should serve well."

"By the fates, I thought I lost that one." The dwarf reached for it, but Cedric plucked it out of reach. "You think I should just do this barefoot or with my boots?"

"Sandals or barefoot, you'll want to be aware of the ground at all times. This is close combat, with very little room to tactically use the terrain anyhow." Some more armor was pulled from the chest and added to the building heap. "Start changing. Time is running out, pup."

"Shit." Cedric started to pull his shirt off and unlace the front of his leather breeches. "I hate doing this here, but…"

Before anyone could say another word, he was bare and exposed. He scowled over a shoulder, narrowing his eyes at a female oni warrior who blew him a kiss. Shaking off the hints of lust he felt from unwelcomed stares, he began strapping the *pteruges,* but began struggling. Romasanta abandoned his search and came to his side, fixing the placement, strapping it tight, hands unapologetic as they touched and groped to put the armored skirt in its place.

A heated stare from Cedric went ignored as Romasanta took up the *galerus* and checked its fit. He paused, staring into the scene etched into it with silver, gold, and copper elements. As he began strapping it to Cedric's shoulder, the scene shifted from a godly scene to one painted to match a view of a decimated battleground. The lustrous shine was gone, the metal darkening in response. This item was something more than enchanted, but it seemed to take a liking to the power Cedric's body held and reflected to match it. Romasanta shook his head and shoved the armor into Cedric, then looked about the table of items.

"Look, I really don't think the *galerus* will be useful." Nicholas Teague began pacing. "I mean, it was purely experimental. It was pure luck I had gotten those items, and it went missing before I could sell it off."

"You don't have any greaves, pauldrons—nothing that's light and flexible enough. Consider it luck of the Oracles." Romasanta circled back and started shoving everything into the chest, double-checking for something, anything, as useful. "You have at least one *manica* in this trash heap?"

Muttering profanities under his breath, Nicholas marched to the other table. Throwing back a cloth, he revealed a smaller chest and turned to Wizard Manny. He nodded and the wizard sighed in defeat. A wave of his hand dispelled the chest and they opened it. It wasn't a junk pile like the other chest. Instead, each item was wrapped in silken cloths of various colors, as if marking each for their type, but it was a mystery whether that was intended for enchantments or craftsmanship level. Manny cleared a spot on the table for the dwarf and frowned.

"Are you sure about this, Mr. Teague?" Manny gave Cedric a haunting glare. "What if they come back asking for this?"

"I don't think they were meant to come back for it." He paused. Reaching into the chest, he pulled out the first item. "Why else would Aether want armor befitting a gladiator? It wasn't meant for him, but someone that would…"

"I see." Manny gave a nod. "His death was untimely, but we all thought…"

Nicholas walked slowly, ceremoniously to the table. "I thought he'd send someone. Maybe he has, and we just don't see what he intended just yet."

Romasanta and Cedric came closer, watching with anticipation to see him unwrap the first item. There laid a *manica* made from a strange colored leather, bluish-black in hue. The metal seemed to have a hint of metallic flakes that moved under the hardened surface. These were not just enchanted armor pieces, but were made with materials that seemed celestial in manner. Cedric frowned, his eyes glowing under the slits of his helmet.

"I couldn't wear something like this." He aimed to walk away, but Romasanta grabbed his hand and shoved it against the armor. "What the hell is the matter with you, old man?!"

"Watch," barked Romasanta. *This is of the same set as the galerus.*

The armor shifted and the shiny metal turned pitch black. Cedric's stomach twisted, and the dwarf gasped. The metallic flaking was more like black sand under the brightest sun. Something about the item reacted to him, to his power, and a chill ran through him. It wanted him to take it, wear it, and if he could, dared him to break it.

This armor is a reflection of my darkest wish. To be broken until I no longer breathe.

Swallowing, he looked at Manny. "You're the magic expert. What the hell is this?"

"That is a rarity among the rare, my friend." He had a sad look in his eyes, staring down at the way the armor shifted in color. "This is legendary living armor. Made with materials of the celestial beings who brought all of the world into being."

"And it likes you." Nicholas snorted, and he circled back to the chest and motioned for the two of them to come and get it. "You will find all you need here, all but a helmet."

"I don't want it." A shudder rocked through him.

He didn't need to be told it was living armor. This inanimate creature made by celestial fires whispered its lust to be his, to be strapped to his body and feed on his power. The idea that it had been sealed in a box by a great magician unnerved him. Celestial armor, on a king incubus, meant to live in the Underworld, a being who preferred to live free in the Mortal Realm, free of the pecking order found in the Otherworld. Taking this would add to his ire about being an abomination who could walk freely among the realms while never belonging to any of them.

"Take it," snarled Nicholas. "To be honest, the wizard and I tried with all our might to find a buyer for a short while."

"It went horribly wrong." Manny turned away, covering his mouth.

"It ate them," Cedric snorted and caressed the scaling layers. "It doesn't change shape until it's found itself a companion, is that it?"

"It hasn't happened before." Nicholas shrugged. "Now get dressed. The drums are starting in the arena."

"Fuck me." Cedric turned to Romasanta, who shrugged.

"We both know nothing comes without a price." He picked up the *manica* and began strapping it on but leaped back. "Living..."

Cedric tensed, his heart racing as the *manica* snaked into place and pulled its own straps tight. He had accepted the offer and it would put itself into place. Glaring at the chest of the remaining pieces, he questioned whether he should abandon the rest. Another thought crossed his mind, in the end, it would hunt him down and find its way to him as the *galerus* had done. Someone had brought the materials, made the request, and by some ill fate, he had become the owner of unwanted treasures left behind by the past.

"What other pieces are in there?" Rolling his shoulder, the armor, light and elated to be on him, unnerving. "I want to know where this thing will be crawling around."

"Fair point." Manny's eyebrows raised high. "Forgive me, good sirs, but I must check on our friends in the stands. It'd be a shame if Mr. Nyctimus was killed in a battle between Fen and Enbharr."

"Well, I hate to say it but…" Nicholas cringed and began rattling out the list, "Sandals, greaves, and…" He stumbled on his words and began coughing until he sputtered, "*Pteruges.*"

"Son of a bitch." Cedric covered his face. "Let's just get this over with."

Reaching over the table, he pulled a gladius from its sheath and cut the current *pteruges* and it fell heavily to the floor. Nicholas shouted at him, snatching it up to address the damage, but Cedric couldn't focus. The armor and the room made his body tense and his skin pimple. He could feel the arousal, the lustful stares, and the sensations behind them. In a room majority male, it annoyed him, but something not unusual nor taboo. He hadn't been one to be bashful, but the anxiety of the armor made him falter on levels he didn't know existed in himself.

If I need to hide my aura, this armor might be the key. It literally feeds on my aura. I'm out of sorts in this realm. The magic in the air is difficult to manage. At least with this godforsaken leech attached…

The armor in the chest rattled, a low wailing humming coming from the wrapped pieces. Cedric cracked his neck, steeling his nerves for what would come next. He was no stranger to the sensation of wandering hands, having had his share of buying out a whorehouse to snuff out past lusting long before Angeline. This was different. He couldn't be sure if he'd ever be able to remove the armor again, but that was a risk he was willing to take if it meant he could achieve his goals faster.

Stiffening, he marched over to the chest. The hum of the screams subsided, and he watched as the pieces of armor snaked out from under their cloths. He held his breath; the sandals spilling out first. In the distraction of shifting to keep balance, he failed to see the quicker element fly from the box. Between his thighs and around his waist, the metal and leather of the armored skirt were cold as ice against his skin. Exhaling, he cursed all involved in his torment, an audience watching as his own armor molested him. It proved far more daring and rougher in strapping itself in place than Romasanta had been.

At least I know this won't fall off.

The greaves were far more forgiving than their counterparts, and when settled, he leaned on his knees. He had seemed weaker after breaking the horn, but this was a level of draining he hadn't expected. Living armor had its fallbacks, indeed. It fed on its host and he was on the menu.

Granted, it had devoured those who had attempted to force ownership. The squirming had faded to feel more like normal armor. He could breathe again, his energy returning as a wave of lust slammed into him from the approaching warrior.

He spun to see the oni warrior approaching. She removed her samurai helmet, her face striking. The stark look of Geisha-style makeup added to the long locks of black hair that escaped the long braid. She bowed deeply, her thin horns tall and black like marble. In her hands, she held out a katana and Cedric raised a brow.

"Um, I don't understand?" Cedric reached for the scabbard but paused. "Why are you offering this to me?"

"It's one thing to come here and fight, but to strip naked and expose all who you are not once, but twice, was quite the show." She met his gaze, her irises a firework of yellow and red. "But to have your armor want to eat you alive before battle is something worthy of a great blade such as this one."

"Thanks, I think." Grabbing it, he pulled it free and smiled. "I've missed this sort of blade. What's your name?"

"Oni Gozen." She stood, placing the helmet back on to hide her face once more. "And that is a blade made from the fang of an *okuri-inu*, blessed by the King of Hell himself."

Cedric turned to Romasanta. "We don't tell Fenrir this is a cousin's fang. He might get riled over that idea."

Romasanta threw up his hands and laughed. "Look, the drums have stopped, and they are about to call you out for your fight. At least you have the weapon you prefer to have, but take something shorter or blunt."

"Right." Cedric turned back to Oni Gozen, bowing in deep respect. "Thank you. This was beyond gracious and unexpected."

She laughed. "I can't say I didn't enjoy the look of your flesh, young one. May you hold your ground against Asterion. But, a word of warning…"

"What is it?" Cedric saw a coy smile on her face.

"Don't use that sword here. It carries miasma on the blade. Demon blades are frowned upon in battle here in the Otherworld."

"Great, a thing I can't use." Cedric looked at the katana with longing. "Perhaps it may prove useful when I get home."

"I hope it serves you as well as it served me." She bowed deeply and he reflected the motion.

The doors opened, horns blowing to call attention to the room. An alfin unrolled a scroll and the two horn-blowing dwarves sidled to the side. The room was quiet, and Cedric tried to secure the scabbard in place, but the armor took over and he flustered at the thought. Nicholas shoved him forward, pushing him apart from the crowd. The alfin with the pale complexion and gaunt face eyed him a moment as if disgusted that this was the one they offered him.

"It seems your fellow warriors said you should face Asterion."

Cedric eyed the warriors in the room and realized none of them wanted to be chosen for this fight. "I guess I'm the only willing participant?"

"Are you sure?" He eyed the crowd behind him. "The last new one you offered didn't make it more than five minutes before bleeding to death."

A toothy grin crossed Cedric's face and he turned. "Quick, someone toss me a one-handed mace."

"Will a war hammer work?" Romasanta tossed it over their heads and Cedric caught it.

"Yeah, this should do the trick." He turned to the alfin. "Now I'm ready to knock a fucking horn off that damn cow. Let me go do what I came to do."

"Tenacious." A wicked grin crossed his lips. "You might be entertaining enough for some hopeful bets to be placed. Fine, I accept... what's your name?"

"Theseus," Romasanta cut into the conversation. "My pupil's name is Theseus."

Really old man? Is this your joke or are you aiming to piss Asterion off?

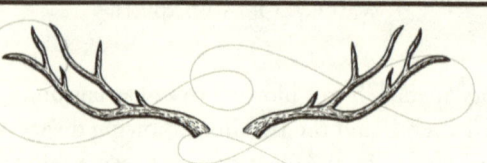

Chapter 14

The Art of Stealth

Angeline

There was little time to rest. Alecto pushed trainees hard and it could be seen even under the ghost-white face paint and black wrappings that made up their clothes. Angeline wasn't alone on this next task. She stood at attention in a line of women, dark rings under all their eyes from the exhaustion pulling at them. This time, they were given dark clothing and sandals with soft soles to help limit the sound their steps would make.

"I'm impressed. The six of you managed to get through the obstacle course without a sound today." Alecto paced in front of them, avoiding their stares. "But be warned, failure will leave you with more scars than you can count. Valkyries will not hesitate to run you through by spear or sword. Many of my warriors have their share of scars from this."

All their eyes spanned the other warriors that stood all around them, the marks across their torsos loud. They had been run through. Angeline's mind flashed back to the busse and again with the way Cedric had impaled Lillith. She had begged for more and so did he when she...

Am I going to have to face the want to be wounded? This is about stealth, not endurance, and I am sure I'll end up with both arms full of Alecto's marks.

It took Angeline a week or longer to manage to pass the initial stealth training. Scores of marks lined her left arm now. Each time they made a noise, wobbled, or even took a wrong step, they had to face a whip cracking at them. Soon, as they were either pulled out or made it to the end, Alecto made quick work of slashing them for each crack of the whip. Granted, Angeline felt uneasy. Most of the girls had already been marked down their other arm or thighs by the time they made it through unscathed. Never had she been so thankful for her former training to hunt and be aware of how she placed her weight in her steps.

They were told not to speak. Angeline could deal with that, but they never said they couldn't share information. Drawing in the sand, making hand signals and nods of the head combined with eye movement, the six of them had ended up teaming up to pass the obstacles as a unit. It seemed to bring a smile to Alecto's face and earned whisperings from those who moderated. Not one whip cracked for these acts of communication, and it made Angeline breathe a little easier.

"I only need one of you to make it to Freya unscathed and leave a mark. I want to see you draw at least a drop of red on that ice queen." The tension building in the room added to the thoughts invading even Angeline's mind as Alecto continued. "That doesn't mean you will fail if you don't. We are looking at how far or close you get to Freya before they run you through. A Fury is swift, but patient in their actions and timing. You need to be very aware of your actions and how they will unfold for not only you and the enemy, but the allies with which you aim to work or even protect. Do you understand your mission?"

"Yes, Grand Assassin Alecto!" They spoke as one shouting force.

"Now, we will leave you to prepare and plan. You have only a few minutes to gather supplies and may use anything and everything within this building only. Consider it a lesson in resources and improvising." The elder Furies left single file, not one word of wisdom whispered to their sisters in training as Alecto added, "Know that we are interested in seeing how this soirée unfolds in a few moments."

The door shut and the other girls dove for the weapon's chest. Angeline had what she needed, the chimeran dagger on her hip as always. Looking through the room, she did a double take. Their normal clothes had been brought and left for them. She rushed to them, pulling hers from the stack, and began changing clothes in a hurry. One of the warriors turned her attention to her.

"What's the matter with you? You look like you're about to make a run for it," Nefeli marveled as Angeline paid no heed to the stranger watching her undress fully. The girl was olive-skinned, much like Artemis, and had curly, brown locks pulled back and pinned tight to her head. Her green eyes were dull and earthy, but it didn't stop Angeline's heart from fluttering at the ache to see Cedric's again. "Are you abandoning the mission? Does Freya terrify you, so?"

"No, that's not it at all. If dealing with Artemis and Kronos for centuries has taught me anything, the answer is far simpler." She rushed to pull on the leather breeches, deciding to keep with the sandals and disregard the boots. "Besides, none of us had access to this hut when we were asked to dress in black assassin regale before the meeting. She also didn't say we all had to make it to Freya. I don't know what will happen."

"You're right. Why would they bring our clothes in here?" Nefeli picked up a pink Greek toga, presumably her own. "This seems strange. I haven't worn this since before the endurance test, so ... these are intentionally picked outfits from before our joining the trails."

"What are you thinking, Sister Angeline?" Another one approached, Sarnai from the orients, had dark hair and eyes. She had been amazing on the obstacle course, and when she saw the attempts at communication had joined Angeline and traded knowledge. All she could get from her after the fact was she had learned much of her skills from her clan. "It seems you have thought of something."

"Yes. Either I am going to make it to Freya or make one hell of a decoy. Look, unlike the rest of you, I can take a hit." A chill up her spine made her shiver as she pulled on the loose lace-up blouse and reached for her leather tunic. "Is there a small dagger, anything like a needle, perhaps?"

"Will this work?" Rati, a shapely woman, though strong and had warm clay-colored skin, intervened, offering a tiny throwing dagger. She had earned the most cuts, but had passed. What made Angeline admire her most was the unfailing smile she mustered, even now, in this panicked rush to prepare for the impossible. "It's small, but it should slip between the breasts or under the tunic."

"Here, let me help lace this up." Nefeli didn't wait for a response and began tying her tight. "What else can we give her? You aren't going in there with just that old thing?" She gestured at the dagger.

"It's not as harmless as it looks," snorted Angeline.

"Here, I found these in my things." Sarnai spun back to her with ornamental hair sticks. She showed how each was sheathed so one could pull them without the hair falling in the way. Let me put your hair up."

"T-thank you." For the first time in a long time, her time with her cousin flashed in her mind.

Swallowing the wave of emotion back, she couldn't stop the burning in her chest. She had dressed her cousin many times like this. Lacing of dresses and corsets, helping braid and brush her blonde locks, but this... Nefeli tugged the air from her and at last tied the tunic. She grunted at the pulling and twisting of her hair as Sarnai worked with Rati as her assistant to brush and sort her hair out. For the first time since she married Cedric du Romulus, she felt like some savage version of royalty.

"There, you are as gorgeous as a lotus flower." Rati sighed and started to check for her own outfits and inventory.

The other two girls eyed them and whispered. They were twins and had taken their advice, but shared nothing back. It could be safe to assume they had their own idea of how to accomplish the goal. Ignoring the way they cleaned out the chest, Angeline and Sarnai glanced at one another and made a knowing expression.

"They are weighing themselves down." Sarnai turned to Rati, who had seemed confused by the expression.

"That, and the more equipment you carry, the more noise you make. One night I will have to put on my Bedleh and dance to prove how noisy even the tiniest piece can be." They laughed as Rati rocked her hips, showing her amazing control and flexibility.

"So, again, Angeline." Nefeli brought them to silence as she cleared her throat. "Speak your mind."

"Look, I'm something ... else." The awkward announcement hadn't been spoken out loud until now. Regardless, her comrades needed to know. "I can heal and take a hit. It's just something I can do. Regardless, if I approach as me, not a Fury or even in training, Freya may grant me an audience."

Sarnai knitted her brow. "And why would she accept?"

"Well, that's something I don't think I should reveal," she swallowed. "Do you trust me?"

"Yes," Rati answered without hesitation, and the others nodded.

"Thank you." The door swung open and they stood at attention.

Alecto stalked in and first looked over the twins. She lifted a brow to see the plethora of weapons crossing their chest, back, arms, and legs. After taking their inventory into account, she turned to the four of them with a wicked grin. And it faltered. A deep frown formed, and she marched across the room and came nose-to-nose with Angeline.

"And where do you plan on going?" she hissed, a glow of red in her eyes.

Steeling her nerves, Angeline forced a smirk and replied coolly, "To see Freya as you've commanded us."

"Then what are you waiting for, Ex-Mortal?" She sidled and motioned for her to go.

Angeline marched for the door. Her friends attempted to follow on her heels, but Alecto stepped in their way. "I wonder. How far you will get without help."

"But, Alecto, she–" Rati's words were silenced as Sarnai hissed.

"We can't go against Alecto's word. She is the queen of Furies and Supreme Justiciar to the gods of the Otherworld and beyond." Sarnai gripped Rati's shoulder reassuringly, giving Angeline a knowing look.

"I've been through worse." Angeline mustered a smile and left through the doors.

It took her a moment to find her way to the Valkyries. As she weaseled into their area of the island, she could see a transition in the warriors. These women had thicker, heavier armor. Some wore layered leather armor to allow some agility teamed with spears and shields. Others wore metal plates with large two-handed swords or war hammers. Angeline marveled over them, the brute force of the training moves bringing her to a stop.

Angeline watched as two Valkyries entered a training circle, one in leather and the other in shining metal with swans etched in bronze. The spearman lunged forward, and the war hammer knight used the handle to interfere the aim of the blade. A ting rang in the air as it bounced off the thick-plated pauldron. As the hammer swung up to counter, the spearman stumbled back, braid and loose hair flowing upward with the powerful wind created from the near blow to the head. Chills rattled Angeline, both a want for her own try against such a foe and the excitement building at taking a blow so strong as that one.

"Sister Svanhvit is one of the few who choose the hammer of all things to battle with." A warrior in similar armor approached, holding out a hand to shake. "I am Alvit, and you are?"

"Oh, A-Angeline." She reached out and the grip tightened and jerked her forward.

Before Angeline could register what was happening, the brute-of-a-woman had shoved up the sleeve of her shirt up to her shoulder, exposing the marks left by Alecto. Angeline's heart skipped a beat, and she locked eyes with the blue-eyed, strawberry-blonde warrior. The grip on her skin burned as she made an attempt to twist from her. At last, Alvit let go, puffing out her plate-armored chest and making Angeline shimmy away. She stood taller than Cedric.

"What is a Fury in training doing here on Valkyrie grounds?" Alvit's stern voice with its Nordic accent sent chills across her.

That's an old dialect seeping into her accent. How old is this woman?

"To see what I can learn from you." Angeline turned back to the fighting ring in time to see Svanhvit swipe low, the hammer skidding across the ground.

The spearman had back stepped out of range, panting already from all the dodging she had done in Angeline's short distraction. Dust rose in a wall between them, yet from where she stood, she could see both sides. Another step back, the spearman searched the dust for movement, knitting her brow and pulling the shield in front. On the other side, Svanhvit gripped the hammer in hand and drove the thin handle through. It didn't stir the dust, and when it hit the shield, the spearman lost her balance.

She fell back, landing hard on the ground. Svanhvit wasted no time, no hesitations as she let the weight of the hammer slide the handle back into her hand and she swung down. The dust blew away, parting like water under a boat's hull. Sunlight caught the armor and glinted brightly across the shield. The hammer thudded hair-raisingly close to the woman's head, the ear-shattering scream echoing from the arena.

"I want to learn to use my strength like that. Smart and efficient." Angeline held her chin high as she met the Valkyrie's judging gaze.

A smile formed. "And who do you hope to take you on, little Fury?"

"I..." Angeline thought a moment, and laughed at herself before braving the name. "I was hoping Freya could suggest someone."

Alvit laughed. "Freya has no time for you, little Fury."

"Ah, but does she have time to speak with Artemis's heiress?" Angeline's quick retort snuffed the laughing.

"You can't be serious?" Narrowing her eyes, Alvit crossed her arms. "Prove it. Cast a spell right now."

Angeline drew her thumb over her cheek and brow. Gathering sweat, she formed a droplet or two and with a flick, it flashed into an ice spear matching the design of the fighters she had passed. A wide grin grew on Alvit's face as she offered for her to take the glimmering magically made weapon. She tried to strike the handle over her knee, but not a crack formed, nor did it give at all. Holding it up, the ice didn't show any signs of melting.

"Oh, we shall show this little gem to Freya." She waved for Angeline to follow. "You must be of Artemis's blood. She's the only one here in the Otherworld who can match Freya's ice magic." She eyed Angeline, pushing her forward as they entered a grand hall much like the one she had arrived in. "But you might prove a worthy adversary."

"A what?" Stumbling into the hall, the room went silent.

A grand banquet had ceased its clamoring to stare at their uninvited guest. The woman at the head of the table stood, a large boar behind her rising to its feet, and Angeline marveled over how on earth it managed to enter the small doorway. Swallowing, she met the woman's gaze. Her eyes were white with nothing more than pupils, her hand motioning for the boar to stand down made Angeline's skin crawl. Her hair was just as snow white, long and braided like the warriors of old, and fell far below the table. She wore a grand fur coat and a white gown with a golden rope for a belt. Simple, but magnificent as it flowed over her stocky, curved body.

"What is the reason for this, Alvit?" Her voice boomed like a giant's, across the way, stirring a cold wind with its magic.

"Look, my queen!" She handed the spear to Angeline and leaned in, whispering, "Throw this at her. If your magic is worthy of her or Artemis, may you draw blood."

Eyes wide, Angeline stared at her ice spear. *Who would have imagined an opportunity this blatant would arise!*

Inhaling deeply, she held it. Cursing herself for not taking up more interest in spears, all she could muster was imagining it as a larger arrow. She considered the weight and the distance to hope to graze the woman, not impale her. The muscles in her arms grew taut. She could overthrow this, but after all the training with Alecto, she understood the muscles in her body more than ever. Aiming back, everyone shifted to watch the woman, who unmistakably was Freya, at the head of their table. A toothy grin formed, and she threw back her coat. Reaching an arm out, she signaled for Angeline to throw.

With all she knew, she tossed it and the spear sliced the wind clean. Angeline watched, holding her breath, stomach knotting as it flew over the table of guests and arched to match Freya's outstretched hand. A blast of cold air boomed from her, but the spear did not slow. Freya's smile dropped, and another blast of cold air boomed. Again, the spear did not waver. Freya's wrist twisted, a shield of ice forming in time for the point to connect. The unthinkable happened.

Freya's shield cracked, and the spear stuck into it. The two ice-made items fell to the table. The pointed edge of the spear had managed to pierce through. In her palm, a red pool of blood formed like a rose petal. She looked at Angeline with a look of shock. The whole room shuffled in a cacophony of chairs and gasps. Alvit's heavy hand gripped Angeline's shoulders, breaking her from her dumbfounded state.

"Well done, little Fury," she whispered before chuckling.

"Who are you?" Freya held her hand over to the boar and it transformed into a muscled Viking with a boar's mask and he wrapped her hand.

"I'm heiress to Artemis."

"I see." She laughed, and Angeline could breathe again.

"Why have you sought an audience with me?"

Taking a knee, she made her request. "I wish to train with the Valkyries so I may use my strength like they do."

"Alvit, I think Olrun would be the best." Freya sat down, drinking her wine.

"But Freya, Olrun has the strength of a giant!" Alvit's panic made Angeline's heart flutter.

"Exactly." Freya's voice had shifted to almost a cooing sound that one would expect from a mother calming her children. "To throw any spear hard enough to pierce a shield, one needed that much strength to start."

Alvit looked at Angeline, confused. "But you are a mere mortal, are you not?"

"No, as Alecto has titled me, I am Ex-Mortal. There's nothing left of me to call human anymore."

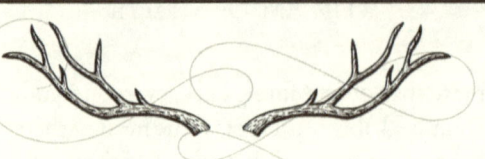

CHAPTER 15

MINOTAUR FIGHT

CEDRIC

Cedric rolled his shoulder, feeling the living armor's *manica* quiver to match his own excitement. The crowds of human and non-human-looking spectators roared and held up betting tickets. Shouts in various languages mangled into everything, some ancient, others, dead languages he couldn't begin to place. Stepping through the last pair of reinforced doors, he at last entered the arena. Dirt, sweat, and blood all invaded his sense of smell, and he shuddered.

I can't believe I actually miss the days of knight tournaments, but this is something far more intense.

In his right hand he held the war hammer, and, in his left, he held the gladius. He still couldn't quite shake the lustful sensations his own armor sent him, but it was just enough to counter the effects of it feeding off his own energy. A shiver ran across him and with a *ka-thud* the opposite doors opened. Red glowing eyes peered out from the darkness, and the scent of cattle and sweat made Cedric's jaw twitch. At last, the minotaur stepped out into the light that braziers and veins of lava and crystal provided in this underground world.

Yeah, this is definitely an unsanctioned fight. I doubt they have rules, just slaughter or defeat the other guy. Dammit, but to be pitched against Asterion is a challenge.

Asterion was double the width and height of Cedric. A large golden bull ring hung from his flared bovine nostrils. Cedric cringed as a thick tongue slipped from Asterion's mouth to lick a nostril. Snot and drool dripped from his snout. His bull head had fur black as night, his ears were long and filled with rings of multiple piercings. The wide-muscled chest made it clear he had strength that could match a dragon's, if not more. Red eyes leered across the arena at Cedric, and that's when he took in the horns. Massive and thick, they curved out to match the width of the creature's shoulders before turning up and twisting forward to reveal piercing tips.

He took a few more steps closer and Cedric matched the motion with his own. Black fur from his waist down was thick and long. Behind Asterion, a ropey tail complete with a tasseled hair whipped to and fro. The legs were thick and matched that of the back legs of a bull. They angled back, then forward until they ended with hooves wider than any cow he'd seen. He could only imagine this was to compensate for the fact he was a bipedal monster carrying an insane amount of weight. The red irises widened until the whites of his eyes caught Cedric's attention.

Fuck, he's charging!

Asterion's maw opened wide, revealing a fanged set of teeth and making a horrific shrieking roar. Cedric backstepped. With a great thrust forward, Asterion closed the gap between them too quickly. Turning, Cedric sidled and held up his *manica*. He had managed to dodge the point of the horn, but not the punch following. The giant fist slammed unyielding into the *manica*, the muscles in Cedric's arm and shoulder taut with anticipation. It sent him flying until his back slammed against the stonewall of the arena.

Blood splattered from his lips. He slid to the ground but didn't fall to his knees. He wiped his mouth with his forearm and glared over at the *manica*. It glimmered, a sense of anger boiling from it, and he smirked. The living armor had kept his arm and shoulder from shattering. Granted, he could have healed even that. He realized he needed to be quicker against Asterion and he didn't need to be injured so soon in the battle. Another howling shriek and the minotaur lowered his head and charged.

Cedric pulled away from the stone, standing tall. He spat blood to the ground, unmoved by the fast-approaching, bull-headed monster. A fanged grin and glint of green shone in his eyes as he leaped up. He managed to plant a foot between the horns. The forceful downkick knocked Asterion off balance and he smashed into the wall. Above them, the crowd scattered, and a dwarf fell over the edge and landed in the arena. Cedric laughed as an elven assistant came rushing from the doors and gathered him up.

Cedric turned his attention back to Asterion, who stood and shook the dust and rubble from his head. He snorted, the dust billowing in a way that mimicked steam from his nostrils. Cracking and creaking came from the stands above and the wall caved a little more under the weight. They were clearing the area. Unsanctioned fights didn't do much in the way to protect spectators. Asterion shook his head once more, the rings in his ears chiming in a musical way. Grunting, he peered over his shoulder at Cedric.

"That was an interesting move, Broken Horn." His voice rumbled out in a thunderous manner. "They tell me you call yourself Theseus."

Cedric snorted, "And who do you think I am?"

"Well, we both know you're not Theseus." He rolled both shoulders back and turned to face Cedric. "And it seems you know who I am by entering under said name."

"The one and only Bull of Minos." They both laughed for a moment. "And it seems we're both in the peculiar situation of being part of an unsanctioned fight."

"I made the mistake of crossing King Frey of the Alfin and owing him this until I lose a fight. Fuck me and my pride for this mess." Asterion cracked his neck one way, then the other. "What's your excuse, Broken Horn?"

Cedric rubbed the back of his neck and at last replied with a smirk, "Would you believe me if I told you I volunteered to help Apollo get his old lady back?"

A great roar of laughter left Asterion. Snot slung to the ground as he leaned on his thighs. It took a moment for him to catch his breath. Cedric couldn't help but laugh too, both of them waiting for the stands to sort themselves out. They had prepared to fight one another, possibly kill, but not take out an entire crowd of bystanders, and there seemed to be an unspoken rule about it. Granted, Cedric was facing a cool-headed opponent, something he hadn't faced at this level since Romasanta handed him his ass in Cerdanya all those centuries ago.

"You just might be a greater fool than I, Broken Horn!" He paced away, looking to the crumbling section of stands before spinning back. "But I haven't had a good opponent in some time. Perhaps, if Apollo thinks you worthy to be on such a journey, you may be the fight to break me from my own imprisonment." He motioned to the arena and his bovine brow creased in an angry scowl. "Prepare Broken Horn. I only know how to battle to kill."

Cedric shifted into an offensive stance, readying the gladius and war hammer. "Then have at it, Asterion. May we both gain what we want from this fight."

Roaring, Asterion launched into yet another charge. A raging bull was a mere understatement as he closed the gap fast and hard. Cedric aimed to leap, but Asterion spun, redirecting in the last second. The turning of the bull-head raked the tip of one horn across Cedric's abdomen before he swung with his gladius. A slice ripped across Asterion's shoulder and he retreated, saving Cedric from the next move to pummel him with one massive arm.

They circled the arena, stealing glances as they assessed their wounds. Cedric could feel the armor quiver and he shuddered. To have it reacting, growing angry at not being able to protect him, felt strange. He shook the distraction as Asterion came charging forward. This time Cedric chose to stand his ground, using a powerful upswing with the hammer aiming for a horn. It missed its mark and the bony forehead connected with Cedric's chest. Both went bulldozing into a new spot of stone wall, screams filling the air.

The wind left Cedric's lungs as his ribs popped under the massive blow. He could feel the hot air blow from Asterion's nostrils. Wheezing to take in some air, ignoring the gurgling and blood filling his senses, Cedric gripped both horns.

Third times a charm...

Asterion pulled away and much to his surprise, Cedric went with him. He shook his head, but Cedric had lifted himself up and with a kick to the back of Asterion's head, he leaped to the ground, running. Cedric wasn't going to make the mistake of latching on like the last time. Coughing, he clenched his teeth to hold back the smattering of blood. His war hammer and gladius had been dropped, and he wasn't quite ready to reveal how monstrous he could be, not with so many gawking eyes. The ground shook, Asterion hot on his heels. Abandoning the gladius, he ran past it and scooped up the war hammer.

Skidding to a stop, Cedric twisted and swung the hammer up and over. Asterion wavered, looking up, and the hammer hit his horn. The reverberation rocked the muscles and bones of Cedric's arms and he lost his grip. Asterion twisted, eyes crisscrossing from the blow as he snorted and shouldered into the dirt. Pumping his fists, Cedric tried to recover the sensation in them. A big wall of dust divided them, and he leaned on his knee with one arm and hugged his torso. Wheezing, he squinted at the sharp pains of broken ribs and punctured lungs.

He could hear Asterion trying to stand and falling over somewhere in the dust as it flowed over and engulfed him. The crowd fell silent, waiting to see what would happen under the cloak of dust. At last, Cedric looked at the war hammer at his feet and picked it up with a look of disdain. It had hit its mark, but neither the horn nor it gave way or cracked. They were equal matches, much like their owners, and he spat blood across the ground in annoyance.

The armor of the *manica* shuddered, and he blinked. "What's the matter with you?"

Another shudder came, and it glimmered blue like a thousand stars as it thinned out and snaked over his hand. It worked its way around and into the war hammer. It grew in size and weight, even length. Cedric gripped it with two hands to compensate for the shift and marveled over the desire to do something more than fail at protecting its host. Cedric grinned, a shudder of excitement rolling through him.

"I see. You want to join the fight. So be it."

He gripped the war hammer tight; the dust settling as Asterion and he both waited with utmost patience. Neither of them wanted to attack aimlessly at one another. This was a fight between prideful monsters. Asterion cracked his neck once more, snorting.

"That one hurt, Broken Horn," he growled and stomped at the ground. "For that, I'll break your other one." He pointed. "We both know those are as real as my own."

"True, but not if I break yours first."

Cedric charged forward. Asterion leaned forward, billowing as he launched toward him to match the assault. The sandals tightened, Cedric took the hint and spun. The move added to his agility and two-handed swing. Like a dancer, he twisted out of the way of the charging minotaur and the improved war hammer met its mark on the other horn. A loud pop and crack rang out. The horn broke free and was sent boomeranging across the arena where it stuck into the ground. His armor abandoned the weapon, leaving it to float away as nothing more than ash as it scurried back to being his *manica*.

Cedric blinked, surprised it had happened so easily. Asterion stumbled to a stop and stood. His hand rose slowly and warily, feeling where the great horn had once been. He pivoted and looked at Cedric wide-eyed. Snarling, his bovine lip quivered, the whites of his eyes scary as he came full steam. Cedric gripped his side. *Nothing.*

"Fuck, the gladius."

He began running full steam in the opposite direction. The armor felt weak, hungry, and was draining him. The ground rumbled an earthquake with every step as Asterion closed in behind him. Scanning the arena, he couldn't see the gladius and cursed the rising dust. Looking behind him, Asterion had caught up. Dropping down, Cedric slid between his legs, hooves striking frighteningly close. The tassel of his tail struck him in the face, adding to his frustration. His cracked ribs had healed enough to speed him up.

Back on his feet, Asterion was slow to turn. Again Cedric ran with long strides in search of his weapon. Under each pant, he cursed the armor, Manny the wizard, Nicholas Teague, and more importantly, Romasanta. Again, the ground shook under him and Asterion had caught up.

"I'm too slow!" he flustered, twisting to raise his *manica* for defense.

Asterion's forehead connected, the remaining horn stabbing his bare shoulder. This time he didn't go sailing as Asterion wrapped his arms around, pulling Cedric onto the horn farther and he screamed in agony. Something hard sliced through his back and Asterion let go. Stepping back, Cedric reached back and found the gladius dug deep into his lower back. Panting, blood dripped from his back and shoulder, and he grinned in a wicked way.

"There's my sword."

"I saw you looking for it, so I returned it." Asterion leaned on his thighs, trying to catch his breath. "You're fast."

With a grunt, Cedric failed to pull the blade from his back. "Not fast enough. Someone should teach you that the kidney makes for a horrible sheath."

Asterion shook his head and locked eyes. "How can you still smile? You must not be right in the head."

"I've been through some shit." Again, he reached for the blade's handle and failed. "Son of a bitch!"

At last, Cedric leaned on his own thighs and the two exhausted warriors stared at one another. The crowd in the stands was screaming chants mangled between "Asterion" and "Theseus." Inhaling deeply, Cedric needed the weapon out of his back. He also needed to find a way to free himself from the armor that slowed his healing. Reaching over, he checked his shoulder and huffed. He had to recover some energy, or he would lose the fight.

I really don't like using that magic, but it might work to finish this and give me a chance to recover.

He scanned the crowds all around. Manny and Fenrir were at the edge, the goofy pride in their faces annoying. Cedric locked eyes with the wizard, and Manny flinched. Cedric stood, rubbing his shoulder, wishing the cartilage would pop back into the proper place so he could use it. The wizard lipped something and pointed at his head. Cedric flipped him the bird and Asterion looked over his shoulder.

"So the wizard put you up to this?" Asterion looked back, a smirk on his bovine face.

"Yea. You could say that. Why?"

"He's the one I hired to get me out of this mess."

"Oh, so I'm cleaning up everyone's shit." Cedric rubbed his forehead. "I just want my fucking wife back. I'm going to kill that old hag."

"Old hag?" Asterion stood shaking his head, the ringing of his earrings filling the air.

"Artemis."

"Look, I don't know if you're aware of this," he nodded to the paneled balcony, "if you make King Frey happy and meet all his challenges, he'll send you to face the Amazonians to challenge his sister's next champion."

"Why the hell would I want that?" Cedric scowled at another failed attempt to retrieve the blade.

"You moron, the three queens of the Amazonians are Alecto, Freya, and Artemis. It's a direct ticket to get you from the far west to the far east islands."

"Really?" Cedric paused, giving up at last.

Don't you dare reveal you're an incubus! You hear me! The wizard Manny's mind invaded his and he glared back at him.

Fuck you! You never said I couldn't reveal the other side, he hissed in his mind, glaring at Manny, who looked flabbergasted.

So, I guess I'm going to have to own up and cave at last. There's no way I can do this without using that. About time I start using my magic. Might make life a hell of a lot easier.

Inhaling deeply, he looked at his armor, curious how it would react to his next move. "Look Asterion, don't take this the wrong way, but you smell delicious right about now."

"W-what?" Asterion tilted his head, but Cedric disappeared in a shadowy cloud.

Asterion took a step back, looking all around. The sword had dropped to the ground, stained with Cedric's blood. A slash of claws opened up on one arm, and Asterion roared and twisted. Shadows twisted, popping in and out of existence. More claw marks struck him, opening wounds across his back and torso. Snorting, Asterion spun, running his tail across the ground to make a cloud of dust. He watched for movement, the dust spinning in the wake of Cedric's masked movements.

"Thanks for the cover." Cedric's words were dark as fangs bit into Asterion's shoulder.

Before the minotaur could smash him, he was gone, and another bite landed on a wrist. This game of sadistic tag continued until the dust fell away, revealing the gladius was gone. Asterion was weakened from the strikes and blood loss; his legs wobbled until he at last fell forward panting. Cedric reappeared and struck him in the back of the head with the pummel of the gladius. Asterion's eyes rolled back, and he fell in defeat.

The crowd gasped... silence lingering for a heartbeat before erupting in a great roar. Cedric walked away, stoic as ever, as he retrieved the horn. The reinforced doors opened and Romasanta gave a quirky grin. All of Cedric's wounds had healed. He seemed unscathed by the events. Wiping the blood from his face, he looked at it on his fingers and groaned.

"Looks like it's back to being the king of vampires again." He marched for the exit and tossed the horn to Nicholas Teague. "After my nap, we'll discuss what you need next. Tell the shady wizard he owes me for freeing the minotaur from the Alfin King."

"Wait, what?" Romasanta caught up, pacing himself beside him. "Since when can you do magic?"

Cedric side glanced and relented. "Since Vlad Tepes. Weren't you and Lillith responsible for making that whole arrangement? You were there, remember? I ate him."

"But I didn't realize you inherit magic from one another. Wait, you hunted down a lot of the royals, so what else can you do?" Romasanta covered his mouth.

"I don't want to talk about it." Cedric licked his fangs. "I fucking hate magic."

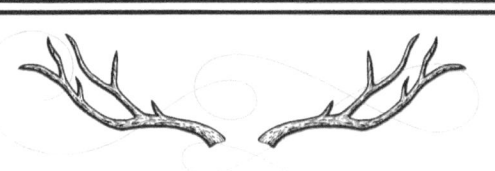

CHAPTER 16

TRAIN WITH VALKYRIES

ANGELINE

Olrun didn't share the blonde hair and blue eyes of her sisters, Svanhvit and Alvit. Instead, she sat on the beach with her red hair flailing in the sea breeze. Her eyes were brown and her was skin freckled as she looked out and beyond the waves. Alvit cleared her throat and she turned to see them with a confused expression.

"And who is this fledgling?" Like her sisters, Olrun's accent carried on her words heavily. "Aren't those Fury marks?"

Angeline had failed to notice that Alvit had ripped her sleeve. "Yeah, they are."

"It seems Mother Freya has asked you to train this one to use her strength." Alvit smirked and shoved Angeline forward. "You two have fun."

"W-wait," Angeline called after Alvit as she faded into a flurry of white feathers.

"Did Freya really ask me to train a little Fury?" Anger built on Olrun's voice and chills ran across Angeline's spine. "Why you?"

"I'm Artemis's heiress. I wish to train under all the factions before I return to the Mortal Realm." Swallowing, Angeline dared to come closer. "And Freya said you might be best considering how strong I am."

Olrun lifted an eyebrow. "Is that so? A mortal wanting to train with all the factions? You must have a death wish."

"Don't worry about that. I heal fast," Angeline smirked. "I was watching your sister fight and how she used the war hammer. It was clever the way she applied her strength to take down an agility-based fighter."

Olrun arched a brow and slid off the boulder she had been perched on. "You choose one weapon. One-handed you get shield training. Two-handed, we double down on strength."

"I want to use the hammer, two-handed."

"Such confidence. So be it. Follow me this way."

Angeline stayed silent as they marched across the sandy beach. They walked for a good hour before a temple appeared beside the rocky cliffs that had grown in size. The water threatened to leave them no room to walk before reaching the stairs carved into the cliffside. Angeline swore if it hadn't been for the endurance training, her thighs and legs would have been aching from the way the sand pulled the ground away and made her feet slide. By the time they reached the temple, the sun began to set. Angeline froze, staring at the red and orange hue of the sinking sunlight. Her chest ached.

The last sunset I enjoyed was in Delphine with Cedric. I want to go back there, back to a moment where can just be together, nothing more and nothing less.

"I know a look of longing when I see one." Olrun caught her attention and led her up the stairs leading into the temple.

"He'll find me. He always does." Angeline smiled, the thought enthralling.

"Welcome to my personal training grounds." Olrun waved her arm out.

Angeline took it all in. The temple columns left the view of the sea intact as well as the flowing fields and forest the separated this place from the Amazonian city. The white marble with black and gray streaks sparkled in the glow of the brazier hanging overhead, the fire blazing high and wild. A dirt arena filled the center and all around weapons lay on tables and weapon stands. In one corner, a forge glowed, an anvil and an array of blacksmith tools close by. On the far side, she saw a hammock hanging between two columns.

"You live here alone?" Angeline followed her down into the arena.

Olrun smiled and glanced back at the hammock. "Yes, I call this home now. I grew up in the country with very little and I feel at peace doing what I've done all throughout my life. Enough of that. Pick a weapon. The hammers are on the table there behind you if you desire to follow through with that decision on the beach."

Angeline spun, pacing toward the table of stacked weapons. The array of designs was breathtaking, from artful with Celtic knots to silver-laden weapons with pictures of stags chased by wolves. Another hammer had the head of a fierce dragon, yet the one next to it was a Viking warrior. Angeline took her time, separating them by size, holding them in her hand or both hands and gauging the pull the head of the hammer had. Some of them were simple, looking like a more exaggerated version of the hammers smiths or carpenters would use.

"Did you make all of these?" Angeline placed one down and reached for the next.

"No." Olrun had turned her attention to an array of shields and spears, riffling through as if paining over which she would be using. "I have friends, you know. They come and we make weapons like the days of old. Many of them leave them here for training or fun. Not all of them are made with equal care, but if it breaks in training, you may pick another."

"A strange custom you and your friends have, though I understand why. I miss my time as nothing more than a companion on the back of the horse and hunting for what I need. The modern world is … overwhelming." Something dark as iron with bronze décor caught her eye, and she dug deeper. "Do you train many Valkyries here?"

"Only those who prove themselves of superior strength." Olrun pulled a shield onto her forearm and bounced it to test the weight. "But many fear dying under a single blow, so you're the first in a long time, Little Fury."

"You shouldn't make light of this one, Olrun." Alecto's voice made them both turn to the forge where she sat on the anvil, eating an apple. "I hear someone drew blood on Freya."

Olrun laughed. "Oh? Was it one of your little Furies?"

"Indeed, it was." She took a large bite of the apple, watching Olrun, who gave her no reaction as she picked through spears.

Angeline left them to their conversation, pulling the two-handed war hammer free. This one proved heaviest of all, but the balance was extraordinary. Leather wrapped the handle in a braided pattern she had seen only a few times, mainly on ceremonial weapons or drawings of legendary weapons. The long handle made of what seemed like wood felt cold as iron. Blossoming from the leather wrappings, it had carved trees, twisting and stretching upward until the vining branch wrapped around a raven, as if plucking it from the sky. The bird's beak and eyes were filled with bronze, making the larger point of the war hammer's head. On the back side, feathers flared out, making the backside similar to a bladed axe. At the bottom of the hilt, a large pommel, looking like a large raven's eye, helped steady the weapon even in one hand.

"Then what brings you here tonight, Alecto?" Olrun placed a spear back and reached for another. "I imagine it's not to battle with me again."

"No. I owe the Ex-Mortal her prize." Alecto earned Angeline's glance and she grinned, biting into her apple.

Chills rattled Angeline, her throat burning with the memory of her last reward. "I'll take this hammer."

Olrun paused, looking over her shoulder, she sighed. "I'll need a better shield and spear in that case." With that, she dropped the one from her arm and circled back. "So, this is the girl who landed the strike. She has good instincts, it seems."

Alecto tossed the apple core into the forge. "Indeed, she does. Though, I think I like her better than Artemis."

"Look, I can choose another hammer..." Angeline gave the hammer another look. "What made this one? It's gorgeous. Reminds me of a bow I lost when I came to this realm."

"That one?" Olrun pulled a shield from the bottom of the stack. "That's Badbh's work. Knowing her, it has some infuriating enchantment on it."

"Badbh? You're friends with Badbh, too?" Angeline marveled at Olrun as she buckled on a larger shield than before.

"Too?" Now Alecto was intrigued, a toothy smirk on her face as she sat on the anvil, straddling it with legs swinging. "Are you implying you know our pal Badbh?"

"Well, I've met her a few times. She's quite the heavy drinker."

Olrun laughed, shaking her head in agreement. "Oh, that she is."

"Look, Ex-Mortal. You've made the stoic Olrun grin and laugh twice now," Alecto teased. "I might stay to watch this little tournament."

"Be honest, Alecto." Olrun strode back to the spears, smiling at the goddess with a sparkle in her eyes. "You wanted to see your swan dance tonight."

Angeline stiffened. A wave of arousal passed between the two women. She turned and saw the playful stare between them. Looking at the hammer, she could feel another wave of it, and she had to inhale and hold her breath. The last thing she wanted was to let that part of her aura react, to do what it had done to Alecto before. At last, she thought of changing their direction.

"So you said I earned a prize?" Angeline shuddered with relief as the arousal broke between them and she could breathe again. "What sort of prize? The last reward I earned proved rather ... dangerous."

"Relax," Alecto snorted. "I promised if you made it through the tribulation, we would take a look at your blade and its curse, no?"

"Cursed blade?" Olrun pulled a spear from the far stand and came marching to the anvil. "What kind of cursed blade?"

"Ask your fledgling, my love." Alecto pointed to Angeline's side. "That is an interesting blade."

Olrun motioned for Angeline to come forth. "Let me see it."

Without hesitation, she gave the blade to them. The two leaned into the blade as Olrun turned it again and again, eyes wide. Her fingers danced over the blacked blade and circled back to the hilt. She swapped hands, gauging its weight, and seemed confused for a moment and balanced it in a flat palm. A frown deepened on her lips and Alecto shot her a curious look.

"Well, what's the matter with it?" she demanded of Olrun.

"A lot," she announced. "It has no balance. The metal blade the curse is sworn into is poorly crafted, something made by a yearling blacksmith or farrier from old. At least the hilt is an improvement. Is this chimeran?"

"Y-yea. It's a gift." Angeline held her arm and bit her lip.

"Really?" Without warning, Olrun pricked Angeline and Alecto. "Strange."

"Ouch." Alecto watched as the tiny wound grew bigger. "I don't feel so good, Olrun. You better fix me."

Angeline had healed, but the sweat on Alecto made her double back. "Why is she struggling? Isn't she a goddess?"

"This blade is something more, perhaps capable of slaying gods." Olrun sliced Angeline's palm and smashed it onto Alecto's wound. "Am I right to think you have exchanged blood at some point with the maker of this curse?"

"Yes, but I'm confused..." She pulled her hand back, the wound closing and Alecto scowling at Olrun.

"You're mean, my swan."

"And so are you. That's what you get for kissing her." She held up the blade. "Don't use this blade here in the Otherworld or you'll attract the wrong attention, Ex-Mortal. Whatever creature you got this from, it's something new and ancient all at once." Turning to them both, she sighed. "Fine, Alecto, I will do it."

"Do what?" Angeline shook her head. "I'm still lost at what *this* is and what just happened to Alecto."

"This blade makes a cut that can only be cured by the blood of the maker. So only you and your lover can heal the wounds, or they will forever grow and bleed." Angeline paled at Alecto's words. "I suspected, but I wasn't going to test that theory without someone who knew more than I could on the matter."

"And she had asked me earlier if I'd rework the blade and make it stronger." Olrun laid it with care on the blacksmith's table. "You see, Furies are awarded a god-slaying weapon when they are accepted into their ranks. Since you own one, we will simply rework it into a stronger weapon for you. Is it okay if I keep the chimeran hilt?"

"Absolutely." Angeline's mind spiraled, wondering if Cedric was even aware of what he had created. "My husband and I slayed the chimera together, and that is his blood that curses it."

The two looked at one another and at last, Alecto asked, "What kind of godly demon is he?"

Angeline's chest ached, searching their faces. "Does that matter?"

Olrun turned away. "No. It's none of our business, is it Alecto?"

"But that won't stop me from looking for him. I want to meet my Ex-Mortal's love and thank him for the interesting turn of events his wife has brought to our little abode." Alecto at last slid off the anvil.

"Enough banter. Let's get you trained and earn your place among the Valkyries." With that, Angeline followed with her new found war hammer and prepared for the next set of tribulations Alecto and Olrun would place upon her.

I will soak in everything they can teach me so I can be stronger for him... No, for me.

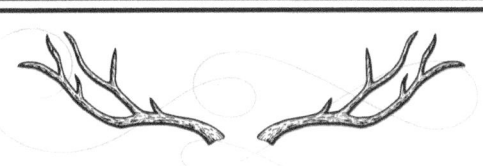

CHAPTER 17

WE THREE KINGS

CEDRIC

Cedric kneeled before King Frey. His pointed ears and pale skin didn't take away from the fact he was practically a giant alfin. Asterion seemed miniature in comparison and second thoughts about the course he had chosen swam in his mind as he stared down at the ground, waiting for the monstrous being to speak.

What the hell have I gotten myself into?

Frey uncrossed his legs and leaned forward. His movements made an icy wind in its wake. Alfin guards lined the walls in their polished armor. Councilmen murmured to one another. Beside Cedric kneeled Asterion. Both had been called to the platform to see the mastermind behind the underground fights.

Either he's pleased, or livid over what happened down there.

"Who are you?" King Frey's voice thundered hard through the air and knocked the wind from Cedric. "Why not use your magic from the start? Who sent you here?"

Swallowing, Cedric dared to meet the white eyes of Frey, the black pupils small and piercing. "I'm just trying to earn my way to the Isle of the Amazonians. I heard this was a direct ticket if I could hold my own."

"I can buy that." King Frey leaned back and crossed his arms. "Answer me. Why not use the magic?"

Cedric bit his lip in contempt for a moment and confessed, "I hate using magic. Plus, I'm a sucker for a challenging fight. Nothing gained unless some blood spills and a bone or two breaks."

Asterion snorted, "You're insane."

"And you're too fucking fast for a cow," spat Cedric.

"Call me a cow again and—"

"Silence!" King Frey roared, a whistling breeze spinning tight around them. "What kind of magic was that? Are you a demon from the Underworld? Has Hades sent you to cause trouble in our realm?"

"I'm the Vampire King. I possess any abilities that I've earned as part of my duties of said title." He swallowed, wondering if he would buy the excuse. *For the most part, it's true...*

Cedric had managed to weasel out that there currently was unrest between all the realms, and they had been clueless. Most of it could be pointed back to Kronos and Gaea's meddling, causing an imbalance in the Mortal Realm. Unlike the rest, it turned out they've been the only obstacles stopping them from completely throwing every realm off balance.

"But you can walk out in the daylight," Frey drawled, making an unamused expression. "Do I look like a fool?"

Cedric licked a fang. "Of course I can. I ate all the others who had that ability long ago."

Asterion shot him a disgusted expression. "You ate your own kind?"

"And I bet you enjoy a juicy steak now and again," he hissed in rebuttal.

"I see." Frey's voice sent them into silence once more. "In that case, I have one more challenge for you, Vampire King."

"One more challenge?" Cedric's body tensed to see the giant smirk. "And if I take this, do I get my ticket to the Isles of Amazonians?"

"Indeed, granted, you'll be titled my champion and face my sister's latest prized warrior." At last, he uncrossed his arms and leaned toward them. "And seeing you did defeat Asterion, it seems you might pass this next task."

"King Frey." Asterion tensed and continued his stare to the ground. "What of our ... arrangement?"

"Ah, Asterion," A long sigh escaped the giant king and at last he relented, "You are free of our contract." He waved a hand and an alfin councilor pulled a scroll from the wall. "In good faith, here is the contract."

Relief washed over Asterion and he stood, happy to receive the dusty parchment. "Thank you, Your Greatness."

"But please, do come back of your own freewill and fight for me..." Asterion's eyes widened and he froze at King Frey's words. "No contract required, of course." He chuckled as the minotaur sighed and slumped his shoulders. "You've lasted longer than I had expected. Next time, don't try to steal another man's food."

Cedric furrowed his brow and gave a bewildered look at Asterion.

"I was foolish thinking I could steal a golden egg from stymphalian. Granted, if I had known you were its owner, I wouldn't have entertained the thought and not acted on it." King Frey waved a hand and Asterion left without another word.

"This challenge," Cedric stayed kneeling, muscles taut over it all, "what is it?"

A wicked smile crested on King Frey's face. "Retrieve a golden egg from my pet's cage."

Cedric frowned and glared up at him. "It's your pet. It seems to make more sense for you to do just that yourself."

King Frey's brow raised high, impressed with the boldness. "Well, true. But when I can charge admission and have several warriors make an attempt to retrieve it... how could I not be so generous to give them a chance, after all?"

"I see." Cedric snorted, thinking for a minute before asking, "And you want me to be the one who completes the challenge though?"

"Exactly, Vampire King." He motioned for Cedric to raise to his feet. "Look, just king to king. I find you likable and mysterious. There's something about you, something you're not sharing, so let's talk plainly." He stood, the room growing cold as a flurry of snow wrapped around him and shrank him to the same height as Cedric. "Leave us at once." Without a fuss or whisper, the guards in clanking armor and the shuffle of councilors left, and the doors shut with a loud thud. "Thank the gods they are gone." Cedric blinked as Frey tossed the crown and robe to the chair. "Let's go someplace ... warm."

He gripped Cedric's shoulder, and, in a flash, they were in a hut, air thick with humidity and a group of female faeries fluttered from them. Frey laughed at them and shoved Cedric down onto the array of cushions. Outside the window, he could see a jungle of enormous flowers and flying types of fae and creatures. The girls had giggled a moment and began bringing food and drinks. Two of them sat with Frey, leaning and fawning over him. One girl started to caress Cedric's chest; he snapped up her wrist, and she yelped.

"Don't touch me..." All eyes and frowns faced him. "It's dangerous."

"Well, now this is a new development." Frey chuckled, taking up a goblet and drinking it.

"Where are we? What are we doing here?" Cedric tried to stand, but Frey wouldn't cede his grip on his shoulder, making it clear he was still as strong as a giant in this smaller, less intimidating state.

"Waiting on my lawyer." Frey plucked some fruit and ate them. "I want to engage in a contract with you, Vampire King."

"Thanks, but no thanks. I don't do contracts." Cedric shoved away the food and wine offered to him. "I'll do it. I'll get the damn egg and fight your sister's champion. No need for me to sign a contract I may not be able to escape."

Frey narrowed his eyes. "We'll see. Just you wait for my lawyer. He's the King of Fae. Perhaps we three kings can come up with a deal sweet enough for all three to sign."

Cedric scowled and crossed his arms. It seemed a solid hour before a man walked in. With wings like a Monarch butterfly, he was olive-skinned with green eyes, a goatee, and a pompadour hairstyle, saying he visited the Mortal Realm often. He disregarded Cedric as Frey stood, hugging one another like old colleagues and exchanging words in a strange language. The faerie women all giggled at something they said, then left as another phrase rolled from the King of Fae.

Do the Fae have their own tongue? Fascinating...

They broke away, Frey sitting next to Cedric and placing his strong grip back on his shoulder. Cedric grimaced, feeling helpless in the situation. Looking back to the King of Fae, he kicked over a cushion and at last looked up. They both paled.

"You can't enter a contract with this man," Pan announced without warning.

"I want to and will," Frey snapped back.

"I don't want to, and I definitely will not with this slimeball as the lawyer!" Cedric broke from Frey's grip and stood in alarm. "YOU!"

"ME! What the hell are you doing in my land!" Pan stood, face flushed. "Oh the gods, you're here about Tony..."

"What about Tony?!" Cedric's anger rose, his voice roaring to life as he took off his helmet and threw it to the ground. "I am so sick of this shit! What have you and Lillith done in my absence?"

"Look! It wasn't us, but we did what we could... but the last bit, that was all Badbh's idea!" Pan panicked and began pacing. "I even went as far as ripping up his registration. I mean, how were we to know it would happen like that?"

"Why would you need to register him?" Cedric's heart raced. *Something did happen...*

Frey sat there in silence. Drinking from his wine and eating grapes slowly in amusement.

"Look, Kronos is making a move. Then the gypsy showed up and cursed Tony. Lillith only could think of one solution, but it was a shot in the dark. Tony's got some balls... let's just start there." Pan covered his face and dropped his stare to Frey. "Wait, why the hell are you here with King Frey?"

"I see you know this Vampire King." Frey grinned and popped a grape into his mouth. "What a delightful turn of events. Are things with this one always so exciting?"

Pan made a face, then nodded. "Him and the rest of his spawn and friends. Anyhow, Frey, you can't do a contract with Cedric."

"Why not?" He sipped his wine, cool and calm.

Pan turned to Cedric and sighed. "He doesn't know..." He paused and pointed at his horns. "What the hell have you been doing to break one? Never mind, I don't want to know. Look, Frey, nothing can leave this room. All information about to be disclosed is now under Fae Curse of Silence to prevent ill-intent." The room darkened as the whites of Pan's eyes turned black and his wings shifted to black and blood red. "Do you accept King of Alfin and King of Vampires?"

"I agree," they answered in unison without yielding.

"Very well." Clearing his throat, Pan's features returned. "Cedric is immune to curses and contracts."

"Wait what?" Cedric snarled. "But what about Angeline and Williamsburg?"

Pan raised a hand and motioned for him to sit. "Look, you were made in a very strange way, and I am still figuring it out. What I do know,

Angeline's recoil was at fault, and as for the other, poor circumstances of maturing to your demonic powers."

Cedric covered his face, muscles in his arms twitching under the taut nerves. "And why are you here? And how did you get here?"

"Ah, yeah, I can see why that would piss you off, but being a son of Gaea, I sort of get the privilege to live here, but I can't bring other immortals around unless they have a right to be here. You've only reached that status recently, thanks to a friend we have in common."

Another huff, and Cedric pulled a hand to cover his mouth and spoke through it. "That stupid peacock of a wizard, I imagine."

"No, that would be my doing." Frey smirked and leaned into whisper, "You're welcome. It also allowed me to bring you here."

Cedric puffed out his cheeks, annoyed by it all. "Since you all seem perfectly content in meddling in my business," his voice growled with the weight of his rage, "now's a good time to update me on all of the shit happening while I'm over here playing gladiator for the King of Elves."

Pan walked over and poured himself a tall wine and downed it. "We gave him training."

"With whom? And you still haven't answered why you would need to register him if he's human." Cedric's mind raced. "And how long have we been stuck in this hellhole?"

"Well..." Reaching for the carafe of wine, he stared at it and the cup. "Which news do you want to hear first?"

"Start with Tony."

He picked up the carafe, taking a few gulps before he spun around to look Cedric in the eyes. "He's fine."

"Enlighten me and tell me what exactly your definition of fine means, Pan," Cedric snarled, his fangs showing.

"He's not dead? Possibly unkillable now," reasoned Pan, swirling the carafe. "And now, uh, he's the King Incubus," he took a swig, avoiding the heated stare, "and Badbh found a great trainer, the only guy who could have done the job besides you. So, now he's on his first quest."

"Quest?" Cedric lowered his brow. "What kind of quest?"

"To see the Salamandre." Pan gulped more of the wine.

"I really should visit the Mortal Realm more often. You have all the fun," pouted King Frey, eating an apple.

"I'll have to deal with that when I get back. He better come back alive." Cedric began pacing the room. "And how long have we been here?"

"A year, maybe a little more…?" Pan went to drink from the carafe and found it empty. "I'm confused. Why are you not mad about sending him to the Salamandre? I pegged that would make you far more upset."

"That's where another god slaying weapon resides, isn't it?" He paused and locked eyes with Pan.

"Y-yea. Did Lillith tell you her plans? I wasn't aware…" Pan knitted his brow as his words faded in thought.

"Oh? Lillith?" Frey perked up, excited. "How is your sister doing these days?"

"Sister?" Cedric's eyes grew wide. "Your … SISTER?!"

"Time for you to go. Please give Manny our regards and apologies!"

Pan snapped his fingers and Cedric's reaching arm fell away in a bundle of rose petals. As he inhaled, the scent of rose was intoxicating. He managed a few steps and blinked. His hand grabbed a shoulder, and he looked up, confused. Romasanta blinked and shot a look around the room. Cedric found himself at Nicholas's forge with the rest, loitering about the place, rising in sudden alarm. Manny paled, looking at the pile of rose petals, and rushed to Cedric.

"Please tell me you didn't sign the contract!" He shook him, dread filling his voice.

"I can't sign contracts, and Pan says it's been over a year." Cedric locked eyes with Romasanta. "And they sent Tony to the Salamandre."

"But he's—" Cedric cut Romasanta's words off.

"He's the new King Incubus."

Confusion twisted his face. "But there can only be one…"

"Right, unless me being here means I'm considered dead to the Mortal Realm."

Romasanta's eyes widened. "Which means if we've taken over a year, she…"

Silence fell on them, and Cedric began pacing the floor. The heat of the forge hit him, and he contemplated the circumstance that could be unfolding in their home realm. Romasanta and Nyctimus whispered back and forth. Manny stood there, marveling over his newfound friends before he at last sidled into Cedric's way. Cedric went to walk around the wizard, but he leaned in the way, earning a heated glare.

"It's been a long day, wizard," he warned.

"Exactly what did you promise Frey?" he demanded.

A smile crossed Cedric's face. "I'll be going into the birdcage, and after that, we have our direct ticket to the Isle of Amazonians. Better still, no contract needed." Cedric leaned into Manny's ear. "No contract or curse can bind me, not even Pan's beloved curse of silence. How long have you been in cahoots with King Frey to bring him entertainment?"

Manny inhaled deeply, holding it a moment before mumbling back, "When the Oracles chose you for their champion, I didn't think I realized it was due to how insightful you can be with little to no information."

"Lust comes in many forms." Cedric chuckled and walked out, waving a hand. "I'm tired. I don't have long before they come back."

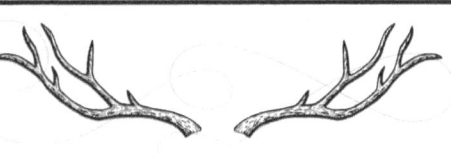

CHAPTER 18

OLRUN'S FORTITUDE

ANGELINE

After several battles in the temple, Olrun had moved them back to the sand beach where Angeline had first seen her. Her body ached; the way her movements had slowed on the unsure footing had added to her frustration. In the temple, she had gained a sense of pacing for how to swing and block with the hammer, but there, it fell apart. Olrun seemed unphased, crouching as she sidled around Angeline. Both women had sand caked on their sweat-soaked skin, Angeline's skin red with sunburn. She had kicked off her boots, bare feet in the sand, proving helpful to regain some of the lost momentum.

Olrun lunged forward, a powerful forward thrust of the spear. Angeline slid her hands apart on the handle, using the new opening to shove the blade off course. She leaned too far, her balance waning and falling backward. It was enough for her to fail to keep the movement going and the spear sliced heavy and deep into her upper arm. The salty sand stung like fire, but it made a quick clotting agent once down. On the boulder, Alecto giggled at the fail.

Angeline shot an angry glare to silence her. Olrun stood ready, unphased but patient enough to allow Angeline to rise to her feet. Shaking the sand from the hammer, she settled back into her offensive pose. Again, Olrun repeated the move and this time Angeline leaned into the attack, driving it away. Olrun spun, pulling her spear away, kicking sand up across Angeline. She couldn't see if the spear aimed high, midway, or low. Her eyes stung with sand and salt.

Instinct riled her, and she kneeled. Considering the momentum Olrun would have, the attack could only come from one direction.

She dropped, planted the handle into the sand, and leaned her forehead against the head of the hammer and let go. The spear broke from the sand and bounced off the handle. With that, Angeline moved toward Olrun, putting her too far inward to be hit by the spear's blade. She pushed forward, knocking Olrun in the chest with the head of the hammer, and sent her rolling backward through the sand.

"Oh, that was an excellent counter." Alecto marveled, chasing Olrun with her eyes.

Olrun wheezed, a line of blood dribbling down her chin from the corner of her mouth. "I... I didn't think..."

"Are you alright?" Angeline stood in alarm as Olrun coughed up blood. "I didn't aim to hurt you..."

"Are you kidding? She's been aiming for kill strikes this whole time, Ex-Mortal," Alecto scoffed, laying back on the boulder.

"I realize that, but I heal so... what does it matter if I get wounded but..." She turned back to where Olrun wobbled to her feet.

"I'm fine..." She wheezed and stumbled to her shield, her legs shaking and giving up. "Dammit, Badbh... that enchantment?" Her eyes rolled back, and she fell forward, passed out.

Alecto was at her side before Angeline could blink. "I'm sorry, we've been fighting for days and I didn't think it had one at this point."

"You're fine, she's fine." Alecto chuckled, wiping sand from Olrun's face. "It seems you found the stipulations. You land square on the chest with the top of the hammer, and it'll drain the enemy's energy. Granted, against me or something more god status and we might stumble, slow down, or even be unable to use magic for a bit in the fight. The problem is, it's not an easy strike to land. Most warriors defend the head and the chest more than anywhere else."

"R-right. What do we do with her?" Angeline sighed, her arm already healed.

"I have her. Look, the lesson was to learn to lean in the correct direction with that heavy-ass thing. You did that and countered. I think I can say you have it." Alecto lifted Olrun in her arms and kissed her forehead. "Let's let her focus on resting and fixing that weapon for now."

"Ok." Angeline went to follow Alecto, but she spun around, stopping her.

"You, you go find Nuha and Manah. Let those girls show you how to use that new fancy bow properly." She chuckled and began walking down the beach. "Besides, it'll look bad if the heiress of Artemis didn't know how to work the bow like a master."

Angeline looked at the ocean. The waves were a calming sound, and she understood why Olrun would stay so close. One can drown their thoughts and longing in that rush. Turning back, she climbed the path that led back to the bustling city of the Amazonians. Her clothes were gritty, sand coming off her with each stride as she hit the marketplace. Looking around, she swore her hut shouldn't be far. The marketplace there was a mixture of the clans, just like the day she ventured from her hut.

"You've changed much since we've met in the marketplace." Nuha's greeting brought instant relief to her.

"That's an understatement." They exchanged a hearty arm-to-arm shake. "I've got the marks of a Fury and a war hammer worthy of a Valkyrie."

"I heard a rumor you drew blood on Freya," she said with a smirk.

"That I can thank Artemis for," Angeline confessed. "The magic training proved invaluable, though it had seemed brief. I was told I should ask you and Manah about proper bow training."

"Ah!" Nuha's eyes lit up, her excitement seemed to make her glow in the sunlight. "Manah would be better. Where is your bow, though?"

Rubbing the back of her neck, Angeline made a desperate face. "In my hut," peering around the marketplace she confided, "which I thought was around here? Maybe?"

Nuha laughed. "Then let me be the light that guides you home."

With that, Nuha hooked her arm in Angeline's and led the way. It took only a few turns past some huts and there they stopped before a particular one. The doorway had been decorated since the last time she visited it. Symbols of the Fury and Valkyries had been hung to the right and left, signifying their locations from where she stood. Above the doorframe was a ceremonial deer skull, much like the one Artemis wore. She took it all in and at last found her words.

"Is this a way of acknowledging my status here?" Angeline knitted her brow, unsure of the mixture of pride and concern it brought her.

"Yes, when one joins a faction, they earn the right to share that on their homes and clothes. Some even tattoo it into their skin." She let go and crossed her arms. "You managed to join three, it seems. Unusual and rare."

"I would imagine so." Her mind flashed through all the ridiculous tests and training she'd endured. "But who left the skull?"

Nuha landed a hand on her shoulder and leaned in to whisper, "They say Artemis herself placed that there. She hopes one day you wear her symbol as proudly as she does."

"Cedric would throw a fit." Angeline's eyes widened at the thought. "Thank you for finding my home. Just a moment while I change and grab the bow."

Angeline dove in and paused, the room still in the form of Cedric's old bedroom from the Romulus mansion. Her eyes paused on the bed; part of her wanted to curl into a ball and sleep. Shaking it off, she shed her clothes as she took long strides across the room. Rushing the barrel, she poured water over herself and the sand rushed off her skin and the sunburn cooled its biting at her. Satisfied she had cleansed herself enough, she spun to pull her garments from a chest and grabbed up Hamadryades's bow. She took only another moment to admire the craftsmanship, before slinging the war hammer onto her back and over her shoulder. Boots on, she left her door with a sense of pride.

"Look at you! More like an Amazonian these days!" Nuha pulled her along, weaving them between people and huts.

At last, they burst through the tight alleyways into an open field lined with archers all practicing at different stations. Nuha kept her moving, no time to stare and observe, until they found Manah. The dark tone of her skin made her muscles look like twisted onyx, gorgeous as she released an arrow and hit the center mark. She turned to them, breaking into a wide smile at the way Angeline looked.

"You train well!" She pulled her in for a tight hug. "And now you must see to it that you're as strong with your bow so as not to disappoint Artemis."

Angeline rolled her eyes. "More along the lines to tighten the talent I made for myself long before Artemis came into my life."

Nuha laughed and smacked her on the back. "So bold! Well, I take my leave, as I have matters to attend with our dear Artemis. Manah, teach her all so she may shine brightly in the Mortal Realm."

"As a sister of the Fates, I will teach her to see in the darkest of places and hit her mark with courage." They bowed to one another, and Nuha ran off. "Let's start at the basics, and just climb the ladder."

"Gladly!" Angeline pulled the bow from her shoulder and pulled a practice arrow from the satchel on a hay bale. "Center target, yes?"

"Yes, but are you not going to take that war hammer off first?" Manah lowered her brow and leaned back to get a better look at it.

"No." Angeline pulled back on the string, aiming quick and released.

"You hit the mark." Manah tilted her head. "Is that not a new weapon? Is your weight not new to you?"

"It is." Angeline grinned, pulling a second arrow across the bow's shelf. "And I find it more meaningful to practice as if I am in battle." She let go, a hissing sound and thud signaling the arrow slid against the first before hitting its mark. "Now, what will you have me do next, Master Manah?"

Manah bit her bottom lip, looking away for a moment. "You have indeed mastered the basics then, and perhaps more than any of these fledglings on the field. How do you feel about some field practice on some busse and help hunt for the feast tonight?"

Angeline looked to the bow, the war hammer heavy against her back. "You know, I think I'd like to see how I handle myself in a hunt."

"Me too." Manah abandoned the bow she was using. "Now it's my turn to go home and get my weapons. Join me, I'd love to hear more of your battles. What happened with the Furies and Valkyries? Do you mind?"

"Not at all." Angeline chuckled, the tension fading, and she allowed herself to feel at peace. "Considering I am waiting for my escort to take me home, please at least confirm the busse are just big stags and not giants as tall as trees."

Manah shook her head as they walked. "No, child. What you faced was rare. These are bull-sized bucks at best."

"Oh, thank goodness."

Angeline looked up at the bright skies. The time there seemed to change slowly.

I wonder where Cedric is right now. How close could he be to arriving, I wonder?

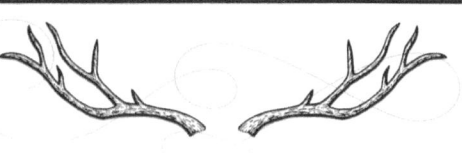

CHAPTER 19

THE BIRD CAGE

CEDRIC

Cedric spat at the ground, standing before the golden cage. It was outside of the encampment and marketplace, far enough away so that the miasma of the bird's feces couldn't kill an innocent bystander. He shot a glare to King Frey, and he waved. Despite the stinging in his nostrils, it was clear the visiting king at his side with the veil was none other than Pan. The lust flowing between the two made him shake his head and roll his eyes. As annoying as it could be to have the awareness when everyone and their mother might feel horny, it did give him the ability to heal and be more powerful.

If he rode up Frey's thigh and higher, I might think they're...

The screaming coming from the cage broke his thoughts. The champion, or the last of the line of champions that came before him, was fleeing. He hadn't even ventured to the egg before turning tail and running for his life. The sound of metal screeching and rubbing against itself meant the stymphalian had taken flight. A barrage of metal feathers rained down on the man, one lodging into his torso, partially seen hanging out of his back and abdomen. He stumbled and Cedric winced.

It had been the failure of those before the warriors that made it clear; don't touch the miasma piles or... The champion reared back onto his feet, part of an arm and half his face starting to melt. His screaming shifted to shrieks. The man was dying. Cedric stood, unmoved, like all the ones who died before him. He watched as he beat at the cage door, begging to be let out, begging to live. The bird swooped down and ate the remaining pieces. Again, Cedric didn't look away. He took in the bird's movements, what is aimed to eat first, and how slow its body had been compared to the metallic feathers it shot across the span of the cage.

Cedric refocused his eyes on the golden egg sitting dead center of the cage. In fact, directly under the perch the bird sat on the majority of the time. Sucking on his cheek, Cedric looked back to the purple and black aura and smoke wafting off the piles of bird shit. He had seen it before, been in it before. Unlike the other champions, he had the advantage of being part demon, perhaps full demon. He could touch it, hell, fall into it, and not melt. The most he'd earn was smelling like shit for weeks on end. The bird choked back the last of the man's remains, swallowing him up like a minnow to an egret on the shoreline. Back it flew, on its perch and ruffled its metal feathers. The sound seemed surreal, like a giant wind chime.

"Ah, Vampire King!" King Frey's voice boomed across the span, clear even over the shouting of the bet makers. "You are the last to go. Please, don't disappoint me."

Turning to face him, he had been given his helmet by an alfin councilor and reminded to wear it at all times. "Forgive me, King Frey, but last I recall, stymphalians don't grow to this size."

"You are right, but we're not in the Mortal Realm." Frey nodded, leaning in to listen to Pan whisper in his ear. "Hmm, yes, he wouldn't know. Please, forgive me, Vampire King. This bird was a gift from the giants where I once lived, and still often visit."

"Of course." Cedric rolled his eyes and approached the cage door. "Remind me of the rules once more, King Frey. I'd hate to disappoint you or your beloved lawyer today."

"Retrieve the golden egg at all costs."

"At all costs?" Cedric met his gaze and smirked. "Are you sure about that last part? I take my verbiage profoundly seriously, you know."

Pan smacked Frey and whispered more. "Ah, well, I want to see him try... no, no..." They paused and looked his way before nodding and whispering some more. "I highly doubt he could... no metal can... ha! You don't think he would after... oh?" Another pause as they looked at one another and at last, Frey sighed and with confidence, repeated. "At all costs."

"I hate you both," he drawled as an alfin guard began to unlatch the door. "You're like a couple of schoolgirls up there gossiping about me when I can hear you perfectly fine from here."

"Can he?" Frey looked wide-eyed at Pan.

"Well, didn't really think he could hear us over all the commotion. He might be bluffing." Pan shrugged.

"I'm not bluffing!" shouted Cedric, rubbing his *manica* to calm the armor.

And dammit, the armor is shivering again, but I can't tell why.

He took a few steps into the cage and the door slammed shut. The bird cocked its head at him, feathers ruffling and chiming as it squawked. Cedric cracked his neck one way, then the other. Looking across the cage floor, he shuddered. It was disgusting, with piles of partially eaten creatures and crap smattered haphazardly all over. There was no straight path to the egg and back. In fact, it seemed the bird did indeed do this in order to protect the egg, seeing none of the trash came close to it.

Rubbing his nose on his forearm, he cursed under his breath. He hated every second of this challenge. Another glance at the two kings over on the throne and his rage flared. Embarrassment took hold. He felt like some plaything for gods he didn't even worship or respect. Cedric turned back to look skyward, and the bird watched him with great interest. He knew she would stay there until she impaled him, or he fell into a pile of her crap. They attacked from afar until the kill was certain and ate before they dissolved. They were just metallic vultures, as far as he cared. He thought back to the first seven champions who tried and wondered how Asterion broke in and got to the egg.

Too fast...

"We need speed." He spoke it out loud and could feel the armor tighten at his feet and calves. "I'm gonna need some sturdy boots for this, something archers would wear for running and climbing, something to give chase in, or in this case, run away on."

The *manica* receded, leaving a simple bracer in its wake. Instead, the resources were reallocated to making the sandals into boots. He stomped and circled his ankles, checking the final details before looking back to pick a path. The minotaur had a soft spot for golden eggs and treasure, and somehow that big cow made his way in and out with the egg. All Cedric lacked was his speed; that was, unless he used his magic.

"You think you can handle that spell again?" The armor shivered. "I hope that's a yes."

He took another look up at the bird; it tilted its head at him. He winked and disappeared. Feathers ruffled, and the stymphalian shrieked, searching the floor for him. Cedric phased in and out of the shadows, snaking his way through the piles of miasma-producing crap. It didn't take him long to weave through the nauseating maze before he at last stood before the egg. He muttered under his breath. The egg was larger and far heavier than he expected. Picking it up, the spell failed.

"Shit, I can't use it while holding this thing." Adjusting his grip, he launched into a sprint.

The sound of metal clanking made him hyperaware that the stymphalian had caught a glimpse of him. Feathers speared down at him, miasma scattering. The bird aimed to change his direction, but he managed to leap over the blockage and dodge another wave of feathers. They stuck in the ground like arrows and javelins. No two were alike, their sizes varying from small daggers to something larger than planks from a barn.

Miasma splattered across the egg, and Cedric stumbled to a stop. Holding his breath, it didn't seem to faze it. He shook it off and started sprinting. Another wave of feathers flew across, one nicking his shoulder. His grip on the egg didn't waver as he took a hard right, diving between two hills of manure. Without warning, the stymphalian swooped down, shoving over a pile in his direction with her talons. Wincing, Cedric prepared for the connection with the flesh-eating miasma.

Manure slapped across his entire right side, hot and sickening in scent. Holding the egg tight, he pushed forward and waited for the pain, for the dissolving of flesh, and burning scent he had endured from those who had failed before him. *Nothing.* He eyed his arm. Nothing but shit-covered skin.

What the hell? Cedric picked up speed, thoughts searching for an explanation. *Incubi are from the Underworld, miasma is associated... well, if King Frey didn't figure it out the other day when I threw my helmet, he's about to find out without reasonable doubt.*

Another pile toppled over. Cedric grunted, sliding to a stop. Reassessing his environment, he now had an advantage. Miasma served no threat, and it opened up more pathways. Already covered and reeking, he ran through a smaller pile. The stymphalian panicked. Cedric bolted down a path, going straight for the gate. Feathers came down twice as thick. One landed in front of him and he backstepped. His torso lit on fire and he fumbled, dropping the egg.

Blood poured to the ground, riding down the metallic feather where it connected and lodged him against the ground. Angry, he tugged it from the dirt and spun to see the stymphalian circle the top of the cage. It locked eyes with him and started to dive for him, talons thrown forward. He gripped the feather and pulled it all the way through, blood splattering the ground and egg. Reaching over, he pulled a few more from the ground. He first launched the smallest in the pile like a spear at the incoming stymphalian and she retreated.

A grin crossed his face. Again, the bird circled back and attempted another dive. This time, Cedric waited until she dove closer and threw the next feather. It tinged off her body and broke her from her dive. Feathers fell to the ground, the impact breaking them free and bending a few. Earlier, he had watched a man toss his sword at her and it bounced off with no reaction other than breaking the blade. Her own feathers, on the other hand, seemed to have the strength to possibly break through and maybe draw blood.

He tossed the helmet down, flustered at the way it limited his ability to see. Shaking his hair loose, sweat flecking off the red strands, he shifted into a better pose. Again, he waited for the stymphalian to dive toward him. Closer, closer still, and at last, he let fly the blood-soaked feather. This one was the heaviest of the pile he had gathered, and it hit the bird with a ping and thud.

The beast screamed, falling to the ground. His strike had broken feathers off until it lodged deep into the bird's chest. Cedric took a moment to gather more feathers as a failsafe. He couldn't see the stymphalian from where he stood, the gateway just on the other side of the last pile of shit heaping behind him as tall as a building. Tucking the feathers under his arm, he hugged the egg back into his arms and sprinted down the only pathway around.

He rounded the corner, the alfin guard paling to see him. The latch was unlocking, the stymphalian screeching somewhere behind him. Swinging open the cage door, the entire array of guards and betters screamed, tickets waving in the air. Cedric scowled, the ground underfoot shaking and his bracer tightening. The bird had managed to climb to its feet. The pile of manure exploded as the great metal beast came through it. Desperate, Cedric tossed the egg to the two guards. They fell to the ground under its weight.

Twisting, he pulled the feathers out from under his arms, wielding them like dual swords. The stymphalian flapped her wings, red blood running down her chest where the makeshift spear still stuck deep into her flesh. She lunged at him, beak snapping as she squawked. Her foul breath slammed hot against him, miasma pouring from her mouth like a chimera's fire breath. It flowed over Cedric, hot and rank. The guards at the gate behind him screamed, running away. Through the black and purple, he saw King Frey and Pan rise to their feet.

Well, my cover's blown. Time to just handle shit my way.

Gripping the feathery blades tight, he ducked under the stymphalian's head and thrust the feathers up and through. They slide through without a snag, sharp and slicing his hands from the power of his strike. The miasma from its beak slowed and sputtered, blood drooling out as the body grew limp and rolled to its side. He stood, sweat dripping off his chin as he sighed in relief. Looking at his one arm covered in shit, he cursed under his breath. The *manica* blossomed back to full size once more, the armor unphased by its own encounter with the miasma.

"Looks like I'm not the only one immune," he snorted.

Kicking the bird for good measure, he marched out of the cage. The entire audience of spectators had fallen silent. He ignored their glares and whispers. Cedric stopped before the platform where Freya and Pan stood in earnest silence. He kneeled, knowing he couldn't hide his entire being from the Otherworld beings anymore. The whole time in the Mortal Realm, he'd managed to feign human for most of his life, but there, he couldn't fool the eyes, noses, and powers beyond even his understanding. This realm made him very aware of how non-human he'd been from the start of his life.

"From one king to another, have I completed my task to your satisfaction." He didn't look up from the ground, very aware of all the eyes staring at him and his mismatched horns.

"Tell me your name." Frey stepped down from the platform and motioned for him to rise. "Tell me who you are, fellow king of the realms."

Cedric's eyes fell on Pan behind him, who gave a reassuring nod. *It seems I might have gotten myself a way to make up for lost time after all. An endorsement from the King of Alfin and King of Fae should get us through the rest of this hellhole faster, I imagine.*

Standing, he locked eyes with Frey. "I am Lord Cedric du Romulus. The Vampire King and King Incubus on the Mortal Realms."

"Not accurate," intervened Pan, stepping down and casting his glare on the gathering crowd. "According to the laws of the Realms, you are the only rightful King of the Incubine kind and the Cursed Ones as we call them here. If I also recall, you brought death to many Otherworld outlaws in the Mortal Realm and sent them to the Underworld. In fact, Slayer of Demons even."

There were gasps from behind them, someone mumbling, "Bringer of Death."

Licking a fang, Cedric's sense of instant regret made him inhale and hold it.

"You don't say?" Frey glanced back at Pan before turning back and cracking a wide grin. "Well, King ... Romulus, was it? I insist you wash up and join us for a celebratory feast!"

"I'd be honored to join." A shudder shook his shoulder upon hearing *King Romulus.*

"King Frey!" A guard pushed through the crowd and rushed to their side. "What shall we do with the dead stymphalian?"

He furrowed his brow. "Well, Pan said you'd find a way to kill the bird, but..."

Cedric shot a glance back, seeing Manny and Nicholas in the crowd. "I made the mess, and I clean it."

"You did enough!" Frey fussed.

"No, really. I have a crew that can take care of this."

"Is that so? Just send us some of the meat. I hear they are excellent." Frey spun on his heels, throwing an arm over Pan. "Now, how about you and I head back to my bed?"

"Are you sure? We only left because you got winded." Pan bit his bottom lip and raised his eyebrows high.

"Hush, someone might hear you." Frey's face flushed and he got Cedric's knitted brow. "Must you listen to everything?!"

Cedric threw up his hands, turning away with a laugh. "I don't need to hear it. The lust between you two is more than enough to make that arrangement loud and clear. Enjoy."

Walking away, Cedric joined the rest of his crew at the cage door. Everyone was there, kelpie and Fen included, as they stared into the manure-covered ground. Miasma still wafted off the piles, making no easy path to reach the corpse, let alone an answer as to how one would retrieve the creature without getting killed in the process. Nicholas and Manny were bickering with two alfin guards charged to stay and obtain meat from the carcass. Cedric shoved past them, marching through the miasma once more unscathed.

Reaching down, he gripped the talons of the bird and dragged it out of the cage and a good distance from the miasma for good measure. Letting go, he wiped his hands on his thighs and turned to the gathering of comrades and onlookers. Seeing he had everyone's attention, he cleared his throat and raised his voice so all could hear.

"Nicholas is in charge of this." He pointed at the dwarf and glanced about to see if anyone would reject. "Make sure King Frey gets his fill of meat." He shot a look at Fen and Enbharr. "You only get what's left over, you mongrels. Not until short-stack says you can."

"Why would I be interested in something dead?" Enbharr crossed their arms in rebuttal.

"Speak for yourself. I love meat!" The excitement in Fen's voice had Romasanta and Nyctimus both grabbing an arm.

"Whatever you intend to do, do not turn into *that form* until we're alone," Nyctimus growled.

"I don't need fangs to eat," he insisted.

With that, Cedric left them to bicker amongst themselves.

Now to face Freya's chosen champion. Just wait, Angeline. I'm almost there.

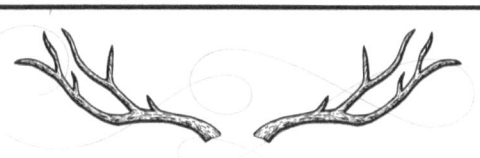

CHAPTER 20

THE CHALLENGER

ANGELINE

Angeline leaned on the table of equipment. She had been given many gifts from merchants and factions which didn't spare any expense. Weapons, armor, and more lay in piles all around. She had been left alone. All her training companions had wished her well, given her their own trinkets and well wishes. Freya herself had approached her while she was still covered in the blood of the busse she had slain with Manah. There had been a cold air weighing down on her until the blood had begun to grow ice crystals. She didn't dare say no.

Shit. I didn't want this, but if it might just give me the chance to test out everything I've been training for, then maybe...

She inhaled deeply and held it. Looking over all the equipment, she began picking out what she favored. Leather breeches, crafted so one could hold throwing blades on the thigh while sewn to allow movement as best as possible. Lace-up leather boots were her favorite, the support on the ankles and the cushioning under her sore bare feet a warm welcome. Olrun had ruined her love of going without shoes, especially after the beach training. She paused, paining over the Valkyrie chest armor and the tight, leather wrapping of the Fury. Huffing, she decided she would double down on her agility with the hammer and go with the more flexible trapping. Plus, it covered her arms all the way and allowed her to hide blades in the wristbands. If that hadn't sold her, she could take the collar over her neck and hide the lower half of her face.

There were leather belts and garters for carrying her weapons and more. She had been gifted many things: the war hammer from Olrun, the bow from Hamadryades, and not to mention the skills to use every weapon imaginable, or even go without. A knock at the door had her scrambling to tuck the thick leather and cloth into place before opening it. Alecto took a bite of an apple against a column just behind Olrun. The Valkyrie seemed breathless, covered in sweat and soot as she kneeled and offered up the blade.

"I'm sorry it's so late..." She at last met her gaze, the dark rings in her face showing her exhaustion. "I had to call in a favor to finish the work, so it seems you have earned this more so than I could imagine."

Angeline's eyes fell to the short sword. The hilt was familiar, the chimeran horn barely changed and familiar in her hand. As she raised the weapon from Olrun's flattened palms, her breath caught. The balance made it far less of a strain on her arm muscles than when it had been a small dagger. The black blade shined like onyx, bronze décor of ravens, stags, and Celtic knots mimicked the war hammer, and her heart skipped a beat. She looked back at Olrun, wild-eyed.

"Your friend, you mean Badbh?" Angeline tilted her head, helping Olrun to her feet.

"Indeed," she smirked. "It seems her war hammer took more energy from me than I had expected, so it only seemed fair she do her share to help me keep my promise. When I heard you had been asked to be the next champion a few weeks ago, I panicked, and, well, Alecto told a birdy of my demise."

"I see." Angeline looked at Alecto, who winked.

"Besides, we got to hear some war stories about your old man." Alecto licked juice from the side of the red apple. "Interesting bedfellows."

Angeline's face flushed. "I suppose it might come off that way considering what he..." Her words faltered, and she redirected her statement's course. "What we are."

"May this blade be able to serve you both well." Olrun sighed as if a great weight had lifted from her shoulders. "I look forward to seeing you battle today and put all that training to good use. Don't be afraid to cut with this cursed blade. It serves you and your blood, and even his at that. It's a rare curse, ancient and raw."

"R-right." Angeline nodded and panicked. "Oh, I don't have a sheath for it though..."

"You're silly, Ex-Mortal." Alecto pulled away from the column, tossing the apple core to the floor behind her. "Olrun and Badbh took care of that matter, too." Unbuckling the large leather straps on her front, a large chest holster of sorts loosened, and she slid her arms out. "This was Badbh's idea, and I added my own touch to it. It should be sturdy enough the hold a sword and the war hammer on your back. I altered it because I want my beloved Fury to be able to pull her weapons out as fast as they can slide back in."

"Oh, thank you, Alecto." Angeline furrowed her brow and smirked. "There's even back and extra sheaths?"

"Exactly. You'll thank me again later." She leaned in, whispering in her ear, "Remember, you do have one chance to call me to your side, but you better save it for a special moment in the timeline. There's nothing you can't handle in this body, but there will come a day you won't have this power to rely on." Angeline blinked, opening her mouth to ask further, but Alecto pressed her fingers against her lips. "Olrun, let's go have a seat. Will you be with me or Mother Freya?"

Olrun twisted her lips. "My sisters are going to throw a fit, but I'll be with you, my love. I may need to use those plump thighs for a pillow as tired as I feel."

"So be it!" And she whisked Olrun away.

Angeline shut the door, looking at the sword that now matched the war hammer. It seemed so artfully done, something worthy of a legendary warrior of old. Granted, nothing about her life seemed anything short of becoming its own legend at this rate. She had fought beside a legendary knight, married a lord of her time, was whisked away by a powerful wizard, and walked the halls of Avalon, though not in the way one would have imagined.

What a crazy life I have. Facing the mother of dragons, befriending gods of the old, and training with female warriors I thought were only fairy tales.

Pulling the holster on, she began buckling it tight. It fit surprisingly well. The runes of the Fury burned into it with snakes and centipedes wrestling for space. Her shoulders shuddered before reaching for the sword and sliding it into place, its weight well balanced, and she started putting the rest on, loading the weapons, and at last, the war hammer made the straps pull at her without feeling as if she would be thrown off balance.

She turned to the table, needing some sort of helmet since it was made clear, no face should be shown on the battlefield during this competition. It was to be a pure display of two warriors.

She had a few options. A variety of tribal masks lined beside Valkyrie helmets, and none of them spoke to her. Picking them up one at a time, she looked them over, tried them on, and fussed over the blind spots they created. She hadn't thought of the idea of training in armor and helmets. Leaning on the table, she scowled at them all. All these years, and never once had she thought to protect her head. She smiled, laughing inside at herself and the careless notion it left her with, even when she had been human and fragile.

"I was hoping..." Artemis's voice sent chills through her. "You would honor me by wearing this."

In a move Angeline could never imagine, Artemis kneeled at her feet and held a mask eerily similar to hers. As if aimed to appeal to her, the deer skull had been stained black like the weapons she had acquired. Bronze horns rose with all the emblems of the factions; braided threads with swan feathers and snake skulls showed her kinship with Valkyries and Furies. The wide skull eye sockets had tears of bronze pouring from them and some part of her felt the sting of the notion that it reflected some truth about herself. From the forehead down the center were Ancient Greek letters.

"What does that say?" She reached out to take it, but recoiled her fingers. "And what magic does this possess?"

Artemis stayed kneeling, unyielding in her offer as she spoke. "*Epimonos... persistent.*"

Angeline shook her head. "Yeah, that seems fitting."

"And the magic is especially important. I didn't survive this long by accident, child." At last, those amber eyes hit Angeline's. "This mask has hidden my presence, my magic, even from Kronos himself for the longest of time. I wish to provide you with this same gift. May you continue to grow, little one. Know I do not harbor ill-intent."

"I understand." Angeline picked up the mask, but Artemis stayed kneeling before her. "But, why be so concerned now of all times?"

A glow came from her eyes and she lipped, *Gaea.*

Angeline swallowed. "Right, I've had enough trouble..."

Nerves taut, she slid the mask on. Much to her surprise, it was light and comfortable. The magic in the totem seemed to make it seem non-existent to the wearer. She turned her head one way, then the other. The trinkets on the horns chimed in a soothing way and the mask didn't hinder her view, though physics made it clear it should have been every bit as invasive as the full-face helmet she tried on earlier.

"You are much like me when it comes to fighting. Would rather go out naked, without any restrictions, especially in the way of sight." Her voice lightened, almost as if hiding a smile behind her own mask. "It's a good sign of a strong archer."

"Now what do I do?" Angeline swallowed, tugging on all her gear and clothes, checking that belts were still buckled tight and in place.

"The horns will blow. A great pyre full of ancient herbs will be lit in the center. Their properties will render your sense of smell and ability to speak useless. In fact, it will go as far as numbing your sense of touch in hopes of making sure the fight starts on even ground, no matter who or what you might be facing." Artemis rose and motioned to two large, reinforced doors. "The warrior you face has been through their own training and tribulations, chosen by the King of Alfin."

"Alfin?" Angeline pumped her fists, trying to steady her nerves and slow her beating heart. "What's an alfin?"

"Elves?" Artemis took a shot in the dark.

"Oh. Okay..." She turned to her. "How big is this warrior?"

Artemis's toothy grin peaked from behind her mask. "You'll have to see for yourself."

A horn blew, loud and long. Angeline stared at the doors, the sound of someone pulling them open making her shiver. She turned to ask Artemis something more, but she had vanished. Her shoulders ached and part of her wished she had her wings back so she could just fly away from this insane match she had been pressured into performing. Today she would be representing all the Amazonians, and she was expected to win.

What have I gotten myself into? Granted, I don't think anyone in the world could say no to Freya, Alecto, or even Artemis.

The doors opened wide and a Valkyrie waved for her to come out into the bright sunlight. She squinted her eyes, blinking and desperate to recover her eyesight. On one side, Manah led a one-horned gladiator to the pyre of pungent, putrid herbs. Nuha grabbed her arm, whispering encouragement as they approached. Through the hot flames, she glared at the warrior, her heart beating fast. He was heavily muscled and broad. Besides the horns that his helmet attempted to hide as his own, he seemed rather human. Inhaling the herbs, she felt faint and Nuha pinched her, making her stiffen. Looking at the stadium, she met eyes with Alecto.

Granted, most of these monsters look human, so this tells me nothing about the powers he might possess and use against me.

"Draw your weapons." A cold wind blasted through, snuffing out the pyre as Freya spoke.

Reaching back, Angeline pulled the war hammer. Her opponent tilted his head and drew out a long blade, a katana of sorts. Black and purple flames glowed off his blade. She cursed his full-face helmet, unable to meet his gaze or gauge his face. He licked a fang, and it made her aware she too had her own set if it came down to that.

I mean, I can bite and drink blood... though I've only done that to one person.

She gripped the handle tight as they circled one another. All around, shouts and whistles filled the air. He rushed in, swinging the sword wide. She backstepped, gauging the strength and movement. Back when training with Olrun, she had made the mistake of not watching her first. She had also made that mistake with the tasks she completed for Alecto as well. He twisted and the sword followed through and swung downward toward her. There wasn't time to dodge; she hadn't expected consecutive strikes so soon.

The katana came racing down, and Angeline dropped to her knees. Rising the head of the hammer up, she used it to block. She held her breath. Metal pinged against metal, but the black and purple flames poured down on her. Tensing, she waited for the pain, for the attack, for... *nothing.* The flames flowed over her and she shot a look at her attacker. Again, the clear tilt of the head and the only facial feature she could see, his lips, said *fuck*. He immediately retreated, but she couldn't let him. In a move much like the one she last made on Olrun, she ran forward, thrusting the hammer to his chest. Then he disappeared in a shadowy puff of smoke.

Pure instinct drove her next move. Hairs stood on end and she pulled the sword free. Unable to change the course of her move with the hammer, she knew she could do a defensive wide strike behind her. It did the trick as he reappeared, and their blades locked. Pressure exploded between the blades, forcing both of them to back down and reassess their opponent. Like a lion, he paced back and forth, his mouth in a deep frown.

He wanted to finish this fight fast and hard like I had planned to do. Whatever magic that black flame was it failed and he's not happy about it. Worse, he seems to have some powerful tricks up his sleeve being able to dodge that strike.

She sheathed the blade and picked up the hammer. He smirked, his grip on the katana tightening. In the blink of an eye, he vanished again like a shadow fading in the wind. Her skin pimpled and she turned, swinging the hammer to her back left. He reappeared, jumping back. The twitching in the muscles in his arm made it clear he hadn't expected her to disrupt his attack. Something about his magic made her own rise in alarm. *Or was that the same level of excitement?*

A wave of lust hit her, and her eyes fell to the *manica* covering one arm. *Did his armor just get turned on?*

Abandoning his magic, he came at her with another powerful and wide swing. She blocked, using the hammer's handle. The force behind them made her slide across the ground with each strike, her muscles jarring. Swallowing, she tried to pay attention to his moves, and a shudder rolled through her. They seemed strangely familiar to her, but the herbs cutting off her sense of smell and the ability for either to speak added to the frustration of being under fire from a flurry of attacks.

Anger rolled forward and she dropped down, dodging the next swing completely as she kicked up the dust with the hammer head skipping across the ground. It was a quick swing, with enough reach to force him back. She heard his steps thudding as he came forward, and she repeated the move she had seen Svanhvit do. The pommel of the hammer hit him in the gut. A big *oof* escaped him and she didn't slow down.

The hammer's handle slid in her hands until it tightened in the appropriate place. She up swung and this time, he didn't have a chance to block. Her first hit had made him lean on the katana, and with the hammer, she hit him square in the chest. Power exploded from the enchantment and launched him backward. His feet left the ground and he smashed into the wall. Coughing, he stumbled away only to reach back to lean into it. She couldn't see his whole face, but it was clear she had pissed him off. The snarl and fangs made her jolt. Blood dripped from the wound and lust filled the air. The wound started to close, and she pulled out the blade.

Shit, I'm going against an incubus.

She shot an angry glare up at Freya, who smirked in response as the man with similar features next to her whispered in her ear. Biting her lip, Angeline returned her gaze to her opponent. Again, he vanished. She swung, but this time, her luck bottomed out. A slice erupted across her back and she stumbled forward. Inhaling swiftly, she cursed under her breath and tried to focus on him. Another cut ripped across her arm. The herbs had numbed her sense of smell that not even blood tinged in her nostrils and the pain seemed duller than it should have for as deep as he cut her. Her arm shook, the cut too deep to support the heavy hammer.

How can he have this much energy? I am quite sure my enchantment hit.

Reaching back, she pulled the sword out and her magic prompted her to raise it in time to block the third strike. He leaped back and she took the reprieve as a chance to slide the hammer into the holster, serving as a means to block attacks from hitting her back again. Another wave of lust left him, and her body reacted, her healing speeding up. His gaze fell to her arm, the wound closing. His posture changed, and again, he began to pace.

Now's my chance, he's thinking too much...

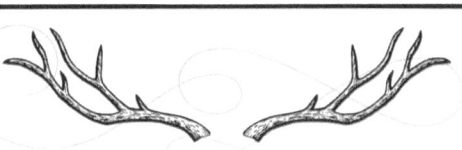

CHAPTER 21

SOUL MATES

CEDRIC

C edric cursed the stipulations and insistence of meddling King Frey and his sister put into place. So far in this fight, his opponent had made it clear she was a demon with her immunity to miasma from the Oni Sword and now, with a wave of lust from him, she healed faster. The deer mask obscured her face, and with the numbing of his sense of smell, he couldn't pick apart how much of her was succubus. If she was a halfling, he could overwhelm her with a wave of lust, but if she was full-blooded, then he could throw his own fight in her favor and feed her power. Rubbing his chest, it still stung where the magic had eaten away all his energy.

Dammit, that hurts. If it weren't for this armor forking up the energy it's been eating off me, I would have been down or struggling by now. I'm running out of energy to cast this spell, but maybe I can...

She holstered her hammer and pulled out a long, black-bladed sword. He gripped the katana tighter, and she launched an attack. Meeting her halfway, their blades connected, sparks flying with each strike. Occasionally she'd managed to dodge, as if her body sensed which way his swing would fall. The mask unnerved him, *one of Artemis's warriors, of course.* It pained him not being able to throw a snarky comment in battle. He swung with harder intent. She blocked, but the blade bit into her shoulder and she growled. A wave of lust escaped him, and he retreated.

What the hell was that reaction?

Cedric felt betrayed by his body for the first time in a long time. *Since when did I have lusting issues again?*

The female warrior came at him, her wound healed.

This was supposed to be over with a single strike, but at this rate, this fight is going to drag out.

He shot an angry glare at King Frey, who waved at him from next to his twin sister, Freya. Cedric flipped him the bird, sending the crowd screaming. The girl had closed the gap and he faded into the shadows, appearing behind her, but his strike connected with the hammer strapped across her back. He cursed the enchanted weapon and retreated. She turned on her heels, arm swinging out and releasing a flurry of throwing knives. He managed to block several with the *manica* but two stuck into his chest.

Pulling them out with an annoyed grunt, he ran at her and she matched the charge with her own. Again, their swords connected with blossoms of sparks. She made a clumsy shift in stance and he took the opening, tossing the two throwing knives. Blocking the one with a hand, it lodged into her palm and the other stuck in her shoulder. She retreated and pulled them out, lust filling the air between them.

We're both struggling. Was it the herbs?

She pulled the knives and tossed them to the ground, her chest showing she was panting. Cedric sucked on his cheek, trying and failing to push the sexual desire down. It seemed his body wanted her, but he had no desire to screw with an Amazonian when Angeline was somewhere on this cursed island. He assessed his opponent. She was resourceful, with a variety of weapons matched with good speed and instincts. Granted, it would only get her so far. She had only managed a few strikes on him, though against any other opponent, she would have had them down for the count by now.

I've read how the best warriors in the world come here, and I believe it.

Again, he rubbed his chest, annoyed at the way it stung and the fact he still didn't have his sense of smell back. They were both healing, but as far as he could tell, she had to be feeling the same effects. Her shoulders stiffened, and he braced himself. She charged forward, making powerful strikes, and he blocked each with confidence. Watching her, he furrowed his brow. She had been more graceful, even struck at him with stronger blows with the hammer.

She's not properly trained to use a sword. In fact, this style brings me back to tournaments against knights.

He dropped down and kicked out a leg. She stumbled, unable to avoid him, but managed to back away and catch herself before a hand hit the ground, costing him any hope for a new opening. The deer mask unnerved him. Feathers and snake skulls chimed in the wind as they reassessed one another yet again. The black mask, tears, and the Greek words for *persistent* sent a chill up his spine. It made him smirk, and so far, he couldn't disagree. She had come at him, worked him, and even landed the best hit in the fight so far.

I'm getting my ass handed to me by an Amazonian, and despite her showing she's one of Artemis's brats, I'm not as pissed off as I should be about it.

She sheathed the sword, and he stood taller, rolling his shoulder. The war hammer and its bronze and black raven eyed him. Again, he rubbed his chest and thought of a way he could avoid another hit. This was clearly the weapon she favored, and his katana couldn't overpower it. She knew how to block, how to counter with accuracy with this item. Being a fellow incubus-succubus demon, he didn't question the ease and strength she had to swing it whether she was a halfling or not. He pumped his grip on the katana, pacing back and forth in front of her.

I need to recover the energy she took with the first hit, but...

Looking down at his katana, he smirked.

Perhaps nothing happens without purpose, but considering what happened last time, what do I have to lose other than making her falter? Look armor, if you can hear my thoughts, I need some kind of sign.

The *manica* shivered, tightening on his arm and he sighed in relief. Again, the tension in her body caught his attention, and she came at him, swinging the hammer. A wave of air flowed over him and he took a step back as to not lose his balance. She didn't stop her rotation, swinging around, dropping lower this time. He blocked with the *manica* and the force of it made him slide across the ground. She inhaled, rising to do an overhead strike. Snorting, he blocked it with the katana, his arms jarring, and he cursed her in his mind.

This is gonna rattle me and start to take a toll. Here's the plan, I'm going to give her an opportunity to land that hit on my chest, but I need you to block it. In fact, I need you to climb your ass onto that hammer and weigh it down.

In response, the armor loosened.

That better be a yes, or this will hurt like hell.

Cedric backstepped again, another wave of lust echoing between them. Both of them flinched, and something deep in Cedric reacted more than enough to make him halt. He forcibly sent her a wave of arousal and the echo that came back tasted sweet and nostalgic.

It couldn't be...

Eyes wide, he had faltered enough to leave himself open, and she ran forward, thrusting the hammer to his chest. The hammerhead stopped short, the enchantment dispersing as his armor piled itself on the weapon and it thudded to the ground. She abandoned it, leaping back out of the way in alarm. A wave of lust hit Cedric from all the gawking eyes. Whistles and catcalls were ignored as he stared at his opponent, picking her apart in a different way, searching for anything familiar.

It has to be...

She reached back for her sword, his eyes snagging on the chimeran hilt.

A-Angeline?

Another charge. She swung wide expecting him to block or step back, especially now that he was completely bare of any armor or clothes, beside his helmet. The blade sliced open his abdomen and he held tensed, grunting. She stumbled, confused, staring at the wound. Both of them dropped their weapons and reached for one another's helmets. Neither deflected the other's intent as they tugged them off and...

Cedric's eyes were wide, his heart racing. She lipped something, but neither of them had managed to regain their voice from the pyre's smoke. He locked lips with her, kissing her deeply. His skin ignited to feel her hands slide over him, clinging to him. She broke the kiss, gripping his wrist tight as she tugged him out of the arena. The Amazonians at a gate opened and closed it, giggling at the naked warrior she had taken with her.

I can't believe she could hold up to me in battle! Since when...

His thoughts unraveled as she began to unbuckle her leather holster. A wave of desire slammed him making his breath catch. Rushing up behind her, he helped slide it off her arms and they both scrambled to tug her shirt off. As it hit the floor, he ran his tongue across her back. Salty and sweet with her blood, the wound had healed but left it covered. She fumbled to undo her breeches, starting to slide them over her hips.

We've been hungering for this moment since we were disconnected...

He dragged her to the table of equipment, bending her over and knocking helmets to the ground. She inhaled sharply as he pressed against her. His hands rode up her body until they cupped her breasts, squeezing them tight. They both moaned, grinding against one another ever faster, their pleasure washing into one another. His eyes caught something under the blood on her back and he saw scars much like his own.

Could it be? She too...

Horns emerged on Angeline's forehead, clawed hands scoring the wooden table as she arched. Her orgasm slammed into him and he lost his balance as he braced himself on the table, grunting. Wrapping his arms under her, he pulled her into him until he nuzzled her neck. Her fingers tangled in his hair. She moaned as he continued making love to her. At last, the want, the need, the desire to connect with her grew too great. Fangs pierced skin, and her body shuddered, arousal peaking once more. He drank deeply as his orgasm peaked and...

Something shifted, their connection rekindled; he could feel the pleasure his bite brought her. She whimpered, panting as she rose to yet another peak. Their bond had been mended in an instant. Breaking away, he spun her around and lifted her onto the table. He wanted to see her face, see the pleasure he felt echoing in and out of both of them. She snapped her fingers, the last of her clothes gone, and he flinched, lifting a brow. Laughing, she shrugged and lipped, *I forgot.* Pressing against her, he kissed her deeply once more, tongues tangling in their moans; her breasts against his chest, fingers clawing down his back as they lost themselves to passion.

Pulling back, he shoved her down, wanting to see all of her as he ground against her. She had worked hard in his absence; her body was stronger, more athletic than before. Part of him pained over what it must have been like, but a stinging in his chest prompted her to reach up and touch the spot. His eyes met the hurt expression on her face, *sorry,* she lipped, and he laughed. Slowing, he released once more, moaning and excited to feel their connection, both physically and spiritually bonded. She arched, her body tensing and shuddering.

He fought to make the words come out, and at last croaked, "You're mine again, my Angel."

They stood still for a moment, tears welling up in her eyes as she smiled up at him. Sweat glistened in the light of the torchlight and she sat up, kissing him tenderly. They broke away and he turned to give her space, but she gripped his wrist once more. He followed without pause as she led him through the door, turning down the hallway and rushing into another room. Turning to face her, she slid the latch and locked the door. The room had a pungent smell; steam filled it and he furrowed his brow at her.

Clearing her throat, she rasped, "Medicinal herb to undo..." She pointed at her throat.

He blinked, and his fang marks were gone already. "I'm sorry, I didn't know it was you out there or I would have..."

Angeline pressed her fingers on his lips, leading him deeper into the room. Stairs unfolded in the steam and soon his feet felt hot waters. He followed her until they both were submerged in the hot water, various herbs floating all around. She dipped her head under, and he followed, enjoying the sensation of grime and sweat being washed away. Coming back up for air, the last of the pyre's restrictions dissolved. Angeline wrapped her arms around him, and he held her tight, his chest aching.

"Did I feel that? Is *it* back?" She pressed her head against his chest.

"Yes, it seems we repaired the bond, but..." He kissed the top of her head, relishing the moment. "I'm sure Artemis and everyone is going to be pissed about it."

"I don't care," she spat.

He chuckled. "That makes two of us."

"Does your chest feel better? I felt the stinging and..."

Pulling her away, he met her guilty expression. "Yes, but don't ever apologize for it again." She blinked and he smirked. "I have to be honest; it never crossed my mind that they would pitch us against each other for this. When it hit me that it might be you..."

"That's why you hesitated in the end, but I don't understand. Did you smell me or..." Her fingers trailed across where she had landed the last cut. "I knew it was you the moment this didn't react."

"React?" He knitted his brow in confusion.

"As a gift, they reworked that cursed dagger into a sword, but I'm not very good with it."

He searched the air. "The hilt, it's the same one, isn't it?"

"It is." She nodded.

"I kept looking at it, couldn't figure out why for the life of me in the fight." He smirked, cupping her jaw to steal another kiss. "I'll need to teach you to use it like a real champion, then. Granted, the way you swing that hammer has me baffled. Where did you learn to use that?"

"Freya and the Valkyries." She shrugged.

"And when you didn't fall after that hit, I can't lie, Angel, I'm impressed."

"And that was Alecto and the Fury training," she confessed.

"You've been busy," he smirked, brushing a strain of her hair off her forehead. "And that move with snapping your fingers?"

Her face flushed. "I hate to say it, but Artemis may have taught me a thing or two about using magic." She lowered her brow. "But what about you? You're missing a horn, and I'm pretty sure you were casting some kind of spell at the start of the fight."

Huffing, he relented. "This place has forced me to do a lot of things against my will. Granted, this..." He pointed to the missing horn and leaned into her ear. "Should give you two matching blades." His fingers trailed down her arm, rippling over the column of scars. "Who did this to you?" Anger rose in his voice.

"Alecto's blade." She reached up and touched the broken horn. "And who did this, then?"

He laughed, pulling her hand down. "I did."

"Why?" She scowled at him.

"So, I could make a weapon worthy of protecting you, my Lady Romulus." He suckled at her ear and began kissing at her neck. She tensed and he paused. "What's the matter?"

"There's something you should know." Her voice was weak, and it jolted him.

"What's the matter?" Cedric swallowed at the pain on her face as tears welled up.

"I remember now... the time that..." She choked on her words, covering her mouth. "I'm so sorry... it's nothing I should have ever forgotten, and I'm so afraid you'll hate me."

Could it be what I've suspected?

His hand slid down her torso and stopped on one of the few scars she possessed. "I've had suspicions..."

"I don't know where she is." Her voice broke.

"A girl..." He leaned his head against hers, soul aching to see how much this tore Angeline to pieces inside and out. "Did you give her a name?"

"Cleo," she whispered.

"The gypsy?" He paled.

"You know her?" Angeline had hope.

"N-not directly. Romasanta has crossed paths with her and..." His mind raced, gathering everything he could fathom. "And she's done something in the Mortal Realm..."

"She's in trouble. Kronos has done something to her ... and if his body dies, he moves on to hers next. He'll take it over." Angeline began shaking, and Cedric pulled her into his arms.

"Listen carefully, Angeline." Swallowing, he spoke firmly to her. "I can rip him out of that body the moment that happens. I've done it before with Morrighan and Beelzebub. The question is, how much of us has she inherited? The power, the..." He stumbled on his words, choking on them and baffled by the sensation. "We'll get through this. We always get through this."

"But it's not just Kronos," she whispered into him. "We will have to take down Mother Gaea."

"I'll face any enemy, whatever it takes to protect our daughter and you."

At any cost.

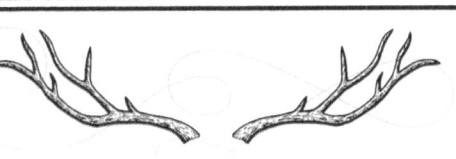

CHAPTER 22

REGRETS

ANGELINE

They finished bathing, but Angeline couldn't come up with words anymore. She stole glances at Cedric's stern face, but his eyes and thoughts were elsewhere. He hadn't been rattled, hadn't been angry with her, but understanding and reassuring at the news of her forgetting she had given birth to *their daughter.*

Manah and Nuha stood guard at the bathhouse door and giggled while offering clean clothes to them both. They barely made it down the hall before they were met with a row of gods and goddesses with unreadable expressions and crossed arms. Cedric slid his hand down and interlocked fingers and Angeline shot him a baffled expression.

He's never done that before.

"Tell me, Vampire King, do you always win a fight with women this way?" King Frey smirked as Freya smacked his arm.

"You dolt, you know exactly why you brought him here and what we *intended* to test between them." Freya bowed her head to them, a quaint smile. "No king should be without a queen that is his match on the battlefield. I give you my blessing, dear Angeline." With an outstretched palm, she blew an icy wind across Angeline. "May you find this helpful."

Angeline shivered, the coldness seeping deep into her as she chattered, "Exactly what kind of blessing did you give me?"

"Knowing my sister, you can probably shapeshift into a wolf or raven or something." Frey waved a hand, unimpressed. "She hands it out in the masses, it's lost it—"

"Dammit." Cedric scowled. "What is with everyone's desire to shapeshift in this place?"

"Aww, the little immortal is jealous," Alecto chimed in, leaning on Artemis's shoulder. "Though I admired the view today, perhaps we should give him some sort of blessing for that majesty of a view."

"Don't you dare bless me with any of your bullshit." He turned to Artemis, pointing at her. "You and me, old hag, we need to talk."

She smirked from under her mask, her amber eyes glowing, "Of course we need to talk, but first I wish to speak to my brother. It's been far longer since I've spoken to him, in person."

"I'm tired," Angeline squeezed Cedric's hand, mumbling.

He tensed, and at last huffed, "You lead the way."

Pushing past the crowd, no one dared to stop them or slow them down. They walked through the huts and marketplace of the Amazonians. Cedric took it all in, his eyes scanning and picking apart everyone and every detail. She tightened her grip on occasion and he would pick up speed. Some part of her felt strange to be holding his hands like she had seen her cousin and the ladies of the court do with their lovers and husbands. A swelling sensation of emotions stirred inside her and she could tell he sensed it, waving lust into her.

Can we do this? Be bound without derailing the other every time we want to fall apart internally, in the silence of our minds.

"It's okay," she muttered and shot a glance at him. "I just, I'm just thinking about my past before you. You don't need to soothe me. Sometimes I need to work out my emotions without... disruption from you."

He inhaled. "You're right. I keep thinking I have to come to your rescue." Cedric looked around and smirked at the gawking eyes, catching her name on whispering lips. "But it seems you can handle yourself just fine these days, Lady Romulus."

"Whatever happened to calling me *pet?*" She smirked and looked away.

He leaned into her ear. "That's for when we're alone, but I do regret not referring to you by your proper namesake, the one you took on against your will and never had the chance to live by."

Another swell of emotions left her, but this time, he didn't try to soothe them. "What other things do you regret?"

"Let us talk in private before I dare speak all my confessions to you in the open, among prying eyes and ears." Again, his grip tightened on her, but she stopped and pulled him back a few steps. "Does it mean that much to you, Angeline?"

Her face flushed red. "I stopped because we're here."

Cedric blinked, looking at the hut's doorway with a baffled expression. "What is all this?" All around, symbols of the various factions draped over her door and he lifted an eyebrow at her. "Did you win over the whole island?"

"Possibly." She tugged him inside, slamming and locking the door. "Come on, before the crowd gathering gets any bigger."

"This is..." Hhis voice failed, walking farther into the room.

Angeline couldn't look him in the face, tucking hair behind her ear. Cedric walked the room, looking at things, pulling items from shelves, and opening drawers. He would inspect something, look back at her wild-eyed, and move on. She hadn't expected him to take close inventory of what she had recreated, nor did she consider dissolving the illusion. The moment he reached the bed, he gripped the covers and inhaled deeply. He turned back with a fanged grin.

"You recreated my bedroom from then." His eyes scanned the room once more. "And in great detail, my love. I'm impressed."

She dared to meet his gaze and her heart fluttered to see a sparkle in his eyes. "I just wanted to feel at home, even for a moment."

"Home." He glanced over it all one more time. "And this is where you..."

At last, she pushed herself to move closer, standing before him. "Home is wherever you are, but this is a close second, I suppose."

"You wanted to know my regrets." The light in his eyes faded, and her heart ached.

Angeline swallowed, nerves tightening. "It was a dumb question..."

"It wasn't." His voice grew deep and soft all at once, his green eyes glowing in the dim light of the fireplace. "I regret," he cupped her jaw and kissed her, "taking away your humanity. I regret," the heat of his hands slid under her shirt, sending goosebumps over her body, "not allowing myself to be honest with you sooner. I regret," he frowned, his brow knitting as he plucked her shirt off and pulled her closer to undo her leather breeches, "not teaching you to use the sword properly. I regret," eyes locking with her own, he searched her face, "not telling you I love you more often, more freely."

Her pants fell to the floor as he locked lips with hers. She could feel the boiling tangle of emotions stirring deep inside him before he let lust swallow it and her up completely. He deepened the kiss, backing her up until she felt the bed against her ass cheeks. His tongue lashed into her mouth, hungry and desperate as he lifted her by the hips, setting her gently on the bed. Breaking away, he shed his own clothes, his eyes on her body making her arousal soar.

Oh, how I've missed him, but this version of him makes me wonder what happened to make him so ... docile?

"Cedric..." She marveled over his words still, but found she didn't know what else to say.

He smirked, softening his expression. "I definitely regret not taking you in my—*our*—bed."

Cedric closed the gap, the heat of his body sending a buzz of excitement through her. "I missed you, my pet."

"And I've missed you," she echoed, her body alive with want as the heat of his hips slid against her thighs. "But you're being so..."

"Gentle for now." His hands rode across her body, sending a wake of magic stirring between them.

"What was that?" Her breath caught as he wrapped soft lips over her nipple, holding her into him.

He didn't bother to answer, but pressed himself into her. She arched, and he suckled hard, grinding against her. Matching the rhythm, she moaned with each deep connection. The pleasure between them shared, and for the first time, without the fog of inner doubts and turmoil. Rising to her knees, she wrapped her legs around him and he grunted. Switching breasts, Cedric's breath washed over her, hot and enthralling.

At last, he began pushing her farther onto the bed, letting her body unfold. Hungry eyes took her in as he abandoned her breasts. Gathering her legs, he moved her ankles over a shoulder. She made a baffled expression, but the wicked grin told her he wanted to make up for all those times he regretted not letting loose in the sheets. Chills rattled her, the provocative desire coming across in their connection making her want him more so.

Leaning forward, he pressed himself against her once more, thrusting hard as she yelped. Both of them moaned and shuddered as orgasms echoed into one another. With each wake, it only energized them to continue to take one another. Twisting her this way and that, at last on all fours, hands gripping the covers as she wailed in pure ecstasy. And when at last Cedric dared to stop and pull away, she threw him down before her on the bed, both panting and feral with passion.

I want to take him...

She straddled him, connecting with him. His eyes rolled back, drowning in the pleasure she took in rocking on him, feeling his body under hers. The heat of his hands explored her body, groping her breasts, trailing down the center of her torso, and squeezing her thighs. Her body was on fire, and when he coaxed her to lean down, to kiss him deep and hungry, she hadn't expected him to take back his control. Arms wrapped tight around her, pulled her into him, and locked her against him as he thrust fast and hard. When she peaked once more, he joined her, and it was only then they let one another break away.

Cedric scooped her into his arms, pulling the covers across them both before nuzzling her neck. She hugged his arms, relishing in the warmth of his body. Every last bit of tension and frustration had left her. Inhaling deeply, she held it and fought the sudden urge to cry.

What's wrong with me?

The swell of emotions made his arms squeeze her tighter for only a second. No bombardment of his lust or emotions, just a physical acknowledgment. She steadied her breathing, inhaling and exhaling, slow and deep. At last, she calmed down and he kissed her shoulder.

"It's okay. We'll find a way to make this right." His words sent chills over her. "And we'll find her soon enough, if she doesn't find us first."

We could have been a family... I could have been a mother ... and they took that from us.

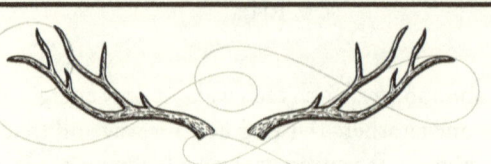

CHAPTER 23

DRYAD'S MESSAGE

CEDRIC

Cedric woke, rolling over, reaching for Angeline. Tension left him as he felt the warmth of her body under the covers. He pulled the heap into him and she wiggled into him, shivering. Both sighed, and he kissed her shoulder. Inhaling deeply, he took in her scent, glad to be freed from the pyre's smoke and to have Angeline at his side. A knock at the door disrupted their moment of peace and he held onto her tight, refusing to let her leave the bed.

"I need to get that," she fussed, and he tightened his hold and bit her shoulder. "Ouch."

"I'll get it." He slid out and strode to the door.

"Naked?" She sat up, pulling the covers up to her chin. "And I'm not dressed."

"I don't care." He smirked over his shoulder at her. "Besides, the whole island got to see what you brought home last night."

Angeline buried her face in the covers. He chuckled, but another more aggressive round of knocking disrupted the moment. With a scowl, he leaned on the wall and cracked the door. On the other side, he met the angry glare of Alecto, her white eyes doing nothing to deter him. She placed a hand on the door, pushing to open it. Cedric's arm muscles tightened, his biceps bulging. A grin crossed both their faces.

"You think you're stronger than a titan, little immortal?" Alecto hissed, her expression growing wild and excited. "Are you challenging me?"

"What do you want, Alecto?" Cedric avoided the taunt.

"Answer me." She pushed harder. The wood creaked, but it didn't budge. "Do you think you have more strength than a titan?"

"I suppose we'll both find out in just a moment," he snarled.

The door creaked, splintering under his hand as she shoved harder. A panel started to bow inward, threatening to buckle under her hand on the other side. Not once did they break their angry glares, both sneering with fanged pride. The door wavered, Alecto at last breaking to stare down in disbelief. It was closing.

"Tell me, are we really going to break this door to find out how much stronger I am?" Her eyes shot back to him and she let go.

"Fine. You are what they claim you to be, I see." Sucking on her cheek, she looked away as if making sure no one had witnessed the test of strength. "I came to drop off all the damn weapons and armor you two left behind. May I come in?"

"Alecto is here..." Cedric pulled the door open, and seeing no one followed her, he closed it. "Hard to return something if you don't have it in hand, Titan."

Winking at Angeline, she spun back to address Cedric. "Well, normally it would be carried but someone was wearing something rather dangerous." She snapped her fingers and clumps of metal and leather items fell onto the table by the fireplace. "Luckily, we Furies know a cursed item when we see it."

"And here they said it was living armor." Cedric looked at the *manica*, curious if it could change shape permanently.

"It is, and it's an interesting mix. Not every day you see something made with the essence of Aether's malice and hope." She narrowed her eyes at him. "But I wonder why on earth it took a liking to you."

"Maybe my middle name is Pandora." He smirked, walking over to pick up his pants off the floor to pull them on. "I did pull the cursed thing out of a box."

"I see. It came to you?" Alecto circled the table, tempted to touch the armor. "In all the time I have walked this world, I've never met two who had such intertwined destinies."

"Alecto, I really need to get dressed." Angeline changed topics, feeling trapped in the bed.

"You should take notes from your man, Ex-Mortal." Cedric flinched hearing Alecto's nickname for Angeline. "Oh, that face," she chuckled. "Be assured, little immortal, you've done nothing that has warranted my attention."

"And why would I care about gaining your attention, Alecto?" He scowled, pulling his shirt on, twisting so his body blocked her view of Angeline.

"It means you've done nothing wrong toward mortals." Another flinch from him made her knit her brows. "And for some strange reason, you disagree with me on this matter?"

"Tell that to everyone who died in Williamsburg," he scoffed. Pulling on the leather tunic, he marched for the table where the living armor began to shake. "Now, if it could be something other than gladiator armor."

"Ah, have you tried asking nicely?" Alecto smirked, heading for the door. "Your posse awaits you and grows impatient. Artemis and Apollo may be twin siblings, but there's an air between them that makes even me uncomfortable. If Gaea found out we've done this much for you two, she may try to take down the whole damn *Tir*."

"So there is a building rebellion against Gaea here in the Otherworld?" Cedric's words brought Alecto to a stop.

She looked over her shoulder with a wicked look in her eyes. "Careful who you dare speak that to, little immortal. She and Kronos still have those who are loyal or have no choice to be as such. I suggest you ask Lillith to join that cause."

"Lillith?" He blinked. "So she has been planning something..." Alecto pushed at the door, and Cedric turned his attention back to the armor. "Ok, look, I'm not one to waltz around as a gladiator. Any chance we can make you into chest pieces, boots, and greaves?"

The armor rattled, glowing on the table. It jumbled itself, tangling into the parts until it seemed to melt into a giant blob of sorts. The black and blue shimmer pulsed and at last, it spread out on the table, as if placing itself on display. Cedric watched calmly as Angeline approached, eyes wide with wonder. At last, the armor had changed, but it didn't stop the indecision building inside Cedric to accept it a second time.

Heaving a sigh, he relented, "I can live with this. Come on back."

Like before, it rattled and crawled across him, finding the places it should be and strapping onto him tight. Angeline gasped, watching as it all settled into place. Her brow knitted, unable to fathom the words to describe what she had witnessed. Pulling her hands down, he kissed her.

"Don't worry, it only wants me." Breaking away, he grabbed the katana and gladius. "We better get going. The sooner we leave, the quicker we can get home."

Angeline scanned the room, and after a moment, turned her attention to getting dressed. He watched in fascination as she at last ended by buckling on the holster and piling on the sword, the war hammer, and at last the bow. Leaning on the table behind him, his eyes bounced between the three, and he smirked.

"So they reworked the dagger, I get that." She stole a glance at him and scoffed. "But that hammer and bow, who gave those up?"

Angeline failed to fight back the smile. "The hammer was pure luck. Apparently, it's one of Badbh's designs. As for the bow, well, that's from Hamadryades."

"And why would she give you a bow? She's not the generous sort. I've only met with the dryads, but never the queen." Pulling from the table, he opened the door for her.

Angeline started her retort, but instead made a squeak as she smacked into Artemis. "You're both wasting time."

"Good morning to you too, Old Hag," drawled Cedric.

"Angeline!" Nyctimus called her attention to behind her ancestor, and she took it as an invitation to scurry away. "I'm so glad to see you safe!"

"Nyctimus!" She hugged the strapping hulk of a man.

Angeline turned and did the same to Wylleam and Romasanta. She spun and flinched. A tall, blond-haired, blue-eyed man held his arms out. His excitement was only matched by the wave of lust escaping him. Cedric gripped him, jerking him well out of reach from Angeline. He spun, brow lowered, and growled at Cedric.

"I want a hug," Fen snarled, the two almost knocking heads as they leaned into one another's faces.

"You want more than a hug, and you're not getting it from my wife." Cedric shoved him back, glancing over at the group. "I see we don't have the wizard, dwarf, or kelpie in tow."

"No, they said this was as far as they could go." Romasanta sighed and glanced behind Cedric's shoulder. "But my sister is coming with."

Cedric scoffed, "Why? It's not like she fights her own battles."

"Mind your tongue," spat Artemis. "I am the chance you have to make sure you make it back to the Mortal Realm intact."

"About that..." Nyctimus scratched his jaw, his hazel eyes narrowing. "Exactly what kind of trouble are we in for trying to get an audience with Gaea?"

"Just keep your mouths shut and follow me." Artemis brushed past Cedric and broke through Romasanta and Nyctimus.

"Who died and made you the leader?" Cedric's jaw tensed, twitching.

"Do you want to leave here sooner or continue to wander the land playing gladiator?" She didn't even slow down her stride and look back at him.

Romasanta lifted his brow high. "Just do me a favor and not kill her until we're out of here."

Fen creased his forehead and smirked, "Do you think her and I—"

"NO," Romasanta, Nyctimus, and Cedric barked in unison.

"Keep your filthy paws off my sister." Romasanta's expression was priceless.

Nyctimus chuckled. "I guess he does like playing the big brother role on occasion. Here it seems more like Big Sis and Baby Brother dynamic."

Cedric reached down and interlocked his fingers with Angeline's. "Let's go."

***

They walked for miles, the Amazon forest fading and by some magic found themselves in a forest. With Artemis as their guide, it seemed effortless to fade from one *Tir* into the next. A thick fog had descended upon them, sending Romasanta, Nyctimus, and Fenrir on edge. If they had fur, it'd be on end, but in their human forms, they narrowed their eyes and sniffed the air. Angeline slid her fingers over the greaves and the armor shuddered.

"What is it?" she murmured, making him unsure if she was asking herself or him.

"Living armor."

"Living?" Her eyes met his and his heart raced.

"And apparently it likes me, so... I'm stuck with it." The air grew silent, the birds and insects no longer making a sound. "Old hag, where the hell are you leading us?"

"A back door of sorts." Artemis didn't bother to glance back.

Still, Cedric paced behind her. Looking back, Romasanta held tight to the new enchanted box holding Gaea's eye. Creaking and rustling came from all around, and they all froze in their steps. The sound came at them like rushing water, and it seemed as if the trees were moving just beyond where they lost focus. At last, a figure appeared, marching slowly and meaningfully toward them until at last, Angeline inhaled swift and sharp.

"Hamadryades."

The dryad queen smiled. "My beloved Angeline. It's so good to see you've found your love again." She met Cedric's suspicious glare, addressing him directly. "I am here to deliver a message to you, King Incubus."

He stiffened. "And who is this message from?"

"Lillith."

Cedric shot a glance back to Romasanta, who gave him a baffled expression. "Are you sure it was meant for me and not Romasanta?"

Hamadryades chuckled. "Trust issues much?"

"I prefer you to take your talk elsewhere." Artemis had crossed her arms, glaring at the box in her brother's arms.

"Indeed, this is a private matter." Hamadryades bowed her head in respect at Artemis.

"You can trust her," Angeline whispered to him.

Gauging her expression, he nodded. "Let's talk in private, Queen of Dryads."

"Oh! We're using official titles, are we?" She shifted, holding a hand out to indicate where they were going. "This way, King Incubus Romulus." He stiffened, but marched between the trees. "For the time being, my dryads will feed you all. Please rest." Tables and chairs blossomed from the ground all around, and women made of wood and plants stepped out from the fog. "Now, let us not dawdle." Hamadryades flowed past him and pointed between two more trees. "She waits for you there."

The muscles in Cedric's cheek twitched at her words. Remaining silent, he marched through the two trees and the fog opened up, making a curtain around the open meadow. Lillith stood at the center, her back to him. It was rare to see her wings and tail, her horns, one still broken, cresting above the top of her head. He stopped a few steps from her, and she turned with a deep scowl on her red lips and her arms crossed.

"I was hoping to catch you in time." She unfolded her arms and gauged his expression. "Pan said he let it slip."

"All I want to know is who you two really are?" Cedric crossed his arms, lowering his brow like a scolding father. "I've already figured out you're trying to take down Gaea and Kronos, but I'm missing the direct link. Something tells me you aren't being honest about who you really are."

She made a face as if sorting her thoughts first. "Well, about that..." Inhaling deeply, she at last locked eyes with him, making no mistake what she would say next was as truthful as she could manage. "My name is Lillith, especially in the Mortal Realm, but my birth is muddled in their history. It is true that I was the first woman to walk this earth. You see, Gaea wanted to love her husband's creation so much, she took a piece of herself and gave it to the first man of humanity. Sadly, that's where the last of her goodwill toward Aether would end."

"I knew you were ancient, but made from Gaea. Why turn on your own maker?"

"You're one to talk," she smirked.

Snorting, he turned away, his back to her. "So what happened next? I imagine something happened and Gaea is to blame?"

"Well, Aether frowned on how much of herself she didn't place into me." Her voice broke a little, and she forced herself to continue. "The things he pressed, was the ability to procreate. She didn't want to do it. In fact, at that time Lamashtu and Kronos were a thing."

Cedric shot a glance over his shoulder. "Lamashtu?"

She managed a smirk. "Yeah, Lamashtu. Granted, Kronos's original body isn't too flattering, so it makes more sense, trust me. Regardless, Aether denied Kronos the Mortal Realm and when he gifted it to Adam and I, all hell broke loose. It was then Gaea decided to give me the ability to procreate, but it wasn't..."

"That. I see." Cedric rubbed his forehead. "And let me guess, Aether got pissed because she wouldn't undo the malice she bestowed you, her jealousy incarnate, so he took a piece of Adam and created Eve, an equal creature to him."

"From there, tables were flipping in the other realms. The worst of it was watching how Aether distanced himself from Gaea more and more with each vile act and move she made. Constantly a sleight of hand to destroy humanity. I was abandoned here, left to breed like a monster, with monsters, and make more monsters if none were to be found. Even Delphyne found herself in the same predicament. She was made from the earth, gifted to Kronos to ravage humankind, but it failed, and he gifted her to his eldest son, Zeus, who gave her a place, a task to protect the Oracles and Phoebe."

"Now things are clicking into place. So, what was so special about Phoebe?" He stared skyward, the tree branches waving in the wind overhead as his mind raced to put the connections together.

"Your direct connection is the fact she's the mother of Apollo and Artemis, and sister-in-law to Kronos, me, and Pan." Cedric spun to face her, the expression on her face told him she wasn't blowing smoke up his ass. "And, at one point, she served as Gaea's personal oracle until she went into hiding. Hence, Gaea snatching up little Artemis the moment Kronos let it out that she had powers that rivaled her mother's."

"Then what is Artemis's aim? She's been pulling my strings more than anyone else in my life." Narrowing his eyes, he paced closer. "Can she be trusted at all?"

"She wants out," Lillith hissed. "But Gaea watches everything she sees and hears. Meanwhile, she practically handed her eye over to Kronos so he could destroy Aether and wreak havoc in the Mortal Realm. If the eye is returned, she has to let Artemis go."

"Why?" Cedric knitted his brow. "What reason does she need? And didn't she task Apollo to bring the cursed thing back?"

"She's been trying to kill Apollo, knowing full well he would come for his sister and his wife. What she didn't count on was Kronos using her eye to bind him to Fenrir and, in doing so, making him almost unkillable." Huffing, she tapped her fingers on her arm in thought. "Look, Gaea lost most of her alliances when Aether was killed and she let it happen. After that, the Celestial Realm was cut off to the Otherworld, and the Underworld was heavily gated after Kronos pissed off Hades. The returning of the eye quest was her trying to maintain what little she had left at the time, but as time passed, many still walked away. She's growing bolder by the day."

"And why should I give a shit about all of this?" he spat, turning away.

"Because her interest has turned to you and yours." She gripped his arm and they locked eyes. "Look, fucking hate me for all I care. Gaea and Kronos are trying to create proper mortal vessels and they are looking at you, Angeline, shit, do you even know you have a daughter?"

With a rotation of his arm, he broke her grasp and gripped her arm. "And when were you going to tell me? Isn't that the reason you dragged me out of my bedroom? How long have you known?"

Lillith broke her glare, her eyes darting to the ground in shame. "It wasn't my place to tell you."

"I figured it out." The bracer shuddered and her eyes grew wide as a wave of malice echoed from it.

"Where'd you get that?" Jerking her arm back, she glared wide-eyed. "That bracer, no..." Her eyes darted to the other bracer, the boots, and the leather tunic. "That armor. Where did you get that?"

"It found me," he declared, muscles taut. "You know something about it?"

"N-no. In fact, I didn't know anything still remained of Aether and..." She bit her lip, despair coming across her face. "Look, hate me all you want. Just know that I am every bit of a victim as you are. We have a common enemy, always have. Right now, everyone is scrambling to locate weapons we can use against her and Kronos."

"So I've heard." He licked a fang. "Rumor has it, something happened to Tony."

"Yeah, and your daughter started that mess. Tony finished it." Her face flushed and a sense of lust escaped her.

"You've got to be kidding me." Cedric shook his head. "So he took the throne from me, after all?"

"Technically, there will be two king Incubi in play when you return." She spun away, wings flaring as if they could hide what had slipped from her already. "He saved me. After I came for Romasanta, Tony ... saved me."

"But that's not the reason you're falling for him, is it?" Cedric smirked.

"No, it's not." Another flare of her wings, and her tail started to swat side to side. "Cedric, he's part titan and part incubus. I don't know how this will work out."

"Something tells me Aether consulted Phoebe and placed a lot more into motion." He leaned on a tree, returning his gaze to the swaying of the branches above them.

"I never took into consideration that my father would seed solutions to take down mother..." She spun back to him. "My time here is up. I need to get back or Gaea will know. Don't take any longer. We may need you for a rescue mission. Tony hasn't returned and we fear the Salamandre may be compromised."

"Why send an amateur?" he scoffed.

"We'll talk later." With that, she flapped her wings and disappeared.

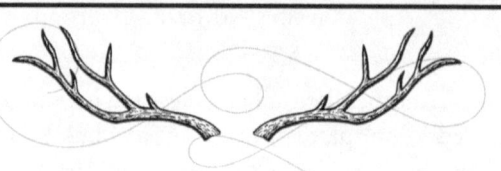

CHAPTER 24

THE AQRABUAMELU

ANGELINE

Time in the Otherworld seemed endless, though it felt no different to Angeline. Whatever *Tir* they currently traversed seemed to have an endless supply of sun and fog as they marched onward. Artemis never glanced back once. Cedric's hand held Angeline's, but the occasional shiver and wave of lust from the bracer made her tense and her heart race.

To wear something alive like that... he really is willing to do whatever it takes to make his way back to me. Maybe next time it'll be my turn to go to him?

She looked up at his face, the chiseled jawline bringing a swell of emotions. At one point she had looked up at the same view and bitterly thought *monster,* but that had been centuries ago. He squeezed her hand, and the emotions calmed. Her face flushed, and he turned to meet her eyes, knitting his brow.

"Is that really all it takes to settle you down on the inside?" Cedric marveled.

"I... I guess so." She laughed.

"When do I get to hold hands with her?" Fenrir shoved forward like an eager little boy.

"Never," hissed Cedric. "Find your own."

"But no one has let me sniff one out?" The apparent confusion on his face spoke volumes.

"Fen, I don't think sniffing a centaur's ass would have ended in the way you imagined." Nyctimus pulled Fen back between him and Romasanta. "You can wreak havoc after we leave."

"Sister." Romasanta's voice made them all jerk, and Artemis came to an abrupt stop. "How much farther? You didn't exactly tell us how long this would take."

"Hush, imbeciles," she hissed, motioning them all to lower their voices and come closer to her. "We are almost upon Gaea's throne. Once we escape the fog here in *Mag Mell*, we will have to gain passage from her aqrabuamelu."

Cedric glanced at the others; no one spoke. "What is that? A monster? A god?"

"They're the guardians who now live in Mt. Olympus on *Mag Mon*. This route takes us past their village, but there will be two you will have to face before we can get through the gates of her throne. I may pass, but..."

"We can't." Romasanta inhaled deeply and glanced at Cedric. "I'm sorry. I didn't realize how much we would rely on you during this stage of the journey."

Cedric smirked. "I can't imagine you enjoy not being able to join the fray, after seeing your face at the arena holding that gladius. I didn't realize how much of a fight junkie you were, old man."

"Don't remind me," gruffed Romasanta.

"Scorpion men," Nyctimus blurted. "The aqrabuamelu. They are scorpion people, famous in Greek and Arabian tales, but..."

"Sometimes I'm secretly relieved we brought the human encyclopedia with us." Cedric turned his attention to Wylleam. "You've been unusually quiet at this point."

Wylleam dropped his ears. "I didn't think you'd want to hear anything I have to say after you discovered..." His puppy dog eyes looked pitiful.

"Look, I forgive you. You didn't act on," Cedric pointed to Artemis, nearly prodding her, "Bitch's request. I need you, I need your advice, old friend. Anything you can give us at this point is better than going into this blind."

Artemis spun on her heel and marched off, but Romasanta gave chase. "Artemis, wait..."

Wylleam waited for her to fade into the fog and his ears perked up. "We've all been let in on the secret of the stone and Artemis by the dryads." He sighed. "And honestly, I've been silent around both, more so."

Angeline furrowed her brow. "The stone is connected to Gaea like Artemis?"

"Indeed," Nyctimus chimed in. "Now what do you know, Wylleam?"

"They are giant monsters with unbreakable skin or armor. Have you..." He scratched his muzzle. "I'm starting to realize my role now in the grand scheme of this, but," his eyes fell to Angeline's hammer, then to Cedric's katana, "we have weapons and the strength of you two to rely on. If Angeline can loosen, smash, or even break their carapace anywhere, then the Oni sword should slice. They are immune to miasma, a majority of titan first generation are. Though the purer they are, the more likely it will at least slow them. Meanwhile, Kronos and the impure will only absorb it and gain power, so you will have to learn to utilize that feature better with time, Cedric."

"You have been holding back," chuckled Cedric.

Nyctimus made fire dance on his fingers. "Will hitting them with fire before the hammer or after would help compromise the hardness? I know it can make steel and iron brittle."

"Strike before the hammer. Angeline, you can aim for his mark, right?" Cedric turned to her to gauge the confidence in her face.

"After the shit the Amazonians gave me, I will hit the marks you layout for me, Nyctimus." She swallowed, heart beating.

Our first battle since I've learned so much. I can do this.

"I don't understand this plan," Fenrir announced, and everyone turned to face him.

"Well..." Wylleam flicked an ear in thought. "If there are two, we will need someone big and strong enough to keep one distracted while we take down the first."

"Me. I want to do that!" Fenrir's excitement and glowing yellow eyes hinted at the wolven form that lay below the surface.

"Well, it seems we all have our roles." Nyctimus shifted, Artemis and Romasanta returning from the fog. "You alright?" His eyes met Romasanta's, who gripped the box tight with an expression of contempt.

"He's fine," blurted Artemis. "Do you understand what comes next?"

"Yes," Cedric answered and they nodded in acknowledgment.

"Very well. Let's not delay this any longer." She turned back to the path and they followed in silence.

The fog dissipated and the forest fell away to barren land, rocky and mountainous. Artemis weaved them through the craigs as the stone walls and jagged cliffs rose all around the deeper they traveled into this new land. Angeline could feel the tension in her comrades, see the stern thoughts in their eyes that matched her own. No one knew what would be in store for them. None of them had faced such an enemy in an ether-rich environment. Everything there became stronger, larger, and *Mag Mon* held a foreboding air.

Artemis came to an abrupt stop, motioning for them to be silent and to peer with caution. Ahead, a large wrought-iron gate of some sort stood massive with giant creatures with spears on either side. The aqrabuamelu were nothing like their centaur cousins. From the waist down, they had everything a scorpion had to offer: front large pincers, six legs, and a long curving tail with a bulbous stinger. A torso and human arms led to a head that seemed more antlike, with eight black eyes wrapping from the front to the sides. There would be no sneaking past them.

They are every bit as large as the golden busse I faced. At least I'm not alone, but how the hell is this man Fenrir supposed to hold one at bay?

"Angeline and I will go out first, pulling their attention. Fenrir, you get ready to hop in the moment they attack." Cedric took charge, whispering his orders.

"Good. Romasanta will need to stay back. Let me pass into the gates before you so I may inform Mother Gaea of your arrival." Artemis walked into the open. The reaction speed of the aqrabuamelus' swiveling heads sent chills across Angeline.

They watched as she spoke something, and one reached over and cracked the gate. She marched between them and, after a few minutes, the ravine echoed from the slammed gate like thunder in the sky. Cedric met her gaze and Angeline nodded, pulling her war hammer from her back. Inhaling deeply, she held her breath as they marched into the open. Again the aqrabuamelu turned to them and she could see their small forms reflected in the array of eyes peering down.

They hissed, readying their spear and snapping their pincers. The motion sent hot, putrid air across them, stirring a dust cloud behind them that slammed into a cliff wall. Even their movements held great speed and power, the ground shaking underfoot.

"You ready?" Cedric whispered without glancing her way.

"I don't think anyone could be ready for this," she scoffed.

"When the giant wolf grabs the one, we pull the other to us."

"Wait, what giant wo—"

A large white creature exploded from where they had hidden themselves moments before. It matched the aqrabuamelu in speed and size, knocking the farthest one from Angeline and Cedric to the ground. Growling filled the air as jaws snapped the spear in half. Cedric waved lust into her, bringing her attention to their own challenge. She tightened her grip on the war hammer and peered up at the aqrabuamelu. It began to twist, aiming to assist its partner as it raised its spear. A fireball slammed into its side, Nyctimus providing support from a safer distance.

The aqrabuamelu squealed, deafening and superseding the commotion Fenrir had made. It rushed forward and Angeline took off running alongside its right side. Cedric matched her on the opposite side. They both had the same target; take out the legs. She ducked under the pincers, and the aqrabuamelu aimed for Nyctimus and ignored them completely. Spinning on her approach, she gained momentum and aimed for the first joint. A great crackling sound matched the force she felt reverberate down the handle.

"The joints are weak points!" Nyctimus's words filled the air, another ball of flame hitting the middle leg joint.

The creature screeched, both legs buckling. Cedric came sliding out from under the monster. His stern expression told her he had decided to change his tactic with the new information. Before she could see what he intended to do, she rolled out of the way of the bulbous stinger. The ground shook and dirt exploded into the air. Another crack and the aqrabuamelu tilted, the pincer lashing out and sticking into the ground to keep it from falling all the way. Eyes stinging from the dirt-filled air, Angeline flicked her wrist.

It doesn't take much magic, but I need to take advantage of every chance that makes itself known. Let's see how you handle this.

Twisting her hand, a breeze rushed across the ground and twisted upward. It pulled the dust into it, tightening into a dust devil of sorts before slamming into the aqrabuamelu's face. It threw up an arm, hissing as it turned its full attention toward her. A pincer swung out for her and she rolled away. As she unfolded, Cedric jumped in her way, knocking into her as the stinger slammed into the katana.

"Thanks." She spun, swinging her hammer overhead and smashing down on the pincer.

The bottom joint snapped. The claw would no longer be able to open and close shut. Another ball of flames hit the torso, leaving the carapace charred. Angeline used the pinned claw as a launching pad, jumping and running her way to the mark Nyctimus had left for her. With an under-swing so as to not lose her balance on the struggling creature, she hit her mark. The carapace shattered. She retreated down its back, its human arms groping for her. Pulling out her cursed sword, she swung at the reaching digits. She managed to lop off the tip of one finger, the black curse staining the wound as it bled profusely.

Sliding to the ground between two broken legs, she landed short of breath. Sweat dripped off her chin, and she shook the moment off, running from the monster for better tactical advantage. She searched for Cedric but didn't see him anywhere. Barking brought her eyes back to the other aqrabuamelu. It had Fenrir pinned to the ground, a hand on his throat as he squirmed on his back. She took a step in their direction, but the stinger struck forward. Angeline winced. That left her open just long enough for her opponent to swing the broken pincer, knocking her across the opening until she slammed into the cliffside.

Her body filled with pain, blood splattering from her mouth as she fell to the ground in a crumpled heap. She could feel how everything felt broken. She fought the nauseating agony, her body unnerving and unable to move. Her eyes rolled back, blood filling her lungs and making it impossible to breathe. A wave of lust hit her, and her body reacted. Somehow, she managed to grin.

I know I can be stronger if I just … let that side out.

Bones were snapping back. Blood retreating from her lungs. She pulled hungrily from Cedric's lust, gobbling it and accepting it as her own. The aqrabuamelu approached, dragging limp legs, clicking and squeaking its insect-like mouth. It rose the spear in one hand. The other arm was black, blood seeping from it. Angeline's body sped ever faster as it healed, on fire, blood boiling. She could feel the horns growing from her fore-head. Her fangs grew longer, hungry for the fight. Her back ached where her wings should have been, adding to the rising ire of her frustrations to have been knocked down.

The spear came down upon her. An explosion of dust as the spearhead dug into the ground, missing its mark. She was winning. The sight compromised and the curse weakening the aqrabuamelu. She ran up the shaft, holding the hammer with ease in one hand and the word in the other. She screamed, a battle cry worthy of any Amazonian. Running up the shaft of the spear, she burst from the cloud of dust, making the aqrabuamelu flinch. It let go, but it was too late. Angeline had launched herself at its torso.

Despite looking humanlike, the skin on the aqrabuamelu's torse was plated with a flesh-toned carapace. Angeline swung her hammer, shattering the plate. Next, she thrust the cursed sword deep into its flesh. She didn't know if she struck a lung or heart, but the curse on the sword would bleed him out. Pulling it out, she lost her balance as the monster reeled and smacked her from its body. She managed to roll back to her feet. Satisfied she had disarmed her threat, she ran for the other, scared of the sight that would unfold before her.

Rounding the corner, she saw Cedric standing there, wide-eyed. He stood, katana drawn. Behind him, the other aqrabuamelu lay dead, head chopped clean off as the giant wolf gnawed on a scorpion leg. A smile formed on his face and he looked back at the creature behind her, sheathing his blade. It gasped for air, clawing at its chest as the black mark grew across its torso. At last, is shuddered and fell to the side with a great, earth-shaking thud. Dust and wind blew past her and waved across Cedric. He closed the gap between them and kissed her deeply, his excitement making her drop her weapons so she could cup his jaw.

"Who knew you were such a tenacious warrior, my pet?"

CHAPTER 25

LOCKED DOORS

CEDRIC

Cedric saw to it that Fenrir changed back, and they gave Angeline time to calm so her horns would withdraw completely. They had been warned to be as human as possible, though he could assume at this stage in the game they could be seen as a threat or enemy to Gaea. Seeing how far she had pulled strings, back door dealing, and aided Kronos, there were no doubts she would do anything to squash out competition to her own throne.

Pushing through the gates led them farther into a ravine, twisting and turning until at last a castle made of black onyx rose before them. Its gothic spires and towers made it look like black claws digging out of the barren dirt and rocks that it sat high above. Not far behind it, an opalescent staircase rose to the sky until it faded into the clouds, sparkling. There was no mistaking that they had at last hit the highest point of the Otherworld and up that heavenly stairway lay the Celestial Realm. A shudder rattled Cedric's shoulders, his armor tightening.

"Behave. I'm almost home and you better not ruin this for me," he muttered before huffing.

The whole walk he kept stealing glimpses at Angeline. She had lost her tension, chatting with Wylleam about her time with the Amazonians and how she missed those days so long ago before... He couldn't believe what she had been able to do. When Fenrir had been pinned and Nyctimus's fireball did nothing to push back the other aqrabuamelu, he had barely made it across the span. The swing of the Oni blade had been powerful and sliced with ease through the creature's neck. Fenrir had twisted to his feet and stumbled back in alarm. Whoever had made the blade had made it to slay all kinds of monsters and deter the rest.

"So, what blade is that?" Nyctimus had found a new interest in it. "It's a Japanese katana, so it seems rather odd for someone so... knightly."

Cedric snorted. "You think I just trained in the broadsword in all my years?"

"You didn't seem too excited to use the gladius against Asteron." Romasanta shot him a smug look.

"And I didn't realize how deep-rooted your bloodlust was until I saw you drooling over that room," spat Cedric before they all started chuckling. "Honestly, I cheated some. When my grandfather gave me my vampiric blood rite, it came with a wide span of knowledge. I saw places I had never been, let alone known the use of many weapons, magic, and..." Cedric stopped, the armor shivering and a voice mumbling, soft and almost mistaken for a songbird. "You hear that?"

"No." Nyctimus narrowed his eyes.

"Y-yes." Romasanta locked eyes. "I... I think I know that voice."

They both strained, trying their best to capture the murmuring of the words reaching out to them. The doors to the cathedral-like palace rumbled open and silenced the voice. As the door widened, the creature on the other side made them tense. The massive mountain of flesh was the size of their former opponent, but that's where their similarities ended. Cedric covered his nose, and the rest of the group did the same. Drool and sweat left the pale skin glossy, the heaps of muscles and limbs untangled to reveal a face, sometimes partially melted into the core as if drowned by what body lay unseen under it all. The feet and legs gave it a spidery centipede sensation, moving in rhythmic patterns as it moved to the side.

They looked at the bouquet of hands that all held weapons, some of them carrying the same. The moaning and wailing sent shivers up Cedric's spine as he took in the cursed thing. Rank body odor seemed to leak from it with every movement, adding to his want to hold his breath entirely. At last, he met eyes with the largest head, and it grinned, teeth jagged and nose seeming as if sheered off. Opening and moving its lips, it took it a few tries to speak to them.

"Mother says Gyges may let you enter." The other faces wailed in response, arms wrestling with one another to be in front as if wishing to greet them. "Please come. Gyges will show you to Mother."

Cedric glanced at Wylleam. "Well?"

Swallowing, Wylleam shook his canine head. "What choice do we have?"

"I say we are safe to follow," Romasanta cut in, pushing past Cedric.

Gyges clattered his feet on the ground, making the floors vibrate. With that he sped off, the swift and smooth movement making Cedric flinch. Everything in this world had proven unpredictable and to see the abomination of clustered flesh so agile added to the danger. He reached out and managed to entwine his fingers and Angeline's. The stir of emotions that rolled for a fleeting moment inside her each time he had done it started to become less worrisome. In fact, it brought calm and a smile to his face. A small inkling of pleasure slipped between them despite the lack of eroticism the notion held.

Again, Cedric strained to listen as they followed behind the anxious creature. Gyges had circled back several times, hundreds of hands coaxing them to move forward. The castle halls twisted on endlessly and, without the rules of physically being possible, reminded him of Avalon. Another ringing in his ears, the hushed whisper barely audible. He shot a look at Romasanta who nodded. He too could hear the voice.

"Do you hear that?" Cedric whispered to Angeline.

"Hear what?" She furrowed her brow, eyes locked on Gyges, who grinned with drool dangling from his mouth. "Gyges?"

"No." Cedric glanced around. "There's someone here. Someone trying to get my attention and Romasanta's." He let her hand go. "I'm going to investigate."

"W-wait." Angeline spun, but the two had vanished, bringing her to a stop.

Cedric had gripped Romasanta, shoving him through a doorway. "You and I need to figure out who the hell is trying to get our attention."

"You're so reckless," breathed Romasanta. "What do you expect us to do?" He motioned to the box.

"Shit." Covering his mouth, he thought a moment. "Fine." He nodded back to the door. "Leave this to me then. Go give that damn thing back."

Romasanta smirked. "Very well."

Cedric watched as he left through the door. It shut, and he stood in darkness. Looking around, it seemed he had ducked into another hallway, less elegant than the one before. He marched forward, searching and listening. After a few minutes, he peered back at the door to discover it gone, and scoffed. Pushing farther into the castle's labyrinth, he tried a few more doors to discover them locked.

Well, I'm not going to knock them down... yet. I don't want to draw attention.

He came to a dead end, forced to travel right or left. Taking a step to the left, his armor tightened. Stepping back, it loosened and he changed direction, stepping down to the right. It shivered, and he stared at it a moment, curious of the reaction. This hallway seemed less curvy, the barren halls changing from the dark onyx and gothic décor to something more on par with how he had the mansion decorated in Williamsburg. Tapestries of stags and knights filled the walls, tables, and furniture made of mahogany placed between the many locked doors.

"You're here." At last, the woman's voice hit his ears, crisp and clear.

"Who are you?" Scanning the hall, he saw no one.

"Please, don't stop... you're almost here." Her desperation made the sing-song voice crack. "Just a little farther, Cedric."

He shuddered. Hearing the voice say his name sent every muscle tense. Jaw twitching, he marched on, the armor shivering again. A door unlike any he had seen stood before him, locks embedded into the wall, frame, and door. Furrowing his brow, he took a step closer. Light poured out from the crack at the bottom. A shadow shifted, revealing someone did indeed stand just on the other side.

"Where is my Apollo?" she questioned.

"With the others, he's carrying the eye back to Gaea."

"Ah, I see."

"So, who are you?" he demanded once more. "And why are you in a locked room in Gaea's castle?"

"Forgive me. Being an oracle, I tend to forget the formalities." There was a long pause as if gauging how she should perform this. "I am Phoebe."

Cedric paled. "As in the Greek goddess?"

"Y-yes?" She seemed unsure and at last added, "Mother to Apollo and Artemis. Former Oracle to Gaea."

The rumors say she left, but if she's here, then everything we know... I gotta get her out of here. We could use an ally of this caliber.

Cedric took a step back and glanced at the locks on the door. "How sturdy are the locks? And is there magic recoil for breaking them?"

"Honestly, if you were Hades, you could just melt them with miasma and resolve both," she flustered. "But it seems Kronos has done something and none of my brothers seem to be anywhere."

"Miasma?" Cedric smirked, drawing the Oni blade. "I think I have just the tool for the job."

The blade sliced and melted through the locks and the door. The blade descended, the door fell away with a great thud, and the Greek goddess stared wide-eyed at him. Much like her children, she carried large brown eyes. Her hair was pulled into a tangled, brown bun on the top of her head with golden laurel hairpins. She wore leather breeches, a small chest plate, and greaves as she contemplated whether to go to battle or at least leave post-haste. Her eyes watched the blade, the miasma dripping from it. Cedric at last returned it to its sheath and she gasped.

"By the gods, you look like him. A younger version, indeed." She stepped out, leather boots completing her battle-worthy look as she circled Cedric. "My, my!" She glanced all around and spun before meeting his gaze again. "We have no time. You need to be back with the others. Don't speak a word of me, not yet. I'll see you on Avalon!"

Phoebe snapped her fingers, a blinding light making him wince. When he managed to crack his eyes back open, he found himself in the back of the group. Gyges spun back, still smiling and waving as he started to open the double doors. Romasanta did a double-take over his shoulder, making a baffled expression. Cedric shook his head as if replying, *Not now, talk later.*

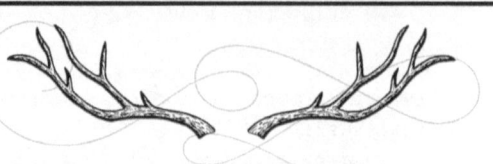

Chapter 26

Gaea's Throne

Cedric

"Mother, Gyges has brought you the mortals." The faces wailed and wept, whether in joy or sorrow, it was indistinguishable at that point.

"Come in," the voice rumbled the air, sounding like the rush of wind and the very earth shaking until a female tone could be produced. "You have something that belongs to me, no?"

The doors widened and unlike the mundane blackness of the rest of her palace, in there it seemed to be on fire. Stories of the Queen of Hearts came to mind with lush red and exuberant golden ornamental decorations littering the throne room. It drew one's eyes to the giantess lounging on the bejeweled golden throne on the platform at the far end. Her eyes were black as night, one having a singular red iris. Artemis stood just down the steps of the platform, bowing before the great ancient goddess.

Her skin seemed to be made of mud and ash, crackling in places before smoothing out in several places. Finger and toes were clawed and stained black to her ankles and wrists. Plump lips and jagged teeth gave her features like a great white shark as she slid something into her mouth, eating it with much pleasure. Her body lacked clothing, almost featureless despite the way her waist and hips curved in and out. Long hair cascaded all around, flowing down from her head and over her shoulders like waterfalls of black until it pooled on the floor. Much like Delphyne, she had a crown of horns that had been carved with designs, golden bands added, and chains strung between them. Diamonds and other precious gems decorated them, making them far more intimidating of a crown than any king could have worn.

"Do not waste my time further, mortals." She shifted, crossing her legs and sitting at attention.

Two more creatures, much like Gyges, stood on either side of the room. A cluster of sounds came from all three creatures. The two didn't share the goofy grin of their companion. One held many spears in its flock of arms while the other had a mixture of bows and swords. In fact, it was this one that made the least amount of sounds and agony; its eyes focused on them and watching with some awareness. Unlike the other two, it wore greaves, helmets on some of the more well-formed heads, and sandals upon the many feet. It was ready for a fight.

"Damn, three one-man-armies seems like overkill, don't you think?" Cedric lifted a brow at Wylleam, who flattened his ears. "Got it, zipping it."

Romasanta pushed to the front of the group and they followed him in silence. He kneeled before the great goddess and pulled the chest in front. He opened it, slow and calculating. She leaned forward, a rumble of a chuckle coming from her. Everyone kneeled behind Romasanta, in fear they would cause any further delay for this quest to at last come to an end. Peering down at the glowing gemstone in the dryad's box, she at last scowled. Her remaining iris glowed, making it clear where the stone had been taken from.

"Mother Gaea, you tasked me to bring this to you and here I am. Apollo, son of Phoebe and Coeus, twin brother to your Oracle, Artemis." He didn't dare look up or flinch as she dipped her claws into the box.

"And you have outdone yourself, Apollo." She stared at the stone in her claws with bitter disdain. "But you shouldn't have risked so much, and for what? A mere girl?"

Cedric watched as the muscles in Apollo's back twitched with rage. Grabbing Fenrir's arm, he stopped him from rising. The rage in his face as blue eyes shifted yellow showed he was very aware of the way this all had gone down, and did not agree with the finale. This monster in the shape of a woman on a throne showed as much compassion as her beloved gate guardians. Worse, the three creatures made of melted flesh seemed powerful beyond anything they could face. If it were just one, maybe the group could manage, *but three?*

Fenrir growled, "She took her from him. Without warning, and did nothing to help him."

"I know." Cedric tugged him back down. "But this isn't the time to take a stand. Not until after he gets her back."

At last, he settled, and Cedric continued to observe the exchange. Reluctantly, Gaea pressed the stone into the solid black eye. It was like watching someone put a contact lens into place. She blinked a few times and lounged in her throne. Tapping her fingers, she sighed.

"I suppose I should return what I have taken, as promised," she drawled and stifled a yawn, before adding, "But I can't return the years she lost."

Artemis spun, backstepping until she kneeled beside her brother. "Mother Gaea, are you implying when you return the girl's humanity that you intend to keep her age the same?" An unnerving chill settled across all of them as they listened to the shaken voice of Artemis. "That would mean she would be nothing more than ash."

"Precisely." Gaea grinned a toothy grin as Romasanta tried to stand to his feet, but Artemis gripped him to stay kneeling.

"May I propose something?" Artemis swallowed, waiting in the lingering silence.

At last, a scoff and frown. "Fine. What do you propose, annoying little sorceress?"

"She remains a dryad, but one who can walk freely like her sisters."

Cedric locked eyes with Wylleam, lipping, *Can she do that?*

Wylleam shrugged.

"Oh, but little one, don't you know Hamadryades and I are no longer on talking ter—" Gaea's words stopped as the doors flew open, knocking Gyges to the ground.

"She has become one of mine, Gaea." Hamadryades's voice was only matched by the large consort that followed on her heels.

Gaea gripped her throne, leaning forward to hiss, "How dare you trespass into my home!"

"We have come to cash in on your sworn word and honor the contract *you* made centuries ago." Freya stepped out from behind one side of Hamadryades. "Alecto, dear, what were those terms again?"

"Ah, there were many things discussed at that last round table." Alecto stepped out from the other side of Hamadryades, Furies and Valkyries pouring into the room and causing the great fleshballs to rethink any action they had intended to make. "For starters, after Apollo so diligently returns her eye from Kronos, who you still swear you have no allegiance to—"

"I don't," Gaea snarled.

"Right. Seeing Apollo has fulfilled the quest, you are to break your curse on Daphne. Changing her back to human after Hamadryades has gifted her the right of being a dryad would be breaking your truce. Ah, but there's more... now if Pan wasn't the contract holder, who was?"

Someone from behind them cleared their throat. "I drafted said contract since I was the only neutral entity available." Manny stepped out between a cluster of Valkyries and unraveled the contract. "My, there were so many stipulations to be undone when, and if, Apollo could get you your eye back. How is your sight this fine evening?"

"Get on with it," she hissed.

Never did I ever think I would be so damn happy to see a purple and yellow peacock enter a room.

"Yes. So, Daphne's curse is lifted?" He eyed Gaea, clearing his throat. "I would love it if you took care of these matters as I list them so we can settle and dissolve this nasty document for good."

Gaea's returned eye glowed for a moment and settled back to red. "Done."

A dryad appeared, whispering to Hamadryades who announced, "And confirmed."

"Ah, next was the freeing of his sister, Artemis. We've outlawed such servitude in this realm, especially after gaining so many rights for seers and oracles alike." He motioned. "Please, do so..."

Artemis stood, stretching her arms out in front of her. Gaea hissed at the watching eyes as a claw came closer and shackles appeared on Artemis's wrists. She tapped it and the manacles dissolved. With that, Artemis reached down and jerked Romasanta to his feet and turned on her heel. She marched, chin high and a grin on her lips. The room that had been vibrant with red and gold seemed to decay to gray, the warmth of it all leaving as Gaea kept her jaw taut with her building rage.

"Rise and stand with them." Artemis motioned as she cut down the middle.

"That's your cue, Fen. Whatever unfolds next is fair game." Cedric released him, making his way forward to meet Angeline halfway. "You definitely made some powerful friends, didn't you? I think they just saved our asses."

"I'm starting to think Gaea didn't mean for Romasanta to make it this far ... ever." Angeline and he rushed to the waiting group of Furies where her comrades from her test winked. "Thank you."

"Has the bond of servitude been broken as promised?" Manny looked to Freya, and she waved her hand over Artemis, who kneeled before her.

"Yes, our trinity of queens has been restored." As Artemis rose to her feet, Freya hugged her. "Welcome back to the free world, my sister mage!"

"Ah, very well. Let's see, next was the dissolution of Gaea's law." Again, Manny cleared his throat. "This was ordained by the Nordic Alliance, Dryad Alliance, the Otherworld Trading Company, the Blacksmithing Faction, the Sibylline Sisters Sorority of Seers, the Trinity Daughters of Calatin, the—"

"Enough. I am very aware of who signed that ridiculous document." Gaea stood, and everyone tensed, prepared for what may come of her next action. "How dare you corner me like some beaten dog!" she howled, the cry blowing wind over the masses of opponents.

"Gaea." King Frey stepped through the doorway and she promptly snapped her jaw close. "I advise you calm down and let the wizard do what he was tasked to do."

"And if not?" A wild look crossed her face and the tension grew.

"I'll devour you!" Fenrir erupted from the crowd, fur rising and his size this time twice fold. "You have wronged this man even knowing he is of your pack!" Anger rolled out of him, growling and barking. "An alpha who turns on the pack will die by the fangs of her pack."

The room fell silent, but Romasanta closed the gap with Fenrir. Giving him a few hearty pats on his legs. Fenrir backed his aggression down a few notches and the tension in the room lightened. Gaea's eyes glowed, the magic in the air growing denser. Cedric's armor tightened. In a matter of seconds, Cedric could feel Angeline stumble. He grabbed her hand, pulling her closer. The ether grew thick, enticing him to grow in size, to let the inhuman truth be revealed.

Shit, she's trying to out us, but why?

"Tell me, have you been honest with me?" Gaea hissed. "Keeping your pact to not create new beings? Leaving that task to me?"

"Madame," Manny smirked. "I assure you, my contract has that spell intact. After all, I am a wizard of my word."

Cedric tightened his grip on Angeline. His armor devouring the power their bodies attempted to produce. Angeline's eyes widened and she peered up at him, bewildered. The unsteady nature had ceased, her breathing calm again. What vibrating heat and friction the thickened, ether-filled air had induced fell away. He could feel the armor pulling her excess energy through their touch. It shivered a sense of delight about the hefty meal the moment had made it. It started to creep to her arm, and he flicked it, making it retreat.

"Fine." Gaea settled back into her throne, regaining her composure. "I will dissolve the curse laid on my children."

"Please do. The moment that comes into effect, this contract shall dissolve itself entirely." Manny walked into the middle of the fray, where all in the room could bear witness. "Please, Gaea, this is the last remaining task, seeing fit that you had only dissolved this for Kronos previously and left your other children defenseless against his attacks."

"Are you accusing Kronos of single-handedly wiping out my other children?" Her eyes narrowed, the tone dark and sinister. "How could a mother sit back and allow such travesties to unfold?"

"Please, the dissolution of Gaea's law and free the rest of your children from servitude per Otherworld laws as promised," Manny demanded, his tone and stare seeming stern.

"Very well." Gaea took a single claw, cutting open her palm. "Here. Take it."

She tossed a key across the floor covered in acrid, black blood. Miasma wafted from the metallic item, sending everyone scattering. There was a wave of whispers and murmurs. She stood, a wicked grin filling her face and her eyes wild, glowing. Again, the room darkened more, and the ether thickened in the air.

Cedric leaned into Angeline's ear. "I'm giving you a bracer. Use it to pull the energy down." He broke away from her and marched up to the key. "Where do I need to take this?"

"Ah, Vampire King!" Manny gleamed. "If you could do the honors, there is a padlock of sort there behind her throne. Unlock that, and the law shall be nevermore."

"There's no Underworlder here—" She inhaled sharply.

Cedric plucked it from the ground, marching past her with a smirk. There, behind the throne, as promised, glowed a lock. He slid the key in, and with a twist, it popped open and crumbled to the floor like dust. A gasp rang out as he retreated, the contract burning up at last. As if sensing their freedom, Lillith and Pan appeared in a flash of roses.

"No time to explain, but we've got to go, now."

Pan snapped his fingers.

CHAPTER 26

War of Roses

Cedric

Rose petals drifted to the ground and Pan winked at Cedric's heated glare. Glancing around, they were back in Avalon. With a deep inhale, the lack of ether in the air was a warm welcome. Turning, he realized more than the original group had come back with them. Romasanta and Nyctimus hugged Fenrir, and that made Cedric's stomach knot.

"Why in the hell did you bring the mutt with us?" he spat at Pan.

"Look, if she's intimidated by him, then he's better off closer to us, where we can keep an eye on him." Pan shrugged. "Besides, it was hard to gauge who all I should grab. King Frey grabbed the rest in case I missed anyone. You have no idea how pissed off Mother Gaea is about this ordeal."

Snorting, Cedric's attention turned to the warm fingers tangling with his own. "Are we really back?"

"It seems so." He sighed and kissed the top of her head. "I'm sorry for all the trouble I've caused you."

Angeline laughed. "And I'm sorry for all the trouble I attract."

Again, he turned to the room filled with people, taking account of everyone. Another scowl crossed his face as Manny waved. Lillith seemed deep in thought, and Artemis seemed to be relaying some sort of message. Shuddering, Cedric took another look at the room. It seemed like an overgrown study of some kind with a desk in the middle. He caught a nameplate reading, *Nomius Panes Silvan, President.* Beyond that, on the opposite wall from the door, was a windowed wall and within it, he recognized the faerie realm. As he spun to see more of the faces standing in confusion, he smirked.

"And look who made it back from the dead." Wylleam spun, ears raised high.

"It is rather strange, but glad to be back, old friend." A grin crossed his face. "So, what are we to do now?"

"Good question..." Again, Cedric took count and at last, approached Romasanta. "Old man, that voice from before."

"Ah, yes, did you figure it out?" He lowered his brow, scratching his jaw. "You were back rather fast. It surprised me."

"Well, she said she would meet us here in Avalon, but..." He gauged Romasanta's face for a moment. "Gaea had Phoebe in a locked room."

He stopped scratching. "My... my mother?" His eyes grew wide. "I thought she ran off?"

"I'm starting to think Gaea needed your sister under lock and key, too." Cedric eyed Artemis, who turned back to him, marching their way. "Speaking of the devil..."

"Cedric." His name left her lips like a hiss. "What have you done?"

"Done?" He blinked.

"We had a plan and you go and waltz over to grab the key, you imbecile." She scoffed. "You painted a target on your back!"

Anger seeped into his voice. "Like I wasn't already a target! Who else could have picked the damn thing up, huh? It was clear to me she thought she was using a power play."

"And so you thought to take it upon yourself to deflate her ego to inflate your own?" she marveled. "It is beyond me how you've survived in this world at all."

"A lot of blood, sweat, and tears... and part of that is your doing, old hag."

There was a moment of silence as they stared each other down.

"Is everyone here, Pan?" The sing-song voice sent the room silent.

"Yes, Phoebe. I think I grabbed everyone you requested." Pan turned to the door and bowed. "It's good to see you, Sister. I didn't think we'd get a chance to rescue you."

"Ah, that reminds me." Phoebe turned, meeting Cedric's gaze, and bowed. "I am in your debt. Thank you."

Everyone in the room turned to face Cedric. The looks seemed baffled and confused. He frowned, unsure how to read the mood shift in the room. Angeline tightened her hold on his hand, and he sighed. What little urge for fight and rise to anger he had left, was gone. The journey, the lower ether, and the churning of thoughts in his mind were draining him.

"I know many of you need to rest," Phoebe addressed the room. "But, I do have one important offer for you all. Gaea must be taken down. She may have followed her contractual duties, but I assure you, she will continue to aid Kronos until he summons her into this realm. We cannot allow this to happen."

"Shit." Cedric's head was spinning, the armor trying to push energy into his body. *Something's wrong.*

"C-Cedric?" Angeline looked him over. "You look pale and..."

"I just... I need rest."

"I implore you all, please join me and my brothers and sisters in our fight against Gaea," Phoebe continued. "She has already placed targets on many of you, as well as has Kronos."

"Then let the War of Roses begin," Manny chimed in, bowing before Phoebe. "I will gladly assist where I can, Goddess Phoebe."

"Everyone out." Lillith cut in, the mood changing from inspirational to dire. "Cedric, Angeline, Pan, Phoebe—you four stay."

The room cleared immediately, and after some stolen glances, they knew why. Cedric wobbled where he stood, holding his face with one hand. His breathing rattled and he couldn't concentrate on any words that hit his ears. Thoughts raced, questioning what could possibly be the issue with him. Angeline pulled him to a chair, forcing him to sit. The muffled words from their lips, his vision blurring. At last, he could hear them clearly again.

"Cedric, listen." Lillith stood, arms crossed with the same intense look she had when they arrived back in the Mortal Realm. "This is my fault. I didn't think about the complications of two king incubi."

"Just re-establish your link with him as the queen," offered Pan.

"Fuck that," Cedric breathed.

"No, if I do that, then my connection to Tony might put him in a similar state. We still don't know where he is." A look of desperation came across Lillith's face, squashing the snarky comment Cedric had aimed to take. "We need those weapons, and we need both of them to maintain their power. I don't know what to do."

"He needs a queen, yes?" Phoebe tapped her lips and looked at Angeline. "And it seems he has one."

They all turned to Angeline, who winced. "But I'm no succubus."

"But you are, my dear." Pan smirked and turned to Lillith. "Looks like you have an apprentice, after all."

"Are you two implying I pass this shit curse to someone?" Rage filled Lillith.

"More like, share it... it might even break it." Pan tapped his fingers on his cheek before a mischievous grin crossed his face. "Oh, why didn't I think of this sooner? It's a rather barbaric way... no, no. This should work wonderfully!" He rushed to his desk, opening and closing drawers. "Oh, you'll hate me for this, but yes. Sometimes a curse can be split and shifted into a yin and a yang effect. Daoists were so clever."

"I am not giving this to her!" Lillith chased him to his desk. "I'm used to it, but she... I can't do this to someone else."

"That curse, was it Father's or Mother's doing?" Phoebe held her chin in thought.

"Mother's." Lillith calmed, the questions throwing her. "Mother made me, but when father insisted on making me fertile like her, she..."

"Right, right." Pan turned and opened another drawer. "Isn't that also how we ended up with *Three's Company*: Gyges, Cottus, and Briareus? Ha! Dad wanted her to give birth to mankind. She agreed to it, and like some botched abortion, expelled it from her body into those three. So gross..."

"Pan," Phoebe warned, and he fell silent. "It seems these two were made with Father's magic."

Lillith and Pan froze, paling.

"Are you sure?" Lillith whispered.

"Positive." Phoebe nodded.

"I don't care," Angeline interjected. "If it means saving him, I am willing to do anything."

Cedric's eye rolled back, and everything went dark.

To Be Continued...

READY FOR BOOK FIVE?

KING INCUBUS: A NEW REIGN
IS WAITING FOR YOU.

I f you enjoyed the book, or something really nagged you about the story, I encourage you to speak your mind about my book in the form of a review. Readers depend on them to know whether they will like the story and characters within the pages.

Where can you leave the review? There are a lot of places! Amazon and GoodReads are great places to leave them, but feel free to visit your favorite online venues and leave them there. Whether it's a one-liner that sums up how you feel, an in-depth review breaking down the book and characters, or a spoiler warning of a rant to follow—

ALL ARE ENCOURAGED.

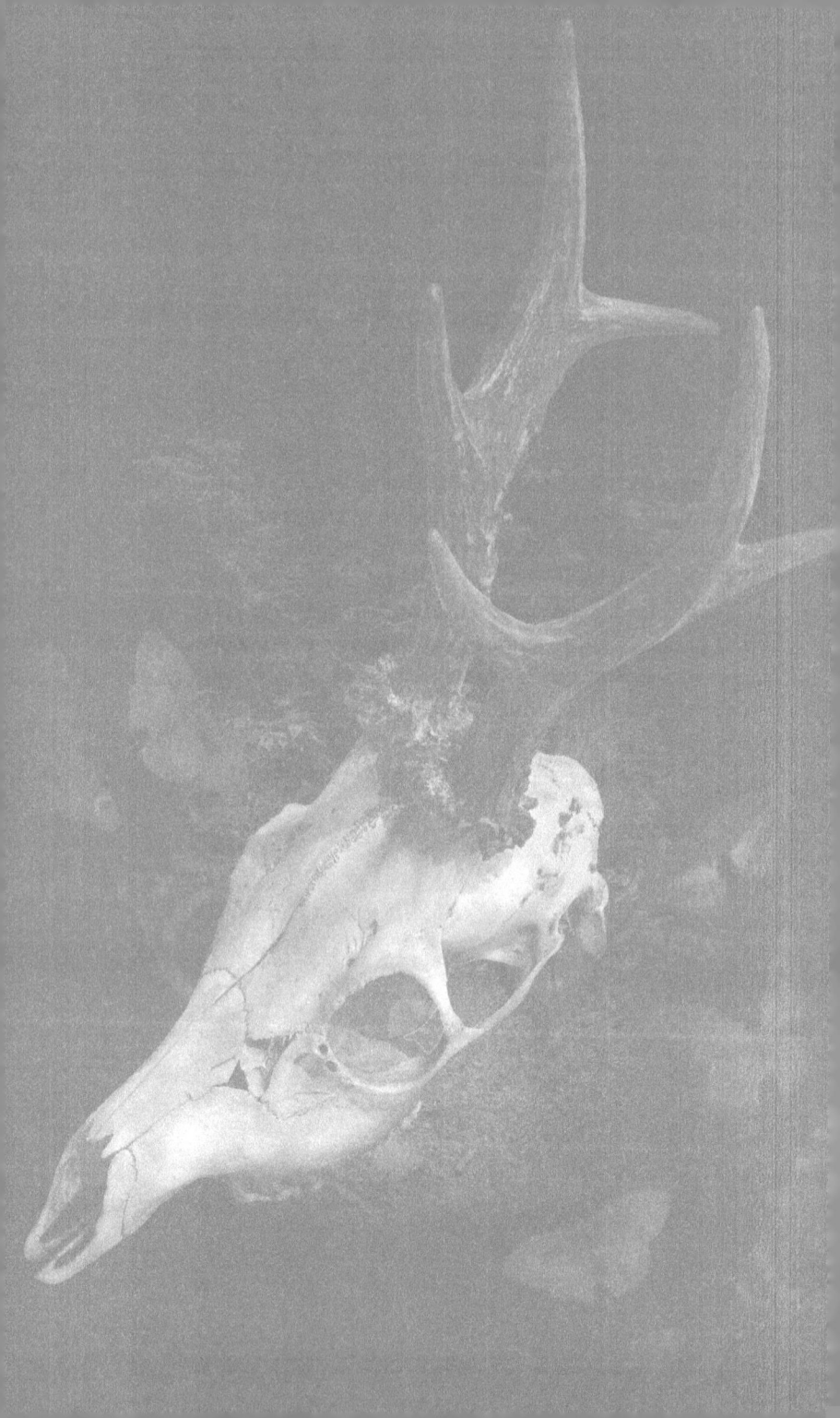

ABOUT THE AUTHOR

Valerie Willis is the Chief Operating Officer for 4 Horsemen Publications, Inc., an expert digital typesetter, and a fantasy romance author based out of Central Florida. When writing, she loves crafting novels with elements inspired by mythology, legends, folklore, fairy tales, and history. As COO, she oversees the design of all books including covers, typesets, and author branding where she pulls in creative print design while making versatile eBooks.

You can find her hosting workshops or attending as a guest speaker at many events (MegaCon, DragonCon, OCLS Writers Conference, Florida Writers Conference, SavvyAuthors, Women in Publishing Summit, etc.). She's been on panels with best-selling authors from Peter David to Delilah Dawson sharing her expertise in writing, research, worldbuilding, character development, book design, reader immersion, and more. You can also find her co-hosting on the Drinking with Authors Podcast speaking with Jonathan Maberry, Heather Graham, Charles Gannon, and many more on their own journeys as an author! Or talking about the spooky stuff over on Eerie Travels with topics such as big foots, mermaids, and even Bloody Mary!

Her award-winning dark fantasy paranormal romance, *The Cedric Series*, is a blend of genres that appeals to a wide range of readers who describe it as "dramatic, lustful, and fantasy fulfilling." The motto here is: "No immortal is beyond the ailments of man" that includes powerful creatures, demons, witches, and deities! Many of the monsters are derived from Medieval Bestiaries adding a fun flavor of new yet deeply-rooted assortment such as Coin Iotair, Shag Foal, Cynocephali, and more.

Like many authors, her writing journey started in grade school and carried her through high school. Many who grew up with her talk often of the traveling binders that were often kept safe in their lockers. This was the precursor to the now complete young adult dark urban fantasy of the *Tattooed Angels Trilogy* starting with *Rebirth*. This alternative historic piece about immortals and a failed reincarnation Hotan covers a wide variety of life lessons such as whether to follow your own lifepath or the one chosen for you, breaking toxic traditions, and the obligations of cleaning up our family's mistakes and destruction. Inspired by her own life tribulations, it has been the beacon to keep her moving toward the world of books and writing even now.

For readers of fantasy MM romance, check out her pen name V.C. Willis with the Traibon Family Saga starting with books *The Prince's Priest* and *The Priest's Assassin*. If you are looking for steamy paranormal erotica, chase down Urban Legends and modern retellings of fairy tales with Honey Cummings. Many have found themselves laughing out loud and fanning themselves while reading *Sleeping with Sasquatch* and *Wanton Woman in White*.

In 2021, she left her day job to join 4 Horsemen Publications, Inc. full time to bring over a decade of typesetting skills and industry knowledge to the table. Nothing is more rewarding for her than making fellow author's dreams come to life in physical format so they may share them with readers. Designing and writing books has been a longtime passion since childhood of hers and she continues to inspire and encourage authors around the world whenever possible, indulging whenever she can to chat about the books folks are reading and writing.

Keep in touch and keep reading!

WWW.WILLISAUTHOR.COM

LINKTR.EE/WILLISAUTHOR

More Books by Valerie Willis

Cedric: The Demonic Knight
Romasanta: Father of Werewolves
The Oracle: Keeper of the Gaea's Gate
Artemis: Eye of Gaea
King Incubus: A New Reign
Queen Succubus: Holder of the Crown

Val's House of Musings: A Mixed Genre Short Story Collection

Rebirth	Writer's Bane: Research 101
Judgment	Writer's Bane: Formatting
Death	

ANTHOLOGIES & COLLECTIONS

A World of Their Own
Work of Hearts Magazine Release
How I Met My Other: True Stories, True Love
It Was Always You: A Thrill of the Heart Anthology

Demonic Wildlife: A Fantastically Funny Adventure
Demonic Household: See Owner's Manual
Demonic Carnival: First Ticket's Free

The Hunted—Thrill of the Hunt 3
Urban Legends Reimagined—Thrill of the Hunt 4
Buried Alive—Thrill of the Hunt 5

PUBLIC DOMAIN REMAKES

Bulfinch's Mythology with Illustrations
Book of Werewolves
The Fairy Faith of Celtic Countries

Writing MM Romance as VC Willis

The Prince's Priest
The Priest's Assassin
The Assassin's Saint

The Champion's Lord: YONDER webnovel
Champion's Love: KU short story

WRITING AS HONEY CUMMINGS

Sleeping with Sasquatch
Cuddling with Chupacabra
Naked with New Jersey Devil
The Erotic Cryptid Collection

Laying with the Lady in Blue
Wanton Woman in White
Beating it with Bloody Mary
The Erotic Ghosts Collection

Beau and Professor Bestialora
The Goat's Gruff
Goldie and Her Three Beards
Pied Piper's Pipe
Princess Pea's Bed
Pinocchio and the Blow Up Doll
Jack's Beanstalk
Pulling Rapunzel's Hair
The Urban Erotica Fairy Tale
Collection

Curses & Crushes: KU short story

Queen's Incubus: YONDER webnovel

ƁOOK ℭLUB ƊISCUSSION ℚUESTIONS

1. What enemy do you think proved the most challenging?

2. What is the significance in separating Cedric and Angeline?

3. What changes internally were unfolding with Cedric?

4. A lot was revealed in this book, which one stood out to you? Why?

5. At last we see Gaea! How did she differ from your initial impression of her?

6. What do you suspect has happened to Tony?

7. Do you think Lillith came personally as a powerplay or a show of honesty?

8. The Otherworld takes its Tir system from Celtic Mythology. What other mythology and legends were revealed?

9. Aether was mentioned many times and in reference to Cedric. What do you think is being implied?

10. This quest was intended for Romasanta, but Cedric did all the heavy lifting. Do you think this was planned out or luck?

11. There is a significant amount of heavy duty weapon gathering happening. Do you think this is foreshadowing for what will be happening in later books?

12. Artemis has been a mysterious force in the previous books. How does meeting her in person differ?

13. Now that you know Cedric and Angeline have a child, what were the hints in the previous books?

14. Which of the three queens of the Amazon would you align with?

15. How do you think Cedric and Angeline's relationship will change after this?

16. Romasanta will finally have Daphne back. How do you think this will change him in future books?

17. Why do you think there weren't any Underworlders in the Otherworld besides Cedric?

18. Cedric has living armor. Do you think this has a significant purpose in this book? In future books?

19. Fenrir is back in action and has his own human form. Do you think Fenrir wants to be in a human body again?

20. Wylleam reveals a lot to Cedric. How do you think his decisions hurt or helped their friendship?